This book is due for return on or before the last date shown below. It may be renewed by telephone, personal application, fax or post, quoting this date, author, title and the book number

NEW CRIME

3 0 OCT 2018

1 0 FEB 2018   1 6 MAY 2018

1 9 DEC 2019

SAFE

Glasgow Life and its service brands, including Glasgow Libraries, (found at www.glasgowlife.org.uk) are operating names for Culture and Sport Glasgow

 Glasgow CITY COUNCIL

ALSO BY JAY STRINGER

Old Gold

Runaway Town

Lost City

Ways To Die In Glasgow

HOW TO KILL FRIENDS AND IMPLICATE PEOPLE

JAY
STRINGER

 THOMAS & MERCER

This is a work of fiction. Names, characters, organizations, places, events, and incidents are either products of the author's imagination or are used fictitiously.

Published by Thomas & Mercer, Seattle

www.apub.com

Amazon, the Amazon logo, and Thomas & Mercer are trademarks of Amazon.com, Inc., or its affiliates.

ISBN-13: 9781503939714
ISBN-10: 1503939715

Cover design by Lisa Horton

Printed in the United States of America

PART ONE
June 6th

'The first time you kill someone, you realise you don't need to suffer fools gladly.'

—Fergus

ONE
CAL
11:00

Fuckin' bawbags.

This is not cool. Not cool at-fucking-all. You think you can trust someone, then they go and screw you over.

'What's this?' I say.

Being all polite, like. Not threatening to stove their heads in with a fuckin' spoon. I'd specifically said to them, get me a wire, like in the movies. Something subtle. Something we could hide in a lassie's clothing, or fit into her bag. Maybe one of they transmitters that sends out the signal to some dude waiting in the next room with the recorder and a swat team.

So, aye, I sent Baz and Nazi Steve out to get me a wire. And the bampots have come back with a Walkman.

'That's all they had,' Nazi Steve says. 'We walked all around the Barras, and that's the closest thing. But look—' He takes the Walkman from me and points to a red button. 'It's got a *record* button.'

'Doesn't need a microphone neither,' Baz says. 'It's got one built in.'

'So yer lassie won't have to worry about all those wires,' Nazi Steve says.

They're nodding at what each of them says, encouraging each other, like a couple fucking special cases on medication day.

'What are yis on?' I say. 'This is boggin. Might as well have bought some fucking Fisher fucking Price kiddies' toy. Look at this, man.' I open the lid and look inside. It's proper old-school. 'You didn't even get a cassette tape to go in the cunting 'hing. Where am I going to get a cassette fae?'

They look at each other. I know what's coming next, but neither of them wants to be the first to go.

It's Baz who fronts up with a shrug. 'Probably get a good deal on one at the Barras,' he says.

The whole thing is going to pot. It had been such a good idea. I just needed this one thing to go right, and then I could pull off my big job.

My masterwork.

Classy and smooth.

My Babycham.

I find the conspiracy of a lifetime, enough information to blackmail half of Glesga. I could be living in gravy for the rest of my days. King of the swingers.

Now I've got to go and meet Paula, send her in without a decent wire. How the fuck is she going to get what we need without it?

I wish Joe was here. Joe Pepper. He'd know what to do. He used to work for my old da, practically one of the family, like. We supported him while he was at uni, started him on the road to being a hot-shit lawyer, friend to the stars. He used to sort shit like this out all the time. Saved my ass loads. Even from my da. Joe stopped me getting a skelping many times fer all the daft shit that I pull.

But now he's got a good job in the city. Wants nothing to do with us.

Fuck it.

Fuck him.

I don't need anyone's help. And deffo not these pure tossers, neither. I mean, who the fuck goes around with a name like 'Nazi Steve'? At least 'Baz' is a wee bit more understandable, since his uncle was called Barry. Steve's not even a Nazi.

I put the Walkman in my pocket. No point chucking it. Right now, it's the best thing I have, and maybe I can find a way to make this whole thing work. I stand up to leave, say, 'See you cunts later,' then head out to the pub.

Aff to see a lassie about some crime.

TWO
CAL
12:00

Paula's nervous. Which is understandable, like. I'm blackmailing her into pretending to be a hooker.

Other than being a total dirty liar, she's probably a nice lass. Cute as fuck, if you like the *rock chick* thing. I do. Well, I like the whole *woman* thing, so she fits the bill.

She's fae Belfast. Or somewhere around there, anyway. A proper tough lass. She makes the people fae Bridgeton look like pussies. I met her about a year ago. She was fresh off the boat.

(Literally. She came over on the ferry. I'm not a fucking moron.)

Paula made on like she was looking fer some fun, join in the scene over here. Played up her connections with the old boys back in Belfast, made herself sound all cool an' shite.

And for a long time, she was.

She got in tight with Gilbert Neil and that lot, doing the property jobs, burning down buildings. She was good at it. Didnae mind getting her hands dirty, and always managed to get away before the polis turned up.

Paula didnae touch drugs at first, and she wasn't always asking annoying questions. She just drank, partied, fucked and crimed it up with the rest of us.

But it's all been a lie.

I know her secret.

Made the mistake of getting stoned and starting to talk too much, didn't she? Told me every'hin'. Told the lads, too, but they didnae believe her. But I do. I've got her.

She's not quite so tough now, and she's going to do this wee job for me, so that I'll keep quiet about what I know. Or, that's what she thinks, anyway. It's just this wee job for now. Then whatever the next thing is. At some point, it'll be worth my while to tell people what she's hiding, but I can get some benefit for myself for a while first.

Paula's waiting for me when I get to the pub. The Pit in Cessnock. It's an old shitey place, full of idiots and piss stains, but it's a cop-free zone, and anything goes.

She's tarted up in a small black dress, but she's got her knee-high boots on and I can see her leather jacket on the chair next to her. It's not quite the look we'd agreed on, but it'll do. Between that and the Walkman, it's time I just get on with things and see how the cookie crumbles.

Paula already has a drink in front of her, so I head to the bar and get a pint of T for myself. I sit down opposite her and give my nicest, least creepy smile.

'How ya doin, ya daft cunt?' I say.

She flinches a little. I know she's fighting back the urge to call me out for saying that to her. I like to needle people like that. Find buttons and then push them regular, like, see how long before someone snaps.

Except, she cannae snap. Not while I'm keeping her secret. So I'm just being a dick, I suppose.

'Did you get a wire?' she says.

I slide the Walkman out of my pocket and on the table between us.

She leans back and rolls her eyes. If there's a way she can put any more distance between her and the Walkman without leaving the room, I'd like to see it.

'No way,' she says. 'Are you nuts?'

'You probably won't need it anyway,' I say, all calm and soothing. 'The guys are going to have the stuff there for you to steal. The recording was just going to be a backup. Dumbo's feather, kinda like, just so's you felt you were doing something more.'

'Something *more*?' She leans forward. 'Listen here, you daft prick. I'm doing this thing because I have to, not because I like being around you. I'm the one going in there. I'm the one who's about to fuck a guy and rob him. You can keep kidding on like you're some kind of criminal fucking genius here, but all you are is a twat blackmailing someone.'

She stands up and pulls on her coat. Stares at me for a second.

'And when this is done,' she says, 'don't think I won't be finding a way to get back at yis.'

She storms out.

Takes the Walkman, though, doesn't she?

Win.

THREE

SAM

15:51

The black cab clipped me as it overtook. Its wing mirror brushed my elbow and then the bullhorn handlebars of my bike. The cabbie didn't even slow down to see if I was okay.

A year earlier, that would have been enough to take me out of the saddle and dump my arse on the pavement. You toughen up fast if you ride a bike in Glasgow. I gripped the bars tight to stop the wobble on the front wheel, and kept pedalling.

That was the first lesson I'd learned on a fixed-gear bike. Pedal *into* the storm. The natural instinct is to stop your legs pumping the minute you hit a problem. Coasting feels like the right thing to do, and a normal bike will allow you to do that. At that point you may as well be on a runaway mine cart. A fixie doesn't let you coast. Nope. Pedal harder. Keep in control. And, even on the streets of Glasgow, don't back down from anything.

Don't show any fear.

It's like Mad Max out here sometimes.

Except I'm better looking. And not Australian. And don't need gasoline. Also, my name's not Max, and I'm not a man. So, it's not really *anything* like Mad Max, but it's a fun thing to say.

The cab dropped into the lane right in front of me, then slowed down to take the corner onto Glasgow Bridge. They were really imaginative when they named that one, right?

I kept the bike under control with my right hand, and straightened up in the saddle. With my left hand, I pulled my keys loose from the pocket, and extended my arm out to the side, stretching the elastic cord that was clipped to my shorts. As the cab slowed down before taking the turn, I let my keys touch the side of the car, and scraped them along the black surface.

This time, the driver noticed the cyclist.

And it was glorious.

He honked the horn and turned to swear at me out of his window. Thick veins bulged on his neck, beneath a shaved, rounded head that carried white scars among the stubble. I waved at him and smiled, then got my head down and picked up speed as I crossed the junction at the bottom of Jamaica Street. On the left, as I cycled under the railway overpass, was a small pedestrianised area. Skater kids and Goths gathered there to do, well, whatever it is skater kids and Goths tend to do. They'd seen my revenge on the cab, and they clapped and cheered as I passed.

My earphones beeped to tell me I had a call. I keep them in while I'm cycling, with my phone strapped into a small pouch on the front strap of my messenger bag. I pressed the button to accept the call.

'You're running late.' My wee brother, Phil. 'You won't make it.'

I was delivering a rush order, and I had twenty minutes to get it from a law firm on the Saltmarket, on one side of Glasgow, to another firm on Blythswood Street, on the other side of town.

I made a fart noise with my lips. 'I'll make it, don't worry.'

'No, you won't. You're still down on Broomielaw and you've only got six minutes left. You should have gone the way I told you.'

We run two small businesses out of an industrial unit in the Gorbals. One is a detective agency that we took over from our father; the other is a courier firm. Phil operates as the dispatcher for both. We have three other part-time riders out delivering packages across the city. I split my time between the courier work and the investigations. Phil monitors all of the riders using the GPS on our phones. It's easier for him to allocate the jobs when he can see where we are.

'Which one of us is out here on the bike?'

I overtook another cyclist. An overweight guy on a shiny new bike. It looked to have a million gears, and he was decked out in the latest cool Lycra from the team that won the Tour de France. I put my right arm out to indicate a turn, and then drifted across into the next lane. I didn't wait for an invitation. Cars don't slow down for cyclists. The trick is to just go for it. Let them adjust.

I drifted again, into the filter lane to turn into York Street. The lights turned red and I pressed back on the pedals, locking my knees to bring the bike to a stop.

'What's that?' Phil said. 'Sounds like you're stopping.'

'Traffic laws, kiddo. Don't worry.'

I disconnected the call and took the chance to take a swig of water from a bottle I kept in my bag. I could feel a car coming up behind me. It was getting too close. Drivers will get right up against the back wheel of a bike in a way they wouldn't dare for a car.

Then the engine revved.

I looked up at the light, but it was still red.

The engine revved again, and this time the car behind nudged my wheel, almost forcing me off the bike. I turned round to swear at the driver.

It was the taxi I'd keyed. He must have taken a turn to come back across the river. Now he was right on top of me.

The lights changed.

FOUR
SAM
15:54

The taxi pushed forward again. The bike jolted beneath me. Another push like that would either knock me off or warp the wheel. I looked at the driver through the sun glare of the windshield. His eyes were flared and his face was pale.

He wasn't acting rationally. This was full-on road rage.

There was a line of cars behind the taxi. I couldn't look to them for help, because all they were seeing right now was a cyclist getting in the way.

I pushed off as the taxi charged forward, skidding my back wheel out of the way just in time. We were in the right-hand filter lane, but I veered left. My pedal clipped the concrete kerb on the other side of the junction as I squeezed between a Volvo and the central divider. The driver blasted his horn and swerved away into the next lane, causing the van behind him to slam on the breaks and let rip on his own horn.

The squeal of more tyres, and the horns grew louder and more insistent. I took a look behind me, and saw that it was the taxi causing the disruption, as my road-rage pal had swerved to follow me, cutting in across the lane of traffic. There was one car between us, but I could see he was already looking to turn into the next lane so that he could draw level with me.

I hunkered low to the frame, and started to power down on the pedals. I swerved into the left-hand lane, which made the traffic behind slow down and block off the cab driver's options for a few seconds.

I'm a good cyclist. I'm fit and fast. For all that, though, I couldn't compete with a car engine over any long distance. It would only be a matter of time before the taxi caught me in a straight race.

A gap opened beside me, and I drifted into that lane before a car could fill it. There were now two vehicles between the taxi and me. The traffic in the left-hand lane sped up. The drivers wanted to put some distance between them and us. I risked another look behind and saw the taxi turn into that lane and speed up.

In a few seconds he was level with me. We locked eyes and I saw he wasn't looking to back down. His hands turned sharply on the wheel, and the cab veered toward me. I moved as far over as I could, keeping a few inches between us, as he drove down the middle of the road now, straddling the two lanes.

There was no divider along this stretch of the road. Nothing to stop me turning into the other lanes of traffic, heading in the other direction. I steeled myself, and did just that, finding a gap between two oncoming cars. Once again I heard horns as the taxi turned after me.

What was it with this guy?

I took a sharp left into McAlpine Street and got a sprint going. I could hear him turn in after me, but I'd figured out a way to shake him. At the top of the road is an MOD building with a gated car park. As I reached the barriers at the entrance, a guard stepped out from the security hut to stop me. I turned past him and bunny-hopped up onto the kerb, squeezing in between the metal fence and the barrier. I heard the guard shouting for me to stop.

I headed straight for the far corner of the car park, where a low wall separates the grounds from the next street over. I climbed off the bike, took a breath, and heaved it over the wall, then climbed after it.

The good news was the taxi was long gone.

The bad news? I had two minutes left to make the delivery.

The extra bad news? The office was a mile away.

I'd been getting faster with each month. I may have given up running, but I still had the same instincts. I was always pushing for a personal best. I'd managed to start doing two-and-a-half-minute miles. I was determined to push on, to try and hit the two-minute mark, but so far it was beyond me. I knew I couldn't make the delivery in time, but I could hear Phil's voice saying *I told you so*, and that was all I needed.

I raced down Argyle Street. My lungs were burning and my heart was still threatening to climb out of my ears. I took the third left, straight into Blythswood Street, then powered up the hill. I mounted the kerb in front of the main entrance to the building I was looking for, and dropped the bike onto the pavement.

The law firm was on the fourth floor, but luckily for me, and my lungs, I only needed to get it signed for at the ground-floor reception.

The receptionist was a petite woman named Tina. She was always neatly styled and hidden away under a layer of fake tan, hairspray and lipstick. I was sure her ideal visitor wasn't a sweaty woman in cargo shorts and a vest, especially one breathing so heavily, but she was used to me by now. This was one of my regular delivery spots, and I'd been to this building a few times in my other job, dressed up much smarter in a business suit.

'Hi, Sam,' she said. 'What we got today?'

17

'A heart attack, I think.'

She pretended that was funny while I rummaged in my messenger bag. I pulled out a heavy package wrapped in Manila paper and handed it across. 'No idea, but it's for Nicolay & Turner.'

She took the package and placed it down out of sight beneath the desk. I handed over the docket for her to sign and checked the time on my phone. I was one minute late.

'What time did they want it by?' Tina said, as she printed her name next to her signature.

'Four.'

Tina checked her watch and then shrugged. She wrote *16.00* in the space for the time the package was received. She tore off the part of the form that needed to go to the client, and handed the docket back to me, offering up a mischievous smile. 'Sod 'em.'

'Thanks, Tina.'

Out on the street I sat down next to my bike and took deep breaths. As soon as I was convinced the world wouldn't start spinning again, I pulled out my water bottle and took a long swig.

My phone beeped a few notifications. One was confirmation on our courier app that I'd made the delivery. The other was from a dating service my best friend, Hanya, had signed me up to.

The website was vLove.co.uk. It sounded like a Swedish car. Hanya had downloaded the app to my phone and signed me up. We'd recorded my profile video in a bar a few nights earlier. She'd needed to get me drunk before I'd play along.

People could watch my video, then decide whether they liked me or not. If they told the app they did, I'd get a notification to watch their video and see if the interest was mutual.

Every *like* I'd had so far seemed to be from a guy who was obsessed with showing me his penis.

No thanks.

My earphones beeped. I pressed the button on the phone, and Phil's voice came on the line.

'I hope you're not skiving,' he said. 'Because we just got another job.'

FIVE
FERGUS
15:00

You're only as good as your most recent kill.

Frankly, mine was a bit of an embarrassment. Some rich old boot paid me to kill her eldest son, ensuring her estate would fall to her youngest.

Families, right?

It's really hard to take pride in settling a stupid domestic squabble with some faked auto-erotic asphyxiation. Even harder when I fucked it up. It took three attempts to strangle the guy, because he was heavier than he looked. I'd tailed him for a couple of days before the hit, but he must have practised using posture to hide the pounds, because, *oh boy* he was a solid lump.

The truth was, I'd been sloppy. I hadn't taken the job seriously. I usually wouldn't have taken something like this on. I mean, I kill people for money, so I can't pretend to be a moral crusader. It's just a job. And I'm good at it. Some people spend their careers developing plagues and diseases. Some people sit in parliament coming up with ways to take money off poor people. Bankers take money off everybody.

They do what they do, with no regard for ethics.

At least I have rules:

No children.

No pets.

No disabled people.

I try to avoid domestics. They're small and petty. I can't pretend that everybody I've killed has been a bad egg. I can't even say they all had it coming. But you want the real truth? We could all be said to *have it coming.* Write down the worst things you've ever done. Just the top ten. The silent little moments of guilt sitting at the back of your eyes in the bathroom mirror.

Did you break someone's heart? Were you a bad husband or wife? Lousy mother or father? Was there a time you stole some money from the till at work? Maybe you just cheated on a test. We've all done things. One day, these things might come to the attention of the wrong person, and you get me knocking on your door.

Morals have to be flexible when you're self-employed. Sometimes I can turn jobs down if I think they're shady, but I've still got bills to pay.

So I took a bad job. I didn't take it seriously. I made a mess of it.

I'm making up for it right now. This one is a more interesting target. Martin Mitchell. A retired politician. 'Retired' is a bit of a euphemism. He lost the election. Martin is the kind of figure who is known by his first name. Say *Martin* in Glasgow, and everyone knows who you mean. If you want to put in the extra wee bit of effort, you can call him *Marxist Martin*, the name the press gave him a couple of decades ago.

Back then he was the poster boy, raging against the establishment with dark hair and a commie cap. But years do funny things to a person, and he's become just another self-serving shill.

If you've been an MP for a few years and you get voted out, you get a thirty-grand payoff. He's been blowing through that with cocaine and hookers at sex clubs, and I think he's been pissing people off with the amount of attention that's been drawing.

Bad for the party and all that.

Case in point for the stupid things he's doing. Right now, at three in the afternoon, in the middle of a heatwave, he's shacked up in his apartment with a hooker. His dealer was the one who tipped me off. Hookers and dealers are fine to work with. They'll sell information, and they rarely rat on a hit man. They talk to the cops all the time, sure, but they're telling tales on each other, not on people like me. It's just basic common sense not to grass on the professional killer.

Martin lives in a secured building in Glasgow's Merchant City. That expensive bit where all the wankers live. (Okay, I tried to buy a place there once. I'm a wee bit jealous.) The door on the ground floor has an electric lock, something you need a key card to open. Unless you're me, and locks are a piece of piss.

He lives on the third floor, but I take the stairs rather than the lift. I like time to think, to plan. Also, I'm a control freak, and I don't like being in a lift on my way to a job. I made that mistake on a job in New York. The lift got stuck between floors for twenty minutes, and by the time the mechanic fixed it, the target had already gone. It was three more days before I tracked her down.

I took her out in a lift, in tribute to the great gods of irony.

When I get to his floor, I can already hear the sex. Insistent and frantic. Most of the noises are male, but I can hear a woman in the mix, too. There are three locks on the door, but each of them is the same Yale design. That's utterly pointless. I spring each in turn, and then ease the door open, covering the lock mechanisms with my forearm to muffle the sounds as each latch springs back out. I listen for any give or wobble that might lead to a squeak in the door, but it's solid.

The hallway is stark, and very white. There's no furniture out here. The only thing is a small bowl full of pebbles on a dark wooden plinth in the middle of the hall. He probably thinks it's Chinese or something. I bet he spent thousands on it. The bedroom door is open a small crack. The sounds are coming from in there.

I take a look in through the opening. The window on the far side, the front of the building, is covered by thick curtains. Good protection against paparazzi. Great cover for a hit. Martin is on his back, being ridden by the woman. She's facing away from me. Her frame is small, with narrow shoulders, and a tattoo of a snake runs down her spine. That must have hurt. She's resting on her knees and rocking back and forth. No excitement or passion in what she's doing, but Martin's into it. There's *bad* sex, and there's *guy* sex. This is both. But for someone like Martin, the sex he's currently having will always be the best he's ever had.

He's making most of the noise, commentating on his own adventure.

It's all:

'Oh yeah, I'm fucking you.'

'Yeah, I'm in deep, baby.'

'You're riding me, bitch.'

What a charmer.

I step back and look to my right. The door to the kitchen is half open. I can see sunlight from the windows falling on the counter top and a large silver fridge. I head into the kitchen and open the fridge. There are twelve bottles of a trendy German beer. I take one out, making sure not to make too much noise, and then pop the top off with a bottle opener that's lying out on the counter, taking care not to rip the plastic of my gloves.

I lean back against the fridge and start taking slow sips from the cool beer. I can let him finish.

Even a fud like Marxist Martin deserves the chance to finish one last time, before he's finished for the last time.

SIX

FERGUS

15:10

I'm halfway down my beer when Martin cums. And he doesn't do it in silence. I hear a loud grunt, almost like he's been surprised by something. Then he starts to announce what's happening. 'I'm cumming,' he says. Then he repeats it several times, as though she didn't believe him before. Given all the build-up, the actual end is disappointing. I just hear a long soft whimper, barely above a child's strangled cry, and he says, 'Yeah.'

I drain the beer and slip the empty bottle into a jacket pocket. I pull out my Ruger.

There's a muffled conversation, and Martin steps out into the hallway. I move away from the fridge and over to the sink, out of sight. He wobbles past the kitchen door and into the next room over. He moves on unsteady legs, like he's just run a marathon. I hear a cough, and then the sound of him pissing into a toilet. Then I hear him start up a shower without flushing.

The bedroom door opens again, and the woman comes out. She lights up a smoke, a cheap-looking brand, and doesn't pay attention to where she's going. I hope she's just going to leave straight away, but she walks into the kitchen. She squints against the sunlight, then let's out a small yelp when she sees me. It's not loud enough for Martin to have heard. I put a finger to my lips and raise the gun; she stares at it and stays quiet.

She's got dusty brown eyes, and her short black hair is slicked down close to her scalp. There's another tattoo winding up her front, but this one is some kind of dragon, with grey wings that spread out over her breasts.

She's a lass with a dragon—

Never mind.

'You professional?' I say.

She nods.

'You been paid?'

She nods again.

'Then pretend you never saw me, and get out of here.'

She doesn't move straight away. Maybe she's not used to people being nice to her. I nod my head to the side, indicating again that she can go. She mouths a silent *Thank you*, then turns on her naked heels and heads back into the bedroom. Just over a minute later she walks, still naked but holding her clothes and a purse in a bundle, out the front door.

I head into the hallway when I hear the shower stop, and push open the bathroom door with my foot.

Martin is stood next to the bathtub, with one foot up on the edge, rubbing his cock with a towel. It's bright red and stood to attention, flapping up and down a little as if there's a passing breeze. He must be popped up on Viagra. He looks up at me and his eyes go wide. I'm used to that. Most people who spend their last seconds looking at me are surprised when it happens. Not because they don't deserve it, but because their egos make them think it'll never happen.

'Hang on, wait,' he says. He puts both hands out toward me, palms out, and the towel falls to the floor. 'I'm not worth it.'

'Probably not.'

I raise the gun.

He does something I don't expect. He gets angry. Indignant. He balls his hands into fists and puts them to his hips, looking like a child having a tantrum.

'Don't you know who I am?' he says.

'Of course I do, ya fud. Joe Pepper sends his regards.'

I fire twice. The gun sounds like a metal bolt slamming home on a heavy door, and my hand recoils between each, but I'm used to it. The first shot cuts through his throat. Insurance that his body doesn't let out a yell before noticing that his brain has stopped talking. The second puts a small red dot on his forehead, and a larger red dot on the mirror behind him.

I wait while he hits the deck. Sometimes I'm paid to make a hit look like something else. For a little extra, I'll even frame a specific person. But for this one the client wants it to look like a hit. He's sending a message.

I walk back out into the hallway, and hear movement in the bedroom.

Shit.

There's someone else in the flat.

How did I miss that?

I stride into the bedroom. There's a blind spot. Behind the door, a whole side of the room that I didn't check out. Basic fucking stuff. A real schoolboy error. I must be losing my edge. In that blind spot, slumped in a chair facing the bed, is a fat guy wearing nothing but a dog collar, and I don't mean he's a priest.

He's got a mobile phone in his hand, and I can hear it dialling out. Whoever he's calling, they'll pick up any second now, and then this whole thing will be out of control.

The fat guy is staring up at me. He's drugged up to his eyeballs, and his reactions are slow, but he's seen me and his brain is trying to figure out what facial expression is appropriate. He looks familiar, but I can't quite place him. And right now, that doesn't matter. He's a witness. I don't like killing people if I don't have to. Usually, if there are bystanders nearby, I walk away from a job and try again later, or figure out a way to do it without being seen.

But I've fucked up on this one.

Like I said, you're only as good as your most recent kill, and my record is getting fucking embarrassing.

I pull the phone from his drugged-up hands. He puts one up to ward off what's coming. I fire the same one-two pattern I used on Martin. Shut him up vocally, followed by permanently. I look down at the number on the phone.

It's not 999.

Someone picks up at the other end. A female voice. Maybe a slight accent. I break the connection and pocket the phone. I'll dump it in the Clyde on the way to my next appointment.

His clothes are on the floor by the chair. I go through the suit trousers and find a wallet. Credit cards. Photo IDs. Dominic Porter.

Shit.

I know the name. I can place him now. My local councillor in the East End. He's a member of a different party to Marxist Martin. They're pretty much rivals. I think I even voted for the daft cunt at the last election. You'd think he had better things to be doing at twenty-past three in the afternoon. Like, say, running a city?

Killing a city councillor was not part of the plan.

Time to get out. Draw a line under this one. The target is dead, and the collateral damage can't be helped.

I'm a professional, though. Even if my current record doesn't make it look that way. I was hired to do a job, and, though I've done it, there were some complications. I need to tell my client. In this game, you're always thinking about the next job, always maintaining good working relationships.

I call my client from my current burner. When he doesn't answer, I leave a voicemail, in a code that I hope he can figure out.

'Joe. It's me. Dropped your passenger off, but there was a problem. Someone else was along for the ride, had to make an extra drop. Call me.'

I step out of the flat and pull the door closed behind me. I pause for a second, listening for any movement around me, or on the floors above and below. Nobody in the building seems to have noticed, and there are no sirens yet.

I take the stairs two at a time on the way down, then walk out onto the street into the sun. I check the time. Perfect. I've got an appointment to meet another customer at four. I blend into the crowded street behind three hot young women in tight clothes, each loaded down with shopping bags. I slip off my rubber gloves and drop them into the nearest of the bags.

I pull sunglasses from my pocket and put them on.

That's two botched jobs in a row, but maybe I can get back on track with the next one.

Please, let it go smooth.

SEVEN

CAL

17:00

Well, this is a fucking mess.

I'm in Marxist Martin's bedroom. Or, his ex-bedroom. Is it still really *his* room, now that he's dead? Or is it just *a* room? Martin's in the bathroom. He's face down in his own blood.

I was glad to find him face down, because it meant I didn't have to see his nuddie little pecker. But then I walk in here, and there's Dom Porter dead on the floor, his brains sprayed across the wall, and his own Steamboat Willie glaring at me through one dead eye.

What the hell happened here?

And where's Paula?

My first sign of trouble wuz when I checked my stash, and saw she'd taken all of my proof. Everything. Then, when she didn't call me by four-thirty, like we'd fuckin' agreed, I came round here.

Getting in was easy, really. My da owns the building, so I've got a key to every door in the place. I'm pretty sure the tenants aren't told that when they sign the lease. That'd be a fun clause for them to agree to. I'm not actually sure my da knows, either. Me and him don't talk these days.

It's a long story.

Well, not that long.

I killed his favourite koi, years ago. I got high, and wanted to talk to the fish. Wanted to ask him how he stopped his skin from going all wrinkly. I mean, look, I'm in the bath for thirty minutes and I look like a fucking prune. This fish? He's in there all the time, looks great.

Well, not great, because he looks like a fish.

But I have nothing against fish.

I wouldn't fuck one, but—

(Well, look, that was just the one time, and for a bet.)

Anyway. So I accidentally killed the fucking fish. He drowned in the air. So my old mate Joe Pepper, he turned up and tried to fix things for me before my da got home. First we tried stealing another one that looked the same, but that didnae work. Then we said, Hold on, why not just make it look like a break-in, steal some stuff from the house, and kill the other fish, too?

Then my da would think that some fuckers had broken into the house, and killed his pets on the way out.

And it worked, too, until we all went out for a drink to celebrate Joe's graduation, and I got drunk and started telling stories about all the crazy shit we'd done down the years.

Haw, howsabout that time I killed yer fish, and the bigyin here covered it up?

Look, we were telling funny stories, and I thought it was a good 'un, okay?

Live and learn, that's what I say.

That's why I have to try pulling jobs like this, find my own Babycham. I got cut off over a fish, you believe that? But now there's two dead bodies, and a load of blood, and I have no idea where my fake hooker has got to.

If only Joe was here.

He'd know what to do.

Hey, that's what I need . . . I'm in a mess here. My Babycham has gone all tits up. I'll call Joe Pepper.

We haven't spoken in years, but he can fix it.

EIGHT
CAL
17:10

The buzzer goes, and when I press the intercom I hear Joe's voice. I click the button to unlock the front door and wait for him to come upstairs. He looks tired. He's dressed all smart, in a suit that looks like someone pressed it around him. He's no' shaved in a couple days and, man, he looks stressed.

'That was fast,' I say.

'I was nearby.' Joe sounds pissed off. But he was never happy. I think he'll enjoy this. Me calling him now. It's just like old times. I'm bringing a bit of fun back to his life.

We go way back.

Joe's parents died when he was a wean, and my da pretty much raised him. Joe was always cleverer than me, so it was his job to keep me out of shite. And I kept pushing that as far as I could. It was like a game, see how much trouble I could cause, and still have Joe to fix it.

Before that thing with the fish.

That was right after Joe had finished a law degree. We'd helped him through it, paid for extra tutors, bribed teachers, all the stuff that families do, aye? He was going to be our guy on the inside, until I fucked it up, and my da cut both of us off.

Joe landed on his feet though. Big time.

He's high up in the local Labour Party now, behind the scenes. He's the guy who pulls the strings, like. Arranges things, sets up meetings, cleans up messes. And he does practise law sometimes, too. Usually it's free jobs he takes.

What's that phrase? Like the lead singer of U2? Summat Bonio?

Well, that's what he does. Because it looks good, and it makes people think he's a good guy. But I know the truth. He'll kill yer fuckin' fish as soon as look at you. Which is why he's my kinda guy.

'How's the lawyering?' I say.

He sighs. 'Busy.'

'Still doing that bonio work?'

'Pro bono. You make it sound like a dog biscuit.'

'That's the badger.'

'Yeah, still doing it.'

'And the politics shite?'

'Yeah.'

Joe walks past me and into the flat. He stops in the doorway to the bathroom, and looks down at Martin. He grunts. It's not quite a surprised noise, more like he's saying, *Here we go again.*

'Anything else?' he says.

He looks at me with tired eyes. I thought he'd enjoy this, but no. His expression makes it feel like I've just walked into his office at the end of the day and put another pile of legal stuff on his desk.

I nod toward the bedroom and he goes to take a look. Even his walk looks fed up, he moves slow, with a great weight pressing down on him. I follow in. He bends down in front of Dom Porter. He's not fazed by seeing the fat fucker's pecker, but then, I reckon Joe likes a bit of cock.

'He wasn't supposed to be here,' he says. He doesn't turn to face me. He's still staring at the dead body. 'Neither were you.'

'It was going to be my fucking Babycham, bro.' Then it hits me and I add, 'What do you mean, *he wasn't supposed to be here?*'

He turns and looks up at me now. 'Your *what?*'

'You know, my big job. My masterpiece. Cal's big score.'

'*Babycham?*'

'Aye. Pure classy.'

Joe looks at me like I've got a screw loose. Maybe the Babycham is too expensive for all those secret lawyer clubs he must go to. Whatever. Fuck it.

I carry on. 'But now Paula's missing, and these guys are, well, spoiler alert an' aw that, but they're deid.'

He stands up and laughs. 'Spoiler alert an aw' that.' Then shakes his head and looks at me again. For just a second, I can see the old Joe in there, the one who used to like listening to my banter.

I hear someone behind me, and turn around. There's a big guy there. Looks like a bouncer, maybe. Has a beard and a flat cap, but he's dressed smart, in a suit. I didn't hear him come in. How didn't I hear him come in?

This isnae good.

I look back at Joe and try again. 'Joe, what did you mean, about him not being here? And who's this guy?'

Joe looks past me to the big guy, and nods. He says, 'Todd,' but it's more in greeting to him than answering me.

I turn to look at this Todd guy. He's wearing black gloves.

'I sorted the other problem,' he says.

I'm all, like, *What the fuck? Is this a code?*

Todd reaches inside his suit jacket and pulls out a gun. The last thing that goes through my brain, before the bullet, is to wonder how he managed to have that in his pocket without ruining the line of his sui—

NINE
SAM
16:20

Phil sent the address for the pickup to my phone. We ran both the courier service and a detective agency from the same office, and had phone apps for both.

Basically, we're Uber for parcels and mysteries.

And I promise, I've only used that line about ten times before.

The address Phil had sent me for the pickup was listed as Virginia Street. I knew a lot of the businesses there from previous jobs. There was a publisher's, a hotel, a place that made corsets and a law firm. A couple of gay bars, too, though they tended not to need a courier.

I followed the numbers in the street. The address I'd been given was the garage for one of the main high street stores. A large sign above the entrance said it was the 'Collection Point'. The entrance itself was hidden in shadows. I couldn't see anybody inside. Had to be a mistake, surely? There was a small hotel directly across from the garage. Maybe that's where I was meant to go?

As I was scanning the address on my phone again, a woman stepped out of the shadow in the entryway to the garage.

'Are you the courier?'

I looked her up and down. There wasn't much to her. She was shorter than me, with a narrow frame and short black hair combed flat to her head. She was wearing knee-high boots and a black dress beneath a biker jacket. Her eyes were hidden beneath sunglasses, and I always get defensive when I'm talking to someone who won't show me their eyes.

'Who's asking?'

'It's, ah, I ordered you. The delivery, I mean. I ordered the delivery.'

She had a strong Belfast accent, but she was nervous and spoke fast. I got the impression the jacket and glasses were a form of defence against the outside world.

'I wasn't expecting . . .' Her words trailed off.

'A woman?'

'A hot one.' She smiled, and then looked away.

I looked away, too. Then down at the bike beneath me. I smiled and looked back up. We both let out a small nervous laugh at the same time. Just like that, she'd knocked me off my game.

She smiled again. 'Sorry.' Then she leaned into the shadow and came back with a large padded envelope. The end was folded over and wrapped in brown parcel tape. I could feel something heavy inside as she passed it to me. There was something off about this job. I knew it straight away. We have some strict rules. We don't do drugs, we don't knowingly pick up crime-related goods, and if a rider feels something is wrong, they don't do it.

Those rules applied to everyone except me.

I've always felt that if I turned down a job, then it might send a different message. The other riders might decide I'm not committed, that I think I'm better than them. As a result, there have been a couple of times I've taken on a package that I wasn't comfortable with.

'Listen,' I said. 'We don't deliver anything dodgy.'

'No, please.' She stepped close and put her hand on mine, resting on the bullhorn. She sounded worried at the thought of being turned down. 'It's important.'

I looked down at her hand and she pulled it away, self-consciously.

There was no address on the envelope, only a name. Robert Butler. I checked the delivery address on the message Phil had sent me. Blythswood Square. I could cycle there in minutes, but it also wouldn't take long for this biker chick to get there herself on foot.

She must have read the hesitation in my face.

'Please,' she said again.

I looked back up at her from my phone, but only saw my own face reflected back in her black glasses. She turned to look down the street, and then up in the other direction. She was worried about being watched.

This stank. I decided we'd come up with the rules for a reason. I started to hand the package back, but she stepped back and pushed her hands into the pockets on the front of her jacket.

'I need your help,' she said. 'I can't deliver it myself, and remembered reading about you in the news. Please, just get it there for me, quickly.' Her right hand came out of the pocket with a roll of twenties. She handed the whole roll to me. The message Phil had sent told me that she'd already paid by debit card, so this was just a nice wee extra. I took the money and looked at it, then made a show of rolling my head, letting her see that I was thinking about it. Then I sighed, put the money into the front pocket of my cut-offs, and slipped the package into my messenger bag.

'Thank you,' she said.

I pushed off on the bike and turned away. I headed down Wilson Street and took a left, heading in the direction of George Square. Glasgow is laid out in a grid, like New York, and it has a confusing one-way system to the traffic that I usually tried to obey.

I took my time and followed the rules. There was no point busting a gut on this one. I'd been on the bike all day, and there was a meeting lined up with someone who wanted to hire me for an investigation job at 6 p.m. I just about had enough time to deliver the package and get home to clean up.

I cycled up St Vincent Street. I could feel the day in my thighs and calves. As the incline got steeper, I needed to get down closer to the bike and really push myself to keep going. I turned up Douglas Street, where the hill rose again, and promised my body I would give it a long hot bath later on.

Something with amazing bubbles.

Maybe even glitter.

I came to a slow stop at the address I'd been given for the delivery. It was empty.

A large 'To Let' sign was bolted to the wall beside the door. I climbed the steps to look in through the door, but it was dark inside. I stepped back and looked up at the windows on the floors above. They were all dark. None of them had curtains or blinds.

I searched the name 'Robert Butler' on my smartphone, but got nothing that seemed to fit. I tried again, varying searches with phrases like 'Law', 'Glasgow' and 'Solicitors' added in, but came up blank.

I got back on the bike and headed down the hill, back into the city centre. I love fixed-gear, but there were moments, like this one, when I would have loved the option of coasting. On this bike, the pedals turned even when I was going downhill, and I apologised to my legs with each rotation of the crank.

I cut down Buchanan Street, the pedestrianised area of the city centre. I drew dirty looks from the shoppers as I threaded between them and their heavy loads of plastic, paper and debt, but I didn't really care. I turned onto Argyle Street and then into the bottom of Virginia Street.

Blue lights bounced off the walls of large old buildings. There were police vans in the street, and an ambulance parked at the kerb, at the entrance to the garage. Paramedics in green jumpsuits were bent over a fallen figure, working furiously.

The motionless figure's legs were all that I could see. They were covered in knee-high boots.

What the hell had I got into this time?

TEN
SAM
16:45

The blue police lights flashed around the narrow street, bouncing off the brownstone walls of the old buildings. I watched as the paramedics worked away at the body. I saw blood covering their gloves as they moved. The police presence was building up around the scene, with more cars pulling into the road, and uniforms starting to put up tape to keep away the passers-by.

I took a few quiet steps back to allow another officer to start cordoning off my end of the street.

The package in my messenger bag started to feel heavy. What the hell was it? A younger version of me might have believed this was all a coincidence. Maybe she was mugged after handing the delivery off to me, and it all meant nothing. A younger version of me also believed in Santa. I'd seen too many of the nasty surprises this city had to offer, and *coincidence* wasn't one of them.

More cars were arriving, pulling into the scene from Wilson Street, to the right. One of them was a midnight blue Audi, and I knew who was behind the wheel even before she climbed out.

Hanya Perera.

My best friend.

Hanya was English, but had been in Glasgow for five years, so she now spoke with a hybrid accent like those rich people in Edinburgh. Her parents were Spanish and Indian, and the most accurate way to describe her looks was *interesting*.

Hanya had transferred up from London back before the regional Scottish police forces were all merged into one. She'd been part of a specialist armed unit, trained in using guns. After the merger, she'd been shuffled around between departments, finally settling in the MIT.

With a Starbucks in one hand and an E-cig in the other, she headed over to watch the paramedics work. She had a terse conversation with them, quiet enough that the words didn't carry down the street toward me. She slipped the E-cig into her jacket and set the coffee down on the road before slipping on a pair of plastic gloves and picking something up off the ground. A purse. She looked through the contents, and then glanced around the street. Finally, her eyes rested on the crowd that had gathered at this end.

On me.

She cocked her head to one side and smiled, just a little. She waved for me to come closer, and nodded to the uniform holding the line. He lifted the tape up to let me through, and I stooped to meet it, wheeling my bike underneath to stand with Hanya on the other side. We moved back down the street a little, far enough away from the crowd.

She nodded at my bike. 'Picking up or dropping off?'

Our friendship was built on many things. Gin. Talking about sex. Watching American TV shows. But, like all good friends, we also lied to each other constantly. 'Just passing by,' I said. 'Caught the whiff.'

Hanya turned and watched the paramedics. She worked murders, mostly. Her being here meant that nobody was expecting a miracle, but she also wasn't on the clock yet.

'Looked at vLove yet?' she said.

When I first started working the detective business, I'd been appalled that cops, paramedics and fire crews could stand and hold such banal conversations so close to tragedy. But that was then. This is now. Violence and blood had become just another thing I was getting used to, like paperwork and flat tyres.

'Nope,' I said. 'Told you, not interested. Swedish car.'

'Personally, I thought it sounded a little vaginal.' She gave me a knowing smile. 'Why I liked it.'

'I don't need any help,' I said.

Hanya fixed me with a look. The same one my brother had been giving me lately. 'Hon, when was the last time you had a guy between your legs who doesn't wear cargo shorts and spend all day on a bike? Someone who knows what a utility bill looks like?'

Crap. She had a point. Okay. Change the subject. I nodded at the victim. 'What's her name?'

That caught Hanya off guard. She was one of the best people I knew, but she'd been at the job long enough to develop a detachment to death and victims.

She looked again at the purse. Pulled out a driver's licence. 'Paula Lucas.'

Then her expression changed. That mixture of suspicion and curiosity that I saw in her whenever she knew I was up to something. I'd achieved three things. I'd changed the conversation away from my love life, and I'd put a name to the victim. But I'd also got Hanya wondering just why I was at the scene.

Hanya's attention was taken away again when the paramedics stopped working. They were climbing to their feet and packing away their equipment. The motionless body at their feet was now officially a corpse. One of the paramedics nodded at Hanya, and she returned the gesture with a heavy sigh.

We both stood in silence for a long few seconds. There's a difference between seeing a dead body, and witnessing someone die. A body is just a thing, it's an empty vessel. It can be creepy to find one, and deeply upsetting if you knew the person, but ultimately there's a numbness to it, an emptiness. But seeing someone *die* is different. It's a moment in time, and it brings a sense of responsibility with it to pay respect to what has just slipped by.

'Well,' Hanya turned back to me, 'I'm on the clock now. I'm going to be sending uniforms out canvassing for witnesses. I get the feeling someone might mention seeing a woman on a bike?'

I was already pushing my way back toward the crowd, getting out of the way so they could all get to work. 'Bikes are getting more common in the city,' I said.

The sensible thing to do was to just come clean and hand over the package there and then. I'd done nothing wrong, and a quick statement to the police would let me walk away from it. But I'm the queen of stupid decisions. I blame my father. Jim Ireland had been both a cop and a private eye in this city, and he had a way of needling authority, a trait he'd passed on to me. The other thing we had in common was that we both hated a mystery, and needed to solve it.

Paula Lucas had trusted me with something. She'd known who I was, and sought me out. It was the last thing she ever did. That didn't sit right with me.

I wanted to know what she'd died for.

I cycled down Argyle Street for a few blocks, putting distance between me and the cops, and pulled into an alleyway called New Wynd.

Great name, right?

I pulled the package out of my bag and used my keys to cut through the tape holding the flap closed at the end. I pulled it open, and looked at the contents.

What the hell?

ELEVEN
FERGUS
16:00

'So, you want me to kill you?'

'No, I want you to pretend to kill me.'

I've spoken to a lot of idiots in my time. Comes with the territory. When you kill people for money, one way or another you end up talking to bampots.

There tend to be two main groups:

People who haven't thought it through, and will back out.

Guys who've seen too many movies and think it's cool to meet a hit man.

But I've never heard anything quite like this. I take a look around the bar, trying to spot if any of my mates are here. This could be a wind-up, with any one of them waiting to jump out and laugh. Except that would entail me having friends.

This isn't a very sociable profession.

I lean in over my pint glass. 'Is this a joke?'

'No.' The guy looks hurt. The only thing worse than an idiot trying to trick you is an idiot telling the truth. 'No, I'm serious. I want to hire you to kill me, but I don't want you to actually kill me. I want to fake my death.'

His name is Alex Pennan. I've done my research. He works for MHW, a financial firm, managing investments and savings for a whole bunch of famous people. They also launder money for some pretty serious criminal organisations.

How do I know this?

Who do you think these organisations hire to deal with their enemies?

But I've never dealt with Pennan directly, and I don't know how he got my details. Until I do, I'm playing it dumb.

'If you don't want anybody to die,' I say, 'why hire a hit man?'

Alex looks around, laughs nervously, makes eye contact with a few people at nearby tables, and then turns back to me. 'Must you say that so loud?'

'What? *Hit man*? We're in a bar, nobody cares.'

It's true.

I do all of my meetings in pubs and bars. The busier the better. People in bars talk all manner of rubbish, and nobody ever pays any attention.

If you're going to have conversations about killing people, whether it's professionally or if you're preserving your amateur status for the Olympics, the best place to do it is in a crowded drinking establishment. And this place is one of the finest in Glasgow. A microbrewery on the edge of Glasgow Green, all dark wood and lots of beers.

Alex gives me an odd look. 'But you're okay talking about . . .'

Holy shit.

I get it. He's not worrying about secrecy. He's asking if I'm ashamed to talk about what I do for a living.

What a dick.

47

'Look,' I say. 'Some people take pride in unblocking drains.
You've made a career out of whatever it is you do. I work for a living,
and I'm not ashamed of it.' I stand up to leave. Forget this rubbish.
Take it from me, the first time you kill someone, you realise you
don't need to suffer fools gladly. 'Thanks for the drink.'

'Wait. Wait. I didn't mean anything by that.' Alex stands after
me. His chair scrapes across the wooden floor.

I didn't mean anything by that. That's as close as these people
come to saying 'sorry'. They can't actually do apologies, because that
makes them sound humble, takes them down a peg.

Now people are paying attention. The bouncer by the door,
the other one at the back of the room who was doing a slow circuit
of the room. The staff. They're all seeing two men stood up, one
apologising. That puts us on a watch list. We're on borrowed time.

I wave the guy back down, in a way that shows I'm going to give
him a second chance. It's rubbish, of course. But there's no point
creating a scene. I can give him another couple of minutes.

I nod at him. Like, *Humour me.* 'Go on?'

Pennan's nervous. There's sweat on his forehead, and he keeps
rubbing at his hands, like they're damp. There's laughter in his
words, and I reckon this is the first time he's talked about his master
plan out loud.

'See,' he says. 'I need everyone to think I'm dead, and I need
it to look real. I don't want any doubts. In fact, I want it so that a
medical examiner could look into the matter and declare me legally
dead. Case closed.'

His plan was possible up until that last part.

'Can't be done,' I say. 'Doctors tend to know what they're
doing. You know that, right? You'd need a body, and they're expensive. *Really* expensive. You're competing with the black market for
organs, and each one is worth thousands.'

'Well, I figured you'd probably have a way of getting a fresh body. Being a—' He pauses, leans in, and whispers the words, 'hit man'.

Right, okay. He's not just wanting me to fake his death, he's wanting me to kill someone else to replace him. It's a bad idea. In fact, it's *such* a bad idea that I'm almost interested.

I start to turn my empty glass around on the table, but stop. I don't want to risk him buying me another drink. 'Okay, but over and above that, any decent medical exam would show up that it's not you on the slab. Even if we figured out a way to fool people's eyes, get someone identical to you, we can't cheat dental records, DNA, fingerprints.'

Shit. I'm putting too much thought into this.

'No.' His words are stronger. Now that he's got over the initial nerves, he's confident, and wants to sell his idea. 'You'd figure it out, do it right, because you're a pro. But don't tell me the details, I don't want to know it's coming.'

'Is this meeting here not a bit of a tip off?'

'What I'm meaning is I don't want to know the specifics. If I do it myself, or if I'm too heavily involved, there would be a trail. A cop or the, ah, anybody else, might notice. They could figure it out.' The *anybody else* is interesting. It's not the cops he wants to kid. There's a scam he's playing. 'If you do it, and you don't tell me when or where or how, then it looks real. There's no trail leading back to me.'

'Alex, have you stolen from the mob?'

He shoots back in the chair, almost taking it off the floor. His act is good. When his mouth says, 'No, what are you talking about?' I almost believe him. Almost. But I've killed too many scammers to fall for lies and bullshit.

If there's one thing I can do well, it's read people.

He almost had me. This job sounds like a fun challenge. But my career is in a bad spot, and the last thing I need right now is to get mixed up in a con job between Alex Pennan and all of the scariest people in town.

That's a fight he can take on for himself.

I stand up to leave. 'Thanks for your time.'

On the way out the door, I feel a phone buzzing in my pocket. I pull it out. It's the one I picked up back at Martin Mitchell's place. I forgot to dump it, and now it has my prints all over it.

I stare at the number.

Same one Dominic Porter dialled.

Shit.

TWELVE
FERGUS
17:20

Back home, I change into a T-shirt and comfortable blue jeans. I never plan on dressing to *look* like a hit man when I'm on the job, but somehow it always ends up that way.

I keep staring at my phone, waiting for Joe Pepper's number to come up. The job didn't go according to plan, and he's got to be pissed off about that. Technically I've done what he paid me for, so I'm not going to go chasing after his approval, but I also did way more, and he won't be happy about it. In the meantime, I'll get on with something more important.

Women.

I've tried so many different ways of meeting the right person. I assumed for years that the first step was to pretend I'm not a hit man. It's funny. As a kid, it was always about trying to seem more grown up and edgy than I really was. I was a working-class kid, of raging lefty parents, with a comfortable home and no horror stories. Just about anything else is more interesting than that. But then I joined the military, and became a spook for a while, and I don't need to pretend to have any extra darkness. I'd rather make people laugh, so it became about pretending to be anything other than edgy. I'd claim just about anything else, as long as I could do it in a way that got a laugh.

I'm an insurance salesman. Not a very good one.

You know the plastic bits on the ends of shoelaces? That's me.

I'm professionally interested in Sweden.

There's no greater drug than making a woman laugh. See, getting a smile, that's fun. Raising it to a chuckle, or a snicker, that's great. Getting a lassie to actually belly laugh? Getting her to struggle for breath, slap her knees, or lean back to belt out the kind of laugh that she usually keeps hidden? That's the fucking boner, right there.

Guys get jealous of a lot of things. We get insecure about our dick size. We get worried being around men who are more attractive than us (we always know). We *hate* seeing men who are sexier than us (and we *definitely* know about that one). But the number one thing that men get jealous about?

Seeing a fella who makes a woman laugh more than we can.

We will *hate* that guy.

But it's also a trap. If I try really hard, if I bring my A game, I can get a real laugh. But then, that's expected all the time. I've got maybe three good jokes a year in me. So it works, but I have to pretend to be someone else to pull it off, and it's exhausting.

I tried something new when I was living in New York. Telling the truth. What the hell, right? Might as well give it a go. I'd be in a bar, I'd be chatting to a woman who looked like fun, and I'd just come clean:

I'm a hit man.

This gun's for hire.

I'll kill anyone, for enough money.

Well, not anyone, I do have a few rules.

They loved it. I was getting so much sex. But I was still pretending to be something else, even though I was being honest, because it wasn't really me they were fucking. It was some myth, some movie that they had in their heads. It wasn't a route to building any kind of lasting relationship.

Truth is, I just want to be myself.

And I'm not a bad guy, if we overlook the fact that I *am* a bad guy.

But I've never figured out how to be myself and meet women. Or how to go to places where being myself would let me meet women. It seems like that would be a very niche place to find.

So I've turned to the internet. The home of niches.

Trouble is, it's full of liars. People on there are experts in cheating the camera. Shooting from the best angle (I'm going to resist the chance to make an obvious joke here) and in black and white. Or pulling just the right facial expression to make you look both witty and skinny at the same time. Raised eyebrows, cocked mouths, jaunty glasses, whatever.

And then there are the people who have no intention of meeting you. They want to have the whole relationship online, telling me they love me without ever actually knowing if we'd get on.

They scare me. And I'm not someone who scares easily.

I'd given up, but my sister, Zoe, found a new site and signed me up. vLove.co.uk. I said it sounded vaginal, but Zoe insisted. Most people use it through a phone app, but I have to be careful about what I load onto my phone. I use the full website version from my computer.

Nice and easy. We all load up videos. As many videos as we want, and on any subject, as long as there's no nudity or porn. Then we can scroll through. See if there's anybody we like.

I load up the newest set of videos and press play on the first one. The picture forms digitally on the screen in front of me, taking a second to focus, probably from a cheap camera phone.

Title card. Name.

Jane.

Strong features, make up, styled hair. No twinkle in the eyes.

'Hi, I'm Jane, I'm 30 . . .'

I click a red button on the left of the screen. Another video pops up.

Title card. Name.

Sam.

Cute looking girl. Embarrassed smile. Her eyes flit between the camera and whoever is holding it, and the subtext is easy: *she's been put up to this.* I know the feeling.

'Hi. My name's . . . Okay, I'm Sam.'

I'm not listening. I'm watching. She speaks for a second, then stops, and smiles. She's uncomfortable on the camera, but looks comfortable in her own skin. She's not posing. Not afraid of looking like herself.

In that second, while she's not even trying to be anything special on camera, I see exactly what I'm looking for.

Hello, Sam.

This could work.

PART TWO
June 6th

'Jeezo, a girl uncovers one massive conspiracy, and suddenly she's Jim Rockford.'

—Phil

THIRTEEN
ALEX
17:00

Alex had always known he was working for criminals. McGoran, Hornor & Wendig clearly handled dirty money. He just didn't know whose money it was.

Sure, the company had legitimate clients. Footballers from both Old Firm teams, a few from the English Premier League. There were actors, musicians, even a couple members of the royal family.

For clients like these, his job was simple.

Investments.

Hedge funds.

Future planning.

Whichever way it was written down, and whatever adjustments were made to his job description, Alex knew he was there to help people cheat on their taxes. And he was fine with that. He paid an accountant a lot of money to do exactly the same for him. Alex hadn't paid more than five per cent tax in a decade.

But when he moved to Glasgow, he found something else going on. Money that didn't appear on the books. Companies that shouldn't have been profitable. Investments that didn't make sense.

Clients would put money into companies that were doomed to fail, and take money out of ones that were just taking off. These decisions seemed so bloody random, until he stepped back and saw the pattern. Alex had always been in the business of making money vanish, of using loopholes and paperwork to let people hide assets away. Once he started working for MHW, he was in the business of making money reappear. Money that shouldn't have been there. In his first year with the firm, they supplied money to help prop up a Greek bank, and none of it had existed on paper before the bailout.

What Alex did next was the most sensible thing in the world.

He started to steal from the mob.

Or maybe not the mob. From whoever. Drug lords, the Russians, terrorists. Does it matter who you steal from, when the money doesn't exist?

It was his own little act of revenge. Something to get one over on the bosses. He hadn't wanted this job, or this life, or this shitty city. He didn't like Glasgow. He didn't like the people, and they didn't like him. He didn't understand the football, or the accents. He didn't like the drivers. They only had two speeds: road rage and stop.

And he didn't like the rain. It rained for 360 days a year. On the other five? Baking sunshine. Every skinny Ned in town takes his top off and worships the strange ball of fire in the sky.

The Merchant City bars were okay. They were overpriced and fashionable. But the private clubs were better. He'd take clients there for meetings, show them the town. He liked to play the part, show off his cash, even though it was always somebody else's money he was spending.

He liked walking round the club, pointing at people, waving, being acknowledged. He liked to look, and feel, connected. And in London, he had been. He knew people, and they knew him. Rolling Stones tracks would play in his head whenever he crossed a room.

The move north had come packaged with a corporate reshuffle, a slap in the face disguised as a promotion. He'd been working as an investment manager for Paterson & Hood, one of London's smaller hedge fund companies. He'd been the best thing to ever happen to them. That's what he told his friends, and what he imagined people said behind his back. Alex was the best in the business at making money legally disappear. He was a wizard with numbers, spreadsheets and tax returns.

He learned the hard way: don't be too successful in the big city. You don't want people to notice you, not really. You want to look important, you want to be able to look rich out on the town and impress your mates. But you don't want the big fish to notice you. They don't look at you and decide to offer you a job; they buy your company because it's getting big enough to get noticed.

A lesson learned when, on a Monday evening, he was taken out for a meal by Ozzy Paterson and Noel Hood, the two retired owners, and told that the company he'd taken so high was being sold to a bank from the Middle East.

'Well done, Alex,' they had assured him. 'It's all down to you.'

Which he'd already known.

'Your job will be safe,' they had said. 'One of the promises we've had is that you will be kept on. They don't want to lose you.'

It was a half-truth. They didn't want to lose him. They wanted to mail him up to run the Glasgow office of another company in their portfolio. MHW. He'd be the boss. The top person in the company, in charge of the most important clients.

He nodded. Took the promotion. Maybe this would be his big break. It would be easier to feel like a big player in Glasgow. It's smaller than London, but still one of the biggest cities in the UK.

Nope. No dice.

He was a nobody up here.

A nobody who handled *a lot* of money.

Alex ran MHW in name only. He answered to a woman named Asma Khan, the euphemistically titled Asset Manager for the people behind the scenes. And he also found out that the official story – MHW being owned by a Middle Eastern bank – was only part of the tale. MHW was a cartel, one that had already moved on Birmingham, Liverpool and Manchester.

Glasgow was just the next step.

They wanted Alex for his skills with numbers, but MHW wasn't really under his control.

Still, he'd been sticking it out for his wife, Kara.

Kara had given up a good job to move with him. She'd been working as the media manager for a Premier League team in London. Alex knew it had been a tough choice for her to walk away. She was the sort of person who could make friends everywhere. Kara had built up a new community around her in Glasgow, and taken a job running the marketing and corporate hospitality for a local team. In three years she'd managed to make herself the centre of a whole social scene, one which Alex didn't understand at all. It involved art exhibitions and shopping, and drinking cocktails made up of funny colours.

Alex didn't understand funny colours.

He really only understood status and money.

And once he realised the status of the people whose money he was handling, the plan began to form. Now he had ten million pounds in an offshore account, and a further five million in cash stored away in an apartment in the Merchant City, a place even his wife didn't know about. Fifteen million, all in.

And who was going to notice? These idiots came to Alex to manage things, he was the one they left in charge of noticing irregularities, and he certainly wasn't going to report on himself.

He was rich.

He and Kara could be set for life.

The only problem was, they would come looking for him if he ran. They would track the two of them down, and kill them. Alex was trapped. He couldn't spend the money while he was alive. He needed to die first.

FOURTEEN
SAM
17:30

Cassette tapes?

Who still used cassette tapes?

That's what was inside the package. Three tapes.

Each one was labelled.

Cal's Log.

The Meeting.

Sexy Time Mix Tape 1999.

There was no way I was handing those over without listening to them first. I mean, come on. Aside from all the questions I already had, about Paula Lucas and a delivery to a fake address, now I had this new question to solve:

Who still uses cassette tapes?

I couldn't get straight to it, though, because I had a paying customer waiting. For all that I wanted answers to the questions, and to find out what this all had to do with Paula Lucas, I had bills to cover. When you're a freelancer, the gigs that pay always come first.

I had a meeting with a client at 6 p.m. Going back to the crime scene had lost me some time. I'd planned my afternoon around being able to head home and shower before going out to meet my client. I didn't really have time for that now. I lived out in Parkhead, to the east of the city centre, and my appointment was at Firhill, a football stadium on the opposite side of town.

I keep some work clothes in my bag. A grey pencil skirt and jacket, rolled up tight. They're creased, and it's not the most professional look in the world, but it's better than rocking up to a meeting looking like a sweaty bike messenger.

I'd gone out with a Partick Thistle player for a few months, at the start of the year. Milo Nardini. Despite the Italian name, he was pure Glaswegian, and had grown up in the shadow of Celtic Park. He was the grandson of Italian immigrants, and he combined Mediterranean looks with a real East End laugh. He was young, funny and good in bed. Beneath the laddish image he liked to show to the world, I'd found a shy little geek. He was obsessed with *Star Wars, Star Trek* and *The X Files*. He had a room in his apartment filled with action figures, still sealed in their boxes. I didn't really like any of those things, but his passion for them gave him a goofy charm.

He'd become Hanya's latest proof that I was avoiding meaningful relationships. The last man I'd really trusted had turned out to be a crooked cop and, worse, a murderer. Since then, I'd stuck mostly to meeting up with other guys on the messenger circuit, and to short-term fuses like Milo Nardini.

Milo had been the hottest ticket in town for the first half of the season. He'd scored fifteen goals in the first ten games, and was starting to attract the interest of Celtic. Not long after we'd hooked up, his form on the pitch took a dip. The more we messed around in the sack, the more he messed up on the pitch. The fans started getting on his back over his performances, and the journalists were questioning whether he was good enough to play for the club. Celtic's scouts stopped going to matches.

I learned where I stood in Milo's priorities when he dumped me to focus on his football. He was worried about losing his big move, and the money that would come with it. He'd played the poverty card, and claimed football was his one shot at making something. Completely oblivious to the fact I grew up in the same part of town, and saw right through his crap.

Milo finished out the season with twenty-five goals, and now a few English teams were rumoured to be after him. I hoped he didn't sign for Celtic, because I didn't want to cheer when he scored for my team.

I took it easy on the ride there. The stadium was only twenty minutes away by bike, so I didn't need to push myself too hard. I chained the bike up in the staff-only car park, and walked into the reception. I knew the kid behind the desk. Chris. He was too sweet and too young, always eager to please anyone he found attractive.

'Hey Sam,' he said, standing up straight when he saw me.

'Hiya, Chrispy. I've got an appointment with the evil one in a few minutes, but I need to change, got a room I could use?'

'Uh, sure, toilets?' He pointed up the stairs.

'Kara might see me, and I want to look professional.' I leaned in and smiled. He met my eyes then looked down. Nervous. Sweet. 'Anywhere down here?'

He opened a door behind the desk and waved me into the small office. I pushed the door closed behind him, and looked around the small cluttered space. There were a couple of chairs and a desk, and a ton of unopened mail. Someone had put a Celtic calendar on the wall. I assumed none of the club's directors ever saw this room, because they'd not be happy about the calendar. I got changed into my suit. My hair was a mess from the day's work, but all I could do was comb it and hope for the best.

I thanked Chris on the way past, and he said, 'S-sure.'

Isn't that sweet?

I headed up the stairs to the hospitality suite, where Kara Pennan was already waiting. Kara worked some kind of magic trick. Despite me never wanting to look anything like the kind of person she was, within seconds of greeting her I always wondered what I could do to look more like her. She was tall and statuesque, with dark skin and a smile that never showed any signs of warmth. She was always smoothly turned out, in pressed, spotless clothes, and carried a glacial poise in every movement.

Kara stood up from one of the round tables and offered me her hand, then the double cheek kiss. 'Sam, darling,' she said. 'Thanks for coming.'

'What can I do for you?'

She lost her poise for a second. She bit her lip, and her face betrayed a youthfulness I'd never seen in her. 'I think my husband is cheating on me,' she said.

FIFTEEN
FERGUS
18:00

Killing people and disposing of the bodies are two different skill sets. People don't always think about that. Some people can take someone out, but are terrible at the clean-up. Others can make a body disappear, but struggle at turning a person into a corpse.

I'm at the top of the game because I'm good at both.

And I charge accordingly.

Joe has only paid me for the hit on this one. He wanted people to find Martin Mitchell. He wanted the death to make the news. So I'm halfway down a homemade burrito when Joe Pepper finally calls about the bodies. Joe is a decent guy. A good client. He always explains why the target needs to die, and most of the time he's telling the truth. He pays my whole fee in advance, which not many people are willing to do in the present financial climate.

(It's getting tough to be a killer in the city.)

The problem is, all clients think they know the job better than me.

Maybe that's universal. I expect someone who hires a roofer will then stand and tell the roofer exactly how it should be done. A plumber probably has to listen to a thesis on how to connect running water from the jamoke who hired him. And so it goes for me. It doesn't matter that I'm the guy you hire so that you don't have to worry about the dirty work, you'll still want to feel like I need direction.

I know Joe's going to call me. My little mess-up changes the game. But he's taking his time, and the idea of a burrito has been calling at me all day. My taste for them comes from the two years that I spent working in New York, when I first went freelance. But now they're everywhere. I think there are half a dozen places within two square miles in Glasgow, and I'm not complaining.

So I'm halfway down a barbacoa, with pinto beans and guac, when I get the call.

'Hi Joe.'

Joe doesn't bother with a greeting. 'Is this line good?'

Joe's with a political party, and those guys are obsessed with the thought that the newspapers might be listening in. And, let's be honest, they've got a point.

I have a contract phone in my own name, and Joe has that number, but it's never used for business. When I'm on the job, I rotate burners, a new one for each hit. I destroy the SIMs once they're used.

'Aye,' I say. 'This one's good, don't worry. I'll be switching it tonight.'

'I'm at the flat,' he says. 'What the fuck?'

Joe and me have a pretty easy-going relationship. But I can hear the nerves in his voice, and this isn't the time to make with the funny.

'Want a hand?'

That's a euphemism, really. Offering to help is *really* me offering to step in and clean it all up. For extra money, of course. When Joe says, yes, I tell him I'll be there in thirty minutes.

It's only a twenty-minute walk, but I want to finish my burrito. Food of the gods.

SIXTEEN
ALEX
18:00

Alex still hadn't told Kara about his plan. He'd been too self-conscious to do it before, too aware that it sounded a little bit mad. But now that he was following through, and meeting with professionals, it was time to fill her in.

She'd be important, after all. She was the one who would need to play along, grieve in public and collect the money.

Kara had been in meetings all day and hadn't returned any of his calls, so Alex decided to turn up at her work and surprise her. He drove out to Firhill, the football stadium where she worked. It was the home of Partick Thistle, a small football club that couldn't help being stuck in the same city as two of the biggest teams in the world.

Alex had found the location confusing when he first moved up here. Partick was farther to the south. It was part of the West End, where the students and hipsters lived. A football team based there could have been like a smaller, more Glaswegian version of Fulham, a club that aimed for some kind of hip boutique status.

Firhill wasn't down in that part of town, though. Almost as if the people who owned the team had wanted some kind of street cred, the football club bearing Partick's name was actually based in Maryhill. This was to the north of the city, and was much poorer and more run down.

It was fun to wind Kara up, though, so Alex still called it the West End.

Alex parked around the back of the stadium, in the staff-only area behind the Jackie Husband stand, and walked into the main reception. The young man behind the desk smiled and nodded a greeting. He had short blond hair and looked to be wearing foundation. The staff here always remembered who he was, because most of them worked for his wife and valued their jobs, but Alex could never remember their names.

'Hi, Mr P. Looking for Kara?'

He nodded that he was.

'She's up in the bar,' the young man said. 'She's meeting with someone, but I'm sure she won't mind if you let her know you're here.'

Alex mumbled a thank you and headed up the stairs. Firhill wasn't a large stadium. Space was limited, and most rooms served multiple purposes. The main bar was used on match days for corporate hospitality and private parties, but on weekdays it was often where staff would hold meetings. Although the bar itself was officially closed during the week, there was always someone around who could serve Alex a drink and find him a seat. And he never knew their names, either.

Kara was sitting at one of the large round tables near the bar. She was talking to another woman, someone who wasn't doing a great job of wearing a suit. It was creased and bunched up around her elbows, and Alex could smell the kind of spray deodorant in the air that he knew Kara would rather die than use. Kara turned to look at Alex as he walked in, and there was a smile that followed a few seconds later.

Kara stood up, and the young woman followed.

'Hi babe,' Alex said. He stepped closer and leaned in for a kiss.

Kara wrinkled her nose and then turned her cheek toward him. She'd smelled the booze on his breath. Alex knew she wouldn't call him on it while she was in business mode, but there would be a slight dig later on.

'Alex, this is Sam.' Kara gestured to the young woman, who put a hand out for a shake. 'Sam, this is my husband, Alex.'

'Hiya,' Sam said.

There was a light behind Sam's eyes. One of those people who've got a lot going on *up there*, Alex thought, that you want to find out about over too many drinks at a bar. That is, if she wasn't standing next to Kara. Alex had never met anyone quite like his wife. She was tall, and had poise, some kind of presence that made people notice when she walked in the room. Her parents had moved over from Kenya before she was born, and even though she was pure south London, there was always a little foreign tilt to her words that drove him nuts. And after three years in Scotland, a touch of Glaswegian had started to find its way into the mix.

'Sam's a private investigator,' Kara said. 'Isn't that amazing?'

Alex caught both the slight patronising edge to Kara's words and that Sam picked up on it. But all three of them moved past it and onto the next thought.

'I've never met a real PI,' Alex said. 'It must be an interesting job.'

'It has its moments,' Sam nodded. 'But mostly it's routine stuff. I serve a lot of legal papers, take pictures of cheating husbands.'

That hung in the air for a second, and Alex couldn't help wondering what Kara was meeting with a PI for. Was someone at the club up to no good? He turned to smile at her, and she read the question that he wasn't asking.

'Oh,' she said. She paused, and looked from Alex to Sam and back again. 'Someone's been mailing death threats to the club. To the players, I mean. Sam's going to look into it.'

'Sounds like fun,' Alex said.

Kara was lying. Alex knew that much. He didn't know the details, but it didn't matter. They each had secrets about their jobs. Alex had never told her where the company's money really came from, and there were things that went on at the club that Kara didn't talk about. That was fine. Alex had worked with enough footballers to know there's a code of silence over certain issues. Football isn't like a normal job. It's show business. There are certain pieces of information that need to be controlled, and if Kara needed to bring in a detective to look into something that was going on at the club, it probably wasn't any of Alex's business.

There was another pause. Alex realised Kara's meeting with Sam hadn't finished.

'Right, sorry,' he said. 'I'll let you kids carry on. I was just wondering,' he touched Kara softly on the arm, 'if you wanted to go out for dinner, maybe?'

Kara leaned in and kissed him on the cheek. 'Thanks, but I've got another couple of meetings after this. I should be home in time for us to get a good takeaway in, though. Watch a film?'

'Sure.' Alex managed to hold his smile in place and not look disappointed. 'No problem.' He put his hand up in a half wave at Sam. 'Nice to meet you.'

On his way back down to the car, Alex smiled. The rest of his plan had just come to him. He'd seen how bad Kara had been about explaining why Sam was there. She'd fumbled, and then told a lie, and there had almost been a sign above her head announcing that she wasn't telling the truth.

No way would she be able to go along with pretending he was dead. She'd give the game away in a second. The cops, the doctors and, especially, whoever it was that came looking for the money, they'd know something was wrong. It would be better if she believed it. Just to begin with, until the heat died down.

So. Okay. That was the plan sorted.

He needed to fake his own death.

And he couldn't tell Kara he was doing it.

SEVENTEEN
SAM
18:00

I'd never known what to make of Kara Pennan.

The club had first hired me to look into some threatening letters sent to them. She'd been friendly and gracious to me at the time. That changed once I started fooling around with Milo. I was a threat to the business. They still wanted my services as an investigator, but she became cold and aloof, and treated me with the kind of polite contempt that I assume they teach at schools down in London.

Standing in front of me at that table, she was shifting between the two. One second, the mask would be in place, the next I'd be seeing something else, something more nervous and tender. Then the mask again. It was like she was fighting to decide which version of herself to present.

I went with the only response I could think of.

'The little shit. What makes you think that?'

She liked that. She gave me a very real smile and then waved for me to take a seat. I pulled back a chair and sat at the round table. Kara sat down beside me. She made a show of picking up her phone and turning it off, so that I knew I was getting all of her valuable time.

'He's been acting odd,' Kara said. 'He's out all hours, and when he comes home he either smells of alcohol and nightclubs or, worse, he smells of nothing.'

'Nothing?'

I understood what she meant, and why it was a bad sign, but sometimes it's best to pretend. Kara liked to be in control, and I would get more out of the conversation by letting her lead it.

She fixed me with an aloof expression, putting me in my place. 'You're single, aren't you?'

'Yep.'

Excellent. That meant she was buying it.

'Well, if he comes home smelling of nothing, at the end of a long day? After being in the office in his suit? And then wherever he's been after that? To not smell of any of it? It means he's had a wash. It means he's covering something.'

'He could just be working late, washing at the office because he doesn't want the first thing you see of him each day to be a tired and sweaty guy.'

'He has a phone that he thinks I don't know about, too. A second phone. It doesn't show up on his bank statements, so I think it's pay-as-you-go. I've seen it a couple of times, it's a small black thing, flip top. It's got *buttons*.'

'Wow.'

'Right? He goes out of the room sometimes, touching the pocket that it's in, like he's about to take a call or answer a text. Other times, I've seen a big stack of mail come through the door in the morning, but later on about half of it's gone, like he's hiding some bank or credit card statements from me.'

Did married people spy on each other's bank statements? Not for the first time, the whole marriage thing seemed alien to me. I'd never been with a man that I really trusted, certainly not one I'd want to share my life with, but I clung on to the idea that marriage should be to someone I *did* trust.

Kara continued. 'He had a couple of travel brochures come through the door recently. Holiday destinations. But he never mentioned it, and the brochures disappeared.'

'And how have you two been getting on? I mean, you've listed a load of stuff there that sounds bad, but it's all in how the two of you are, aye? It could all be innocent.'

'He's been distant in the last couple of months. He's always looking over his shoulder when we're out, and he doesn't talk much. It used to take a gag to get him to shut up, he always wanted to share his opinions.'

'He's from London, too, aye?'

'Yeah. We came up for his work. He's never liked it here. He thinks everyone's out to get him, because he's English. But I keep telling him, I'm English, too, and I love it here.'

There was something off in what she was saying. More to the point, it was in the way she was saying it. The confusion I'd noticed at the start, between the two different personas, had carried on. She was switching in and out, sometimes in control, sometimes nervy. The more she did it, the more it felt like a performance. Was she playing me?

The door at the far end of the room opened, and a man in a suit walked in. He looked familiar, like maybe I'd met him at a club party or something. He seemed tired, and a little empty, but he hid it all under a fake tan. He saw Kara before me, but then I couldn't help but notice he kept looking at me more.

Kara stood up, and after a few seconds so did I.

He looked from me back to Kara. 'Hi babe.'

When he leaned in to kiss her, I figured out he was the husband. See, I'm a detective. I pick up on clues like that. Kara offered her cheek for his lips, then turned to bring me into the conversation. 'Alex, this is Sam. Sam, this is my husband, Alex.'

'Hiya,' I said.

There was alcohol in his eyes. His jawline was starting to soften with a couple of extra pounds, and he carried himself like he was in denial about it.

'Sam's a private investigator,' Kara said. 'Isn't that amazing?'

There was a patronising edge to Kara's words that I didn't like. Maybe she'd not meant it. She could have been trying to mask the awkwardness of Alex coming in, but all I heard was, 'This is Sam, she has a funny little career, isn't that cute?'

'I've never met a real PI,' Alex said. We shared a look that told me he'd noticed the edge to Kara's words too. For just a moment, we were on the same side. 'It must be an interesting job.'

He looked me up and down again. I sometimes wonder; are men even aware of how often they check out our boobs? Like, is it a conscious thing, or just the way their eyes work? Kara's tone, plus Alex's wandering eyes, were putting me in a bad mood. I decided to play rough. 'Mostly it's routine stuff. I serve a lot of legal papers, take pictures of cheating husbands.'

I watched for their reactions.

Alex looked blank. He didn't seem to be aware that there was any relevance to what I'd said. A guilty man tends to act guilty. Hit them on whatever they're hiding, and you'll see it in their eyes. I got nothing off him. Kara, on the other hand, shifted her feet a little, changed her stance. It was a reaction I'd been expecting off Alex, not her.

Interesting.

EIGHTEEN
FERGUS
18:30

I have a moment of panic when I walk into the flat. I mean, I know I've been fucking things up a wee bit lately, but I definitely remember killing *two* people, and there are *three* stiffs on the floor.

I go for the only response I can think of as I look down at the third body. 'Huh.'

It's a bloke. Looks like a Ned. Wearing a trackie and Adidas trainers. Too many stripes. There's a small bullet hole beneath his left eye, and a much bigger entry wound at the back of his head. None of that surprises me, of course. Once you've seen one daft idiot shot in the head, you've seen them all.

The odd thing is that it was a damn good shot.

And it wasn't me.

Joe sits down on the bed. I notice he's wearing black gloves, which is handy because so am I. Neither of us are going to be leaving prints in this place, we're not fucking amateurs.

'Who?' I point to the third stiff.

'Cal. Cal Gibson.'

'Gibson?' I don't believe in coincidences in Glasgow. 'Any relation?'

Joe nods. 'Son.'

Mike Gibson is a bit of a name. There have been a lot of changes in Glasgow over the last few years. A lot of the old guard have retired, or been pushed out. A whole bunch of them died last year when the media got hold of a cover-up gone wrong. MHW had paid for me to help in the clean-up, I took out a lawyer who was trying to blackmail them. But Mike Gibson survived. He was one of the big men in the Southside when I was younger, before I left for the military. He was a loan shark, and shared in a lot of the prostitution and gambling businesses with Rab Anderson and the Washer Lady. Now he's semi-legit. He just operates as a landlord in the city centre, with buildings he bought from the council on the cheap, then received grants from the same council to renovate the properties at taxpayers' expense.

That's all well and good, but—

'Why is Gibson's son here?'

Joe looks like he's struggling a bit with all of this. His mouth keeps flexing, biting back on emotions. He's pale, sullen and gulping a lot. I've seen this reaction before. Grief. I just about remember it.

'He was up to something. Some scam. He said this was his Babycham.' He looks up at me with a face that says, *Yeah, I know, stupid*. 'His masterpiece. He knew Porter was going to be here.'

I don't like this. Joe's talking as if he spoke to Cal, which means that Joe was here before the kid died. There are two different scenarios here, and neither one is good.

First, it could mean he bought someone else in to clean up my work. If one pro comes in to fix a mess left by another, then the first guy's days are numbered.

Second, it could mean that Joe did it himself.

It's a *really* good shot. Professional.

'Joe, you got someone else hitting for you?'

He doesn't answer.

If there's someone else in the game, I need to find out who. Two contractors on the same turf can lead to problems. Clearly, this other killer isn't as good at the clean-up as me, otherwise I wouldn't be here. That buys me some time. Joe still needs me.

But there's a clock ticking.

'Uh, Joe? What's going on here?'

He shrugs. 'I don't actually know. This was supposed to be simple. You do Mitchell, we let someone find him, huge press story, and the right people get the message. Porter wasn't part of the plan. Cal wasn't part—' He pauses. I see a light go on behind his eyes. 'Shit,' he says. 'Cal mentioned someone else. Pauline? Paula? Said she was missing, which, baws, he thought she would be here.'

Shitey shitey shite.

If Joe hadn't dropped Cal himself, I'd be tempted to fess up. Tell the truth and say, crap, sorry man, there was a woman here but I let her go. He knows that hit men tend to leave prozzies alone. Like a code.

But now? No way. He might drop me, and I don't know where his gun is.

'There was nobody else here,' I say.

He stares at me for a second, but there's no real heat to it. He looks like he's already moved on to the next thing, to figuring out what the hell this mess is, and to how he's going to fix it.

That's what Joe does. He fixes Glasgow's messes.

Joe looks down at Cal. 'What did you do?' Then back at me. 'This changes the plan. I don't know why Dom was here, or who else was working with Cal. I can't have anything unexpected before the ninth.'

'What's happening on the ninth?'

He looks up at me. I can see he hadn't meant to mention the date. He's let something slip. 'Nothing,' he says. 'Forget it.'

Joe walks around the flat in silence for a while, moving from room to room. His hands in his pockets. He's doing that thing where his mouth twitches from side to side, like he's sucking on a sweet. I stand and watch from the bedroom doorway, giving him the time to think. He opens the front door and leans out into the hallway, as if looking for something, then shuts the door and comes back toward me.

'Okay,' he says. 'I need to figure out what happened here. Why the fuck was Dom here? Jeez. Look, clean them all away. Then torch the place. Make sure the fire alarms go off just before the flat goes up, so everyone else in the building has time to get out. I'll pay you for getting rid of Mitchell and Cal, but Porter's on you.'

That seems fair.

NINETEEN
SAM
18:30

My gut told me something was wrong with Kara's case. Phil called this feeling my *Spidey sense*. I couldn't put my finger on why, but I felt she was holding something back. Kara is slick and professional. Everything she'd said had convinced me her husband was cheating on her, but there was more to it.

Still, it was a paying job, so I told Kara I'd look into it. I didn't need to quote prices or hourly rates, because she already knew the details. The phone app allows clients to keep track of how many hours I've logged on their case.

Chris let me into the office to change back into the cargo shorts, and I rolled my suit up back into the bag. Chris worked really hard at acting like he wasn't trying to look. I gave him top marks for the effort. I cycled back out onto the canal path and rode for a few hundred yards, enough to make sure I was out of earshot of the stadium. Then I called my brother.

He answered straight away. 'Take the job?'

'You don't even know what it is yet.'

'True. But I know the client, and they pay on time. So, take the job?'

I shook my head, which was pointless on the phone. 'It's not the club. Kara's hiring me privately.'

Phil didn't answer straight away. He was thinking it through. 'Okay. So, there's gossip, then?'

'She says her husband is cheating on her. But, I don't know, something feels off.'

'She's good for the money though, aye?'

'She'll be good for all the extra hours we charge her, totally.' It was my turn to pause. 'But I want to keep my eyes on her for a while. Something feels a little off here.'

Phil saw what was coming. 'Oh no, no no, nu uh.'

'Phil—'

'Not happening. You do the legwork, not me.'

I changed my tone, went for the pleading sister trick. It usually worked. 'Please, Phil. You can keep all the money for the hours you work. I just don't like the idea that she's playing us. I want to see what she's up to, and you can follow her husband for a while.'

I could hear in his response that my tone change had worked. He hadn't said *Yes* yet, but he was getting there. 'Not that you're letting your previous get in the way here.'

I played innocent. 'What do you mean?'

'Well, she did tell your boy toy to dump you, right? In some worlds, that would mean the two of you are now mortal enemies. Locked in a rivalry that can only be settled by a fight to the death. I saw a movie about it, *The Hunger Games*.'

'That wasn't a documentary, Philomena.'

'Aye, I suppose. But what I'm meaning is, I know people who would pay good money to see that. Can we talk about broadcasting rights?'

'You're not helping.'

'No way. The fight would be all down to you. I'd hold the camera, though. Do some commentary.'

'You know what I mean.'

'You know what I mean, too. You and Kara have previous. I know you don't like her, but are you sure that's not influencing you here? Just because she's a bitch, doesn't mean she can't be right about this. Especially since a man is involved. A man will stick his dick in anything. Well, anything except me, it seems.'

'Phil—'

'Sorry.'

'But I take your point. You're right, I don't like her, and I'd love for her to be wrong about this, or trying something on. But, you know, I still think I'm right. My gut says something is off here, and I want to stick close to her for a while.'

'Jeezo, a girl uncovers one massive conspiracy, and suddenly she's Jim Rockford. Okay, I'll play along. But remember, I'm getting the money for these hours.'

'Thanks, I'll owe you one.'

'Yep.'

My phone had vibrated a couple of times while we were talking. The sign of either a voicemail or SMS. My handset was on its last legs, and the screen was prone to freezing. I sat for a couple of minutes while it still said I was on the call to Phil, even though he'd hung up. I used all the skills I would have picked up on an IT course, and switched the phone off and on again. Once it had restarted, I could see the three text messages from Hanya.

Three witnesses describe a woman on a bike.

And:

It's going to take 24 hrs for me to get all the CCTV.

Also:

Let's go for a drink tonight.

It was unusual for Hanya to play this game. We're best friends, sure, but she still has a job to do. Of the few times I've strayed into one of her cases, she's usually pulled me in straight away to get the statement over with. There was only one case when she'd given me the room to do my own thing, and that had been when her old partner, John Cummings, had been in trouble. She hadn't been sure whose side her bosses were on, and she'd let me snoop around.

Why was she giving me the leeway on this one?

I pushed that away. I had more pressing mysteries to deal with. One, Paula Lucas was dead after handing me some cassettes. The other, Kara Pennan was playing some kind of game.

But she was paying me for it, so this was a game I was willing to play.

TWENTY
FERGUS
19:00

The actual clean-up is pretty easy. Always is. The trick, as with anything else, is to get the professionals in.

Undertakers deal with death every day. Nobody bats an eyelid to them having corpses in their vans, and cops almost never stop them. They're allowed to go anywhere and everywhere, and they're experts at making dead people vanish. In every city in the world, if you need to get rid of a stiff, there will be an undertaker that will deal with it. For the right price.

I have a regular subcontractor in central Scotland. They have branches in both Glasgow and Edinburgh, and several towns in between. A couple of quick calls to my contact there, and a half hour wait, and then two guys are in the flat with me cleaning up the mess and carrying the bodies away discreetly in bags, down to a waiting van. They may as well be invisible. If passers-by see paramedics, cops or firemen, they're going to rubberneck. If they see an undertaker, they look the hell away.

Once the cleaners are gone, I head out into the hallway and set off one of the main smoke alarms. It's loud and insistent, an electronic beep that pulses around my brain and makes my ears try and shut down for a while.

Back inside the flat, I listen as people in the building start to make their way down the stairs, grumbling that this better not be a drill. Fire crews can take around four minutes to arrive in the city, and a few well-placed flames will take this place up in roughly the same time. Factor in that they'll need to get up the stairs, identify which flat the alarm originates from, and evacuate the remainder of the building.

I have time.

I don't start the fire in the bedroom or bathroom, though. That would be amateur hour. The fire investigators will focus on the room where the problems started, and I can't have that be the same place where they might find forensic traces of death.

I start in the living room. There are two bookcases stuffed with an odd mix: Marxist tomes and spy novels. Everyone thinks that books are a fire hazard. They're not. They burn, sure, but most things *burn*. What you want is something that will spread the fire. Something like, say, a wooden bookcase. I take my Zippo to the nearest shelf and pull out a couple of books, lighting them, then dropping them back onto the shelf.

Then I look around at the furniture. An expensive-looking leather couch isn't going to help me much. But the cheaper-looking fabric chairs on either side? Bingo. I take a few seconds to get each one burning. They go up straight away, spilling chemical fumes and smoke into the air around them.

The building is old, but the inside looks to have been renovated more recently, and the flat has fire doors, with small chains that are meant to pull them closed. Fortunately, Mitchell has each one propped open with a small plastic door stop, so the flames will spread.

I watch from the hallway as the walls start to go. Mitchell's cheap and bland landscape photographs start to curl and blacken. The smoke is climbing out of the living room now and crawling along the ceiling toward me. I need to get out, but I want to make sure the flames are spreading. At the first sign of their red and amber edges eating into the doorframe, I turn and head out the front door.

I pull it shut behind me and feel the Yale locks click into place. This floor is deserted now, but I can still hear people moving about elsewhere in the building. The fire alarm drills into my skull as I stand beneath it, but it doesn't stop me hearing fire engines out in the city, trying to make their way here through the one-way system.

A different sound makes its way through the electronic pulse in my ears. Someone breathing heavily, struggling to move. I turn to look down the stairs behind me, but can't see anything. There is another flight of stairs at the end of the small hallway, this one leading up to the next floor. I run to the bottom step and look up. There's an old lady struggling at the top, making it down one slow step at a time with frail-looking legs. I can see a walking stick on the floor at the top, abandoned. She has a cat carrier in each hand, and is fighting for control of them as the animals inside run around, terrified of all the noise.

What the hell is a woman so frail doing living up so high?

I head up to her, taking the steps two at a time. I start to talk, but she looks at me with a firm squint and shakes her head. 'Deaf as a post,' she shouts. 'Need my kids.'

It takes me a second to realise she's meaning the cats.

Right.

Okay.

I smile at her and take both carriers, one in each hand. The animals are heavy, and not at all happy about any single part of the current situation. They're threatening to pull my hands clean off at my wrists, so I don't know how she was managing. I stick out my elbow, and she takes the hint, looping her arm through mine. I guide her down to the ground floor, taking each step slowly, but quicker than she was managing on her own.

As we hit the lobby, the firemen are coming in. They step aside to let us out, then run up the stairs, shouting out commands and calling for anyone left in the building. There are cops outside. I hand the two carriers back to the woman with a smile, then slip away into the crowd.

Okay.

I've killed two people, disposed of three bodies, and torched an apartment.

I think it's time to go visit my parents.

TWENTY-ONE
ALEX
19:00

Alex drove home. The Pennans lived in a decent-sized house in Westerton, north-west of the city. It looked like a single-storey building from the front, but from the back the upstairs was visible, looking out onto a large garden, and to a small wooded area behind the property that crested the hill.

There was a note pushed through the front door. A clumsy scrawl written on the back of an old betting slip. Alex had hired a builder named Keith to do some renovation work in the back garden. They were installing decking at the back door, where a big gas barbecue could be kept for summer nights like this, and a water feature in the far corner, a fountain that ran down to a small brook.

They'd given Keith a key to the garage, for full access to water and tools, but Alex hadn't been dumb enough to let him get into the house while they were out, and he communicated in a series of notes written on ever more random slips of paper. The note asked for Alex to give him a call as soon as he got in.

Keith had an odd accent. He'd been living in Glasgow for a couple of decades, but he grew up in Fife. It was as if someone had purposely designed a dialect just to confuse Alex. Keith ended every other sentence with, 'Ken?' Alex had only just learned that meant, 'Understand?'

It seemed a pretty flawed approach. If you want to ask whether someone gets what you're saying, you should probably phrase the question itself in a way that people can understand.

Talking to Keith was going to be a struggle. Alex would need a little more in the tank first, to take the edge off the meeting with that prick of a hit man. The guy had called him on it. He'd figured out Alex's plan, and now he'd feel like he could hold it over him.

Alex knew that meant he should find someone else, but he didn't know how. He'd only found Fergus by accident, following a trail of numbers on a few of his clients' accounts. He could ask Joe Pepper. Joe was working with him on a big project for Asma Khan. MHW was buying out the old guard across the city, everything from gang leaders and drug dealers to law firms and money launderers. The cartel behind MHW wanted to own the city, and they were close to getting it.

Which was precisely why he *couldn't* talk to Joe about it. He was one of the very people he needed to keep out of this.

He'd need to figure out a way to convince Fergus to reconsider. And a way to keep him from talking about it.

Bollocks. Well, first things first. He crossed the living room, a large white space decorated to Kara's tastes with sparse furniture and a few weird pieces of art on the wall. *Conversation starters*, that's what Kara called them. Well, anytime Alex had invited people around, they'd consciously avoided talking about the art, so how did that work?

Between the living room and the large open-plan kitchen was a wooden bar, the kind that millionaires had in movies. It was stocked with whisky, gin, vodka and a few bottles of flavoured stuff that Alex had never been desperate enough to try. The bar had been part of the deal he'd made with Kara about the decorations. She could have everything else just the way she wanted, as long as he could have this.

Alex downed a generous finger of Talisker, and prepared a second, this time with ice. He liked a fast first hit to take the edge off the day, but afterwards he'd slow it down, take his time and sip at the drink. Maintain a gentle buzz.

He read through Keith's note a second time. Something about needing a special kind of hosepipe to install the water feature. Bollocks to that. Alex picked up the phone and dialled Keith's number, just about legible in the note.

'Howya,' Keith said, in a slightly drunken Irish lilt. Apparently adding a second accent to his collection. 'Thanks for calling, neebor.'

'How are we getting on?' Alex took a look out through the French doors at the back, which opened out onto where the decking was supposed to be. 'I don't see decking. Or a water feature.'

'Aye, well, here's the 'hing.' Keith's voice dropped, making this sound like he was letting Alex in on some secret. 'It's gonnae need a different kind of hosepipe.'

Alex knew for a fact there were five different hoses in the garage. Each of them thick enough, and long enough, for what Keith needed. Alex had looked the specifications up on the internet before they hired the guy.

'We have hoses,' Alex said. 'You said they'd be fine.'

'Aye. I know. Well, I wis wrang. See, it needs to be a special kind of rubber, aye? One that'll hold out through the winters without cracking, like. Ye ken? And one that moles can't chew through.'

Alex looked out again at the back garden. The lawn was perfect. The only marks were patches of mud trailed across by Keith himself. 'We don't have any moles.'

'Well no' the noo, no. But if they find out you've got a hosepipe in there . . .'

Was Alex hearing this right? Was Keith trying on some kind of protection racket, with moles as his mafia backup? Jesus cocking Christ. Half of Alex really wanted to lay into this guy, tear him apart, verbally. The other half wanted to go and get Kara, ask her to do it. Alex preferred to leave confrontation to her, because she handled people so well. Kara could speak to an idiot in such a calm and controlled way that she would get things done without a fuss.

But Kara wasn't here, so it was going to have to be option A.

'Fine.' Alex said. 'You go and search for this special hosepipe. I'll drive down to B&Q and buy a normal one, then pay someone *half* what we're paying you to fit the cocking thing. Or, better yet, I'll type it into Google, find the instructions, and do it myself. How's that?'

Keith clearly hadn't expected this. There was a pause on the line.

'Look, I'm no trying to scam you.'

'No. You're just trying to trick me out of money, which is a whole different thing. Now, are you going to finish the job tomorrow or am I finding one of the thousands of people round here who can do it?'

Keith grunted something. Alex couldn't tell sometimes whether the noises were words or simply sounds. He could hear Keith moving around, away from the phone, and guessed that he might have been asking Alex to hold.

Alex smiled. Dammit, he was enjoying this. Maybe he should thank the builder for the entertainment.

'Sorry about that.' Keith came back on the line. 'I was just looking for the 'hingmy, you ken?'

'What?'

'The hose. Aye. I've just found one on my shelf here that'll do the trick just fine. I'd just forgot I had it, aye?'

'Funny that.'

'Ach, one of they 'hings. Just bein' daft, you ken? But I've got one the noo, so it's all sorted.'

'Excellent. Those magic hosepipes must be very popular. It's so good that you had one spare.'

'Aye, and it'll no' cost you anything extra, don't you worry neebor.' Keith waited for a moment, as if he thought Alex would acknowledge his generosity. Then he said, 'Aye, well. That's us sorted, then. I should get back to this thing, I'll be back round the morra.'

Alex disconnected the call and drained the glass. He stood up and poured himself another drink, then set the glass down and laughed. That call had been perfect. It had let him feel in control again.

And now he knew how to get Fergus onside.

TWENTY-TWO

SAM

19:35

'Hello. Hey. Where are you?'

What? Oh right.

I'd met Hanya at her favourite bar. Taking her up on the offer of a drink. But my mind kept drifting back to both Paula and Kara.

'Sorry, Han. It's been a strange day.'

'You're telling me.'

I'd tried to follow Kara, but lost her. Surveillance on a bike is a tricky thing. You can't do a stakeout, because people in the street will notice a cyclist standing around for hours. On the other hand, it's a good way to tail a driver. Once someone is behind the wheel of a car, they pretty much forget that cyclists exist. I can get right up close behind a driver, and they won't notice me. There is one obvious downside to this, though, and it was exposed when Kara pulled out into the road in her car. She turned the other way, and drove uphill at speed.

Crap.

I'd texted Phil to let me know when Kara turned up at the Pennan house, then headed into town to meet Hanya.

Hanya looked great. She'd changed out of her work clothes and into a sleek silk-looking blouse under a cream jacket. Hanya could be a bit of a clothes-horse at times.

We met outside The FuBar, a small bar down from street level on Bath Street. It was in a good spot, but had never really taken off. They played low jazzy music during the day, then switched up to a mix of nineties' indie and pop in the evening. It had a steady flow of customers, usually cops, lawyers and hangers on, and it was a good place for someone like Hanya to meet guys who understood the score: *Nothing serious, we all have work in the morning.*

We sat outside on a small metal table that had one leg shorter than the other. It wobbled every time we set our drinks down, so we'd agreed the only sensible thing to do was to keep holding them. And drink quicker, just to avoid the temptation to put them down.

'It's a joke,' said Hanya.

Crap. I'd drifted off into my head again, and had no idea what she'd been saying. I judged from the tone that this *wasn't* a joke. She was annoyed. I bluffed a response. 'You're kidding on.'

'I wish I was. Anyway.' Hanya sipped from her drink then leaned forward. Her shoulders squared, and she gave me a look that said, *Listen, I'm getting serious now.* 'So, listen, I logged into your vLove account today. After we talked.'

Wait, she wasn't talking about the case? No. She meant the dating site. Great. Hanya had the log in details because she'd been the one to set up the account and download the app to my phone. It had been here in FuBar that we'd recorded the video, and I'd had just enough drink in me to go along with it.

'After we talked? Before or after you started a murder investigation, Han?'

Hanya stiffened. 'I'm not on that case. It's weird.'

'What do you mean?'

'I ran her name into the system. Came back with nothing. No national insurance, no address, absolutely nothing. But it must have flagged *something* because the feds came in and took it off us. I've been moved over to some arson job.'

The feds was new cop slang. An in-joke aimed at the people working up in Gartcosh. The Scottish government had reorganised the police force in Scotland, merging all the regional forces into one organisation, *Police Scotland*. Gartcosh was the site of the new organisation's big white bull, the *Crime Campus*. They would send detectives out to major cases, parachuting in to take over the investigations. Local cops around Scotland had come to see these visiting officers like the FBI in America.

'So her name was on some list?' I said. 'Must've been.'

There's a look cops sometimes give me. Hanya's old partner, John Cummings, had been a master of it. It was a signal to do the opposite of whatever they were saying. If his mouth was telling me to *Stay out of the case*, his eyes might be saying, *Keep in the loop*.

Hanya gave me that look as she said, 'Don't get involved, Sam. And whatever you've got, hand it straight over to them.'

She was as interested as me. Hanya was a professional, and policing was simply her job. She didn't take work home the way I did. But territoriality was different, and the feds had made it personal by taking it off her.

'Anyway,' Hanya continued. Moving us both on. 'Sam, you've got *loads* of guys liking your page. Have you looked?'

I rolled my eyes hard enough for people to see them two streets away. 'No, I told you, I'm not interested in any of that. Han, I'm fine. I don't need help.'

'When was the last time you had anything between your legs that was old enough to remember Euro '96?' The problem with Hanya being English was that all of her football references were

English, too. I swear she mentioned 1966 every other time we spoke. She also kept forgetting the age difference between us.

'Han, *I* only just remember Euro '96.'

'Okay, wean, take a look at the site.'

She wasn't going to give up unless I humoured her. I could make a show of it, at least. Look at a few of the pages, pretend I was thinking about contacting any of the guys. I picked my phone up off the table and loaded the app. A number glowed red at the bottom of the page, showing how many people had liked my profile. It was now down to me to decide whether I was going to return the gesture to any of them, which would then put us in contact.

Each member had their own page, where we could upload videos. Blogs. Links. Whatever. Hanya had been using it for a couple of months, and her page was filled with short clips of her trying to be funny and opinionated.

My page just had the one video. The one we'd filmed here.

I pressed the icon for the first profile. A video started to play. The guy was cute. Brown hair, stubble that looked to be carefully maintained, and a lopsided smile. He was talking about himself, telling me his name was Billy, and he was twenty-six. He looked poised. Too poised. I didn't want someone who was going to be reading a script when he spoke to me. Even in the hypothetical world where I would follow up on these leads, I wanted it to be someone I liked the look of.

I swiped the screen to the left, which told the dating service I didn't want any more from Billy.

'What was his username?' Hanya was typing into her own phone. 'I want to look him up.'

'BillyAndWhizz22.'

'Ah, okay, maybe I won't.'

The second profile loaded. A guy with a goatee trying to be way funnier than he could manage. No way. I swiped him to the left.

The third person popped up. He was okay looking. Not a stud, by any measurement. Billy probably had him beat on that score. But there was something else there, something, I don't know, *hurt?*

No way, Sam.

Not happening.

You're not taking on any more fixer-uppers.

Hanya giggled, and I looked up. 'You've got that look on your face,' she said.

'What look?'

'The *patron saint of whoever* look.'

I made a *phsssst* noise, and pretended not to know what she was talking about. I clicked the video again, and this time listened to the words.

'Hi my name's Fergus. I'm thirty years old, and I, ummm. This is daft, aye? Look, my sister put me up to this. I have a hard time meeting people. I like action films, I like the music I listened to when I was a teenager. I like trying to make people laugh.'

My finger hovered over the screen.

I paused, laughed at myself, then swiped.

TWENTY-THREE
FERGUS
19:33

My parents live in a modern house in Barrowfield Street, in the East End. Celtic Park sits at the end of the road, which is kind of funny because my old man, Ronnie, is a Rangers fan. I didn't follow him into that faith, which is just one of the many small acts of rebellion I've carried out over the years.

I'm not sure where he'd sit on the whole 'killing people for money' thing.

That's not true. I do know. It's why I don't tell him.

Sometimes I think I should feel guilty for lying to my parents about what I do for a living. But my best mate is thirty years old and still hides the fact that he smokes from his mum, so I reckon I'm probably doing the right thing.

My folks used to live in Shawlands, on the Southside, which is where I grew up. They moved to Barrowfield Street for my sister, Zoe. She has cerebral palsy, and they got a grant from the Scottish government to make some renovations to the old house for wheelchair access, but it was easier to convert this newer build. The move also put them within walking distance of the new Emirates Arena, and the council gym there has exercise programmes specifically for disabled people, so my sister is getting to have more fun these days.

I earn enough that I could have paid for the renovations myself, but my parents refuse to take any money from me. Joke's on them, really, because I've been topping up their pension payments for years and they've not noticed.

I park out front and let myself in. I've got a key, but the door isn't locked. I keep telling them about that. Anybody can walk in off the street. And they do, but usually for a coffee or a bottle of beer. The Fletcher household has always been an open door to people who want to drop by. My old man used to be a union leader back in the old days, and people across the Southside always knew they could drop by at any hour of the day and Ronnie or Irene Fletcher would make sure they had a drink and some food.

These days it's mostly people my parents' age, pensioners who drop in for a coffee and some warm nostalgia.

I find them out in the back garden, sat on the new patio enjoying the evening heat. Heatwaves might be rare in Glasgow, but we have that shit down. The minute the sun comes out, we're in a garden or a field, layering on the suncream and looking for the nearest raincloud to judge whether we've got time to get a barbecue on the go.

True to form, my folks have a barbecue on the go.

Dad greets me with a handshake; then his attention goes back to the meat on the grill. Blackened sausages and a couple of burgers that are heading in the same direction. They smell great, but they'll taste like arse. Their version of a barbecue is just old-school British grilling: stick some meat on a grill and cook until black, then cover with red or brown sauce and some bread. The taste, and smell, of summer.

'Grab yersel' a beer, son,' Dad says, in his croaky old voice. 'Plenty in the fridge.'

Mum's sat in a folding lounger, reading a book. There's no sign of my sister.

'Where's Zoe?'

Mum doesn't even look up from her book. Must be a good one. 'She's up the gym,' she says. 'Her club's got a special night on tonight, Olympics theme.'

'She liking it there?'

Dad answers without looking up. 'Aye. Course. But you know Zoe, she has to pretend like it's a chore. We see her smile, though, right enough.'

He hands me a hot dog. The sausage is buried in sauce. I haven't got the heart to tell him I've already eaten. Besides, what kind of idiot says no to a hot dog? I bite into it, squirting sauce across the patio floor, and start to chew my way through the layer of charcoal.

I look down at the book my mum's reading. *Girl Meets Boy on a Crime Spree,* by A.N. Smith. It's the one everyone's talking about on the TV. 'Any good?'

She shuts the book, with her thumb pressed between the pages to keep her place. 'Don't know, do I? Someone just stopped me reading it.' She waits for my smile before carrying on. 'It's good, aye. Too much swearing, but that's just the way now. Like on the telly.'

'What's it about?'

'I'm not really sure. Mostly about house-cleaning so far. I think she's got some dark secret, and she doesn't like her husband. It's part of a series, they were all on display in the shop. This girl, she gets trains, has tattoos, kicks things, all sorts.'

'I don't think it's a series, Mum. They just call all books the same thing now.'

'Like you're the expert on reading, all of a sudden?' Dad comes and sits on the empty lounger next to Mum. He hands me an open bottle of beer, and mumbles about me being too lazy to get one myself.

'I've read whole books,' I say, a little too defensively.

Dad smiles and bends down to pick up his own book from beneath the chair. It's a biography of Leon Trotsky. I half expect it to be called *The Girl Who Met The Revolutionary.*

My phone goes. My real one, the contract in my name. It's a text message from Alex Pennan.

I didn't give him my real number.

What the hell?

TWENTY-FOUR
ALEX
20:40

'How did you get my number?'

Fergus, who had given his name to Alex as Ross Douglas, sat down at the bar. Alex had arranged to meet him at a small place just under a mile from the house, somewhere he could walk to, without bringing Fergus too close to his home patch.

As Fergus sat down, Alex noticed a small blotch of ketchup on the guy's T-shirt. An extra little humanising detail that helped take the edge off the first impression. Alex wasn't scared of this guy now.

'That's not important, Fergus.' Alex smiled. He watched as it registered across the prick's face that Alex knew his real name. 'What *does* matter is that I have it. And your address. And your parents'.'

Fergus leaned in close. He smelled of charcoal. 'You think it's a good idea to threaten someone in my line of work?'

Alex nodded, raised his pint in a mock salute. 'It's your line of work that means I can threaten you. All I'm asking is that you do this job for me. And I'm offering you your usual going rate. But if you don't, and I have to get someone else to do the job, I might give him a few extra hits to carry out. Real ones. Or maybe I'll be nice, and just let the cops and press know what you do for a living.'

Alex had found out about Fergus by accident.

While he'd been following the trails of money that didn't exist, and working out how much of it could easily *not exist* in his own bank account, he started to notice who his clients were paying money *to*. It didn't take much to figure out what some of those payments were for. Once he accepted that he was working for criminals, well, it didn't take much to figure out what kind of people they would be paying.

He had a file on his hard drive full of the contact details for the businesses, private contractors and 'consultants' that money was sent to. He'd noticed one particular insurance firm received payments from more than half of his clients, always in multiples of five grand. Joe Pepper had made payments a number of times recently. The real kicker was when he found payments going from a company that had been set up for Asma Khan. It was a small investment firm on paper, but in reality it was a way for Khan to pay people quickly and quietly.

A quick check with Companies House down in London also confirmed that the insurance firm itself was clearly a front. But it was easy to follow the trail. Alex pulled on the thread, and it led right back to a small security firm in Glasgow. There were three board members, and two of them had the same surname. Fletcher.

One other bolt of inspiration had struck Alex as he looked at all of this information. He checked the dates of the payments, and then started searching the news in internet caches. Newspapers, Google, the BBC.

People died around those dates.

Some of the names were famous, some were nobodies. Some had been found dead, some had never been found at all. Khan had made a number of payments all around the same time, the previous summer. Alex remembered there had been a local gang war around then, triggered when a detective had gained fifteen minutes of fame and uncovered an arson scam that most of the old guard had been in on.

Holy shit.

This guy was a hit man.

A real life, bona fide, hit man.

Like in the movies.

That was when Alex had known he could make off with the money. And the perfect guy to help him do it. Now the hit man was sitting next to Alex at the bar, slumping in his seat, and caving in.

'Okay. So, I'm going to kill you. And you don't want to know where, and you don't want to know when, or even how. And you don't want me to actually kill you.'

'Well, I suppose—'

'What?'

'I suppose I've always wanted to go out with a bang. Something big. A death that makes people wonder how well the guy lived. You know, like if I was given an hour to live, I'd love to get absolutely loaded on drink or drugs. Get an absolute skinful of all the things you're too scared to take normally. Then, I think, get in a car and drive. Really go for it.'

Alex liked that. Hell, maybe someone would make a film about it. Or a TV movie, at least. And the best thing? He'd be able to watch it.

'Car explosion,' Fergus said. 'Easy enough.'

'Don't tell me.' Wait, there was something else. 'Oh, and nobody can know about this.'

Fergus gave him a *No shit, Sherlock* look. 'I had assumed that.'

'Yeah, of course. No. Um. What I mean is my wife can't know. Not until afterwards.'

'And are you sure you can trust her?'

Wait, what?

'Wait, what?'

Fergus leaned back and smiled. His anger and nerves had gone. 'Well, let's be honest. We both know you're stealing from some *very* rich people. I assume you've got accounts ready. If you're technically dead, all of your money belongs to her. Are you sure she'll share it with you, once you're dead?'

That hung in the air for a while. Alex knew Fergus was just messing with him. Fighting to regain a little control. Fuck him. Kara was his rock. She'd own all of his public money. The life insurance and the house. But she didn't know about his *real* reserves. The money he'd been stealing. And she wouldn't mess him about when her told her. Sure, she'd be pissed at him for lying, for not letting her in on the plan. But once she calmed down, she'd be golden.

Fergus smiled again, and Alex got a bad feeling. 'Your other problem,' Fergus said, 'is that if you *did* try and expose me to the press, or the cops, then you'd be selling yourself out, too. Because the obvious question would be, why were you having business dealings with a hit man?'

Alex tried a bluff. 'I've been recording our conversations. I can just say it was a sting, that I was leading you on in order to get a confession on tape. Besides—' He was thinking on his feet, but his voice got stronger, he was sure he had the winning hand now. 'What would they try and get me on? I'm hiring you to *not* kill me.'

'Aye.' Fergus shrugged. 'Maybe. Maybe you'd skate on that, if they overlooked the whole conspiracy to commit fraud. But even still, you'd have a bigger problem than that. Whatever it is, this thing you've got planned, the pay-out you're looking for, you wouldn't be able to do it. Selling me out would ruin whatever you've got cooking.' Fergus paused. Scratched his nose slowly. Easy. Letting Alex know he was in charge again, just like the last meeting. 'But I tell you what. I'm interested in this now. And even if it's just to shut you up, I'll take the job. But I'm charging double. And you're paying me up front.' He stood up to leave. 'I'll be in touch.'

As Fergus turned to leave, Alex got the urge to get the last word in.

He pointed at Fergus's T-shirt. 'You've got ketchup on you.'

TWENTY-FIVE
FERGUS
22:10

I get home and change my T-shirt. Sauce all down it. It's almost embarrassing that it had to be Alex who pointed it out, but I don't care what he thinks, so it doesn't quite sting.

It's going to be a pleasure, not killing him.

I know the broad strokes of how I'm going to do it, but there are some things to set up first. I'm going to need a spare body. Someone fresh. Within a few hours of Alex's fake death.

I need another job, and fast.

The thought of the next job, though? My hands shake a little. That's a new thing. I don't get guilty about what I do. I'm an atheist, so I don't worry about heaven or hell, and I don't need redemption. And yet, right now, I'm feeling—

I don't know.

I can't describe it.

Fuck it. Stop being a wee pussy, Fergus.

I take a couple of beta blockers to numb whatever this crap is, and then call my agent. Yes, hit men have agents. Of course we do.

We're not in a profession that demands high interpersonal skills. We need someone else to do all the nicey-nice stuff.

There are a few agencies around the world. Most pros who go into my job, at the serious level, do it after stints in intelligence or the military. The agencies have scouts who spot good talent and hook them up with steady work. I first went professional in New York, and I've stayed with the agency that first spotted me. I work with Stan Decker at the Hit List. They were the best team to be with in the States, and the geek in me just likes having a business card with a Manhattan address on it.

Stan answers on the fifth ring. It's not until he says hello that I bother to check the time. The East Coast of America is five hours behind Glasgow, putting it at a little after 5 p.m. over there. The truth is, agents have their phones surgically attached to their hands. It doesn't matter what time you call, they'll answer.

'Hey,' he says.

He sounds a little out of breath. I can hear just the edge of a pant through the words, and there's a distant sound to his voice, like the phone's not held to his ear.

'Are you, Stan, are you *running*?'

'Yeah. I'm at the gym.'

'So, the Mitchell job went a bit tits up.' I push on past the whole *gym* thing. I hate them. I love running, but out in the real world, not on a machine. 'I dropped an extra package, and had to do some of the cleaning up out of my own pocket.'

'Yeah, I heard,' Stan says. 'These things happen, though, right? I wouldn't worry about it.'

'Yeah, I dunno.' I leave that hanging there.

Truth is I don't even know what I'm trying to say. I think back to the small mistakes I made today. To the bigger ones on the previous job. When I take a longer view, I can see my work has been getting sloppy for a while now. Since I came home to Glasgow. I had a couple gigs last summer that I almost ballsed up completely, but nobody saw it so I hadn't mentioned the mistakes. If I was a footballer, people might say I was out of form. In a slump. But can people in my line of work afford to hit a bad streak?

My hand starts to shake, making the phone wobble at my ear.

Even through the pills, I was jittery.

What the fuck?

Stan can hear something in my voice, or maybe in my pauses. 'What's wrong?'

'Stan, do you ever see people get burned out on this?'

Stan doesn't answer straight away. When he does, his tone's changed a little. He's still upbeat, but I can hear the effort that's going into it. 'Hey, everyone goes through a slump sometimes. Happens to the best. Have you started shaking?'

'No,' I lie.

'Then you're okay,' he says. 'You just need a break. It's only if you start to get things like shakes or blackouts that you need to worry, that's the time to get out.'

'People can become blackout killers?'

'You'd be surprised. Listen, you know, yeah. It's okay if you want to take a break. Have the rest of the summer off. Christmas is when things get busy again, and you know there'll be some work lined up for you then, so just take it easy for a while.'

'And what if it's more than a break?'

'You have the shakes, don't you?'

'Maybe. I'm feeling like this isn't me anymore.'

'Well,' there's a pause, and I hear a loud noise and a sigh. Then when Stan speaks again it's calmer and he's no longer running. 'You've got investments. Savings. Plus, we'll be getting royalties on that coup in Cambodia for a while. You're in a good spot. People like you can usually retire with no problems.'

'And the ones who don't?'

'Well, it's not a great job if you don't want to make some enemies. Especially the Cambodia thing.' He pauses, and comes back with the optimism high-beam back in place. 'But that's not going to be you. Maybe you just need a break. You've been hitting it really hard this year.'

Hitting it. 'Nice, well done.'

On the table in front of me, I hear my computer beep. The screen is flashing something up, but I ignore it. I need to stay focused on this conversation. Letting my mind drift has been causing too many problems already.

I've got to find one more body. 'Well, first things first, I've got a weird one on.'

'That business guy? Yeah, he sounded weird. Taking the job? He hasn't got back to me to arrange anything. I could chase him down?'

'He knows who I am. Called me on my own cell.' I always unconsciously switch into US terms when speaking to Stan. 'And he tried blackmailing me.'

'What? Like, you said no, right?'

'I've taken it on, but I'm charging double. Make sure that's what comes through. No pay, no job.' It's time to start getting the details of the job lined up. 'I'm going to need another body, though. Part of his thing. He wants me to fake his death.'

'Why would anybody hire a hit man to not kill them?'

'Aye, right? I know. Anyway. So I need a fresh body, tonight or tomorrow morning probably. I could ask around at the morgue, but I'd prefer to have control over it all myself. You got anything I could take on?'

'I'll have a look.'

'Make it a scumbag,' I say. 'A real arse. Someone who really has it coming.'

'They all have it coming, Fergus.'

For the first time I'm wondering, *What do I have coming?*

'Oh, Stan? Joe has another contractor. Could you ask around, see who else is working Glasgow? I don't want any surprises.'

My computer beeps again. I put the phone down and look at the screen

Holy shit.

Sam has liked me back. The website now loads up a new screen, a private messenger app. It shows my face on one side, and Sam's on another, next to a little bubble that's flashing to say that she's typing me a message.

My stomach turns over.

The shakes stop.

TWENTY-SIX
ALEX
21:30

Alex stayed in the pub for another drink after Fergus left. That prick had looked all in control when he left, getting up and walking out all cool. Other people in the bar had seen that, and this was on Alex's turf.

Well, 'turf' might be pushing it.

He'd been in here once since moving up.

But still, it was local. It *could* be his turf.

He *could* learn the bartender's name. He could have people wave at him when he walked in, or at least a drunken nod. So he needed to save face. He shrugged after Fergus left, and made it look like he was in no hurry. He ordered another drink and leaned into the bar, like he was there for the long haul.

Halfway down the pint, he started to count how much he'd already put away. A few pints in the afternoon, to build up courage to meet with Fergus first time round. Three generous whiskies when he got home, and now on to his second pint since walking in. He yawned, and it followed through with a burp.

He looked around to see if anyone had noticed.

He'd got away with it.

Smooth.

He finished the drink and got up off the stool. The warm evening air made the alcohol wash around his eyeballs like a warm blanket. Yeah, he was drunk. But it was a pleasant kind of sauced, and it matched the evening perfectly.

Just after 9.30 p.m., and the sun was still out. The air was warm. There was an amber glow in the sky, like a giant pint of lager. This was like living in London. Alex smiled. If every day in Glasgow was like this, he wouldn't mind living here.

Well, if it maybe didn't have quite so many Glaswegians. That would help.

He turned and walked up the road. His house was at the top of a hill, and he'd never regretted that decision until now. Slogging up the steep incline with beer in his system and the sun on his back. He was sweating through his shirt by the time he reached the front door.

His wife's car wasn't in the driveway. Odd. She hadn't mentioned being out this late. Alex let himself in and headed straight for his bar. He poured another whisky. A Lagavulin this time, sixteen years old. He may as well finish out the day in the manner it had gone so far.

He was taking his first sip when the front door opened. Kara walked in carrying her briefcase and a bag from the Chinese takeaway down on the main road.

'Hey, babe,' she said. 'I guessed you wouldn't have eaten, so I got us something.'

Two things:

Alex realised for the first time that he was *starving*.

Was she wearing a different top?

Alex wasn't the most observant guy in the world when it came to noticing what his wife was wearing. Other people, sure. Like young women. He noticed what they were wearing, because he noticed what they were *not* wearing. But his wife? Not so much. And the real problem now was that he couldn't ask her about it. Because there was every chance he was wrong.

He might *be that* guy, but he didn't want to *look* like *that* guy.

He headed into the kitchen and picked up a couple of plates, forks and a bowl to put the prawn crackers in. He carried them through to the living room, and he and Kara met at the dining table.

Alex leaned in for a kiss, and their lips met for a few seconds. She wasn't really into it, but that was fine, she'd been at work all day. He could understand.

Except—

'Hey, did you have a shower?'

She smelled clean. Too clean. Soap and fresh perfume.

'Yeah.' She busied herself dishing the food onto plates. 'It was a long day. You know how it is. Meetings. I get hot in the suit, but it looks unprofessional if I start dressing down.'

'You showered at work?'

'Yeah.' She met his eyes. 'Don't worry, there was nobody there to watch me. I locked the door.'

Alex felt something in him relax. He hadn't been aware that he was suspicious, but clearly, seeing her so clean had made him worry. It must have been that cock, Fergus, messing with his head. Kara had looked him in the eye, and told the truth. He knew his wife. He could tell when she lied. So could everyone else, that's why he knew he couldn't tell her about the plan.

But, oh boy, did he want to.

He wanted an audience. He wanted someone to tell him what a great idea it was. And Kara would be impressed, but it would have to wait until afterwards, when he rose from the dead with bundles of cash. It would be hard on her. She'd be grieving for him, for real. But he was sure she'd understand. Really get into the spirit of things, when she saw why he'd done it.

He had the plan.

He had the money.

Now he had the hit man.

He smiled. This was going to work.

TWENTY-SEVEN
SAM
22:20

I called Phil when I got home.

I was drunk, but not wasted. I'd cycled back after the bar, and promised myself it was the last time I was going to do it. I made the same promise every time. It never lasted. Cycling after a few drinks wasn't all that difficult. The physical exertion forced me to be alert.

But that was the gin speaking. I knew I shouldn't do it.

I lived out by Celtic Park in the East End. I wasn't as hard core a fan as my father had been, but listening to the crowd each week made me feel closer to him. I used to live a mile closer to town, in Bridgeton, but it had become uncomfortable when the wrong kinds of people had targeted my address after a previous case.

Phil picked up straight away, 'Yes, Commissioner?'

'*Commissioner?*' I said.

'Yeah. Gordon. You get upset when I call you Robin, but I'm pretty sure I'm The Batman, so I made you the Commissioner instead.'

'Isn't he, like, ancient?'

'Nah, he's cool. Second toughest person in the city.'

'Next to you, I'm guessing?'

'Well, duh.'

I could hear people talking in the background, but it was quiet. He was listening to one of his podcasts in the car. Ifanboy, or Movie Fights. He'd tried to get me to listen a few times, but what do I care?

'Still outside the Pennans' house?'

'Yeah. They're both there now. Wife turned up a few minutes ago.'

I checked the time on my Fitbit. 'So, about twenty to ten, you think?'

'Sounds about right.'

Interesting. I lost her just before seven. She didn't get home for another three hours. Where did she go?

My gut was telling me I was right, that Kara was up to something.

'Put trackers on both cars,' I said.

Our detective agency owned four GPS trackers. They were surprisingly cheap to buy, and a huge leap forward from the way my dad would have operated the business. He was all about going down those mean streets, talking to people, whiling away tax deductible hours in the pubs building up a network of informants.

Me and Phil?

We had smartphones and GPS.

'And don't forget to log all these hours on the app,' I said. I was going to hang up when I thought of something else. 'Phil, do you have a cassette player?'

'You know this is 2016, right? Nobody uses cassettes anymore.'

That's what I'd thought, too.

I hung up and changed into the T-shirt and pants that passed for nightwear. I grabbed an open bottle of red wine from the kitchen, along with a clean glass.

On the sofa, I tapped the contents of the package out onto the cushion and stared at the tapes. The riders for our messenger service would probably have tape players. If there was a perfect hybrid between the hip and the obscure, between people who loved obsolete technology and people who liked to be cool and cutting edge, the fixed-gear bike messenger was it.

I was sure at least two of the lads I knew on the deliveries circuit would be able to lend me a player, but those were two of the guys Hanya had been talking about, and I didn't want to ask them for favours. They'd give me those puppy dog eyes and use it as a reason to follow me around for a few days.

The Barras market would definitely have some tape players for sale. You can get anything there, as long as by 'anything' you mean, 'old stuff'. But the market wasn't open on weekdays, and I didn't have time to wait until Saturday.

My phone buzzed.

I opened up the vLove app to see that Fergus had replied to my message. I'd sent him a simple, 'Hi.' I'd done it on impulse before leaving the bar, because I knew I would have talked myself out of it if I'd waited.

FergusSingsTheBlues – Hi. Thanks.

FergusSingsTheBlues – For liking me, I mean.

FergusSingsTheBlues – (That just made it sound worse, didn't it?)

I'll be honest. A wee part of me was tempted not to reply straight away. See how much nervous gibberish he would talk in the silence. But then, that was the part of me that was covering for my own nerves.

Truth was, I was scared.

I'd never really done something like this before.

I went for honesty.

TheSamIreland – Ha. Don't worry. I know what you mean.

FergusSingsTheBlues – Thanks for not saying LOL.

TheSamIreland – LOL.

I'm not sure what it was, but something about talking to Fergus took my mind off the cassettes enough to figure something out.

When I'd taken over the detective business from my dad, I'd inherited all of his files and equipment. None of it was any use to me, because he'd never really joined the twenty-first century.

But that meant—

Maybe—

I opened the closet where I stored all his stuff. I lifted the biggest boxes out of the way, mostly full of paperwork and old invoices. At the back was a small box, where I'd kept his old electrical equipment. Including, yes, a tape recorder.

I pressed the buttons but the batteries had died long ago. I checked the size, and then opened up my TV remote to steal the AAs from inside. I clipped them into place in the tape machine and pressed the buttons again. The little black spools turned.

Bingo.

I lifted the first tape off the cushion, slipped it into the deck, and pressed *play.*

FIRST INTERMISSION

Cal's Log

CAL'S LOG

>click<

Cal's Log. Stardate whatever-the-fuck.

How do they work those out? I don't fucking know, do I? I'm no a geek.

If you're listening to this, well, you're a nosy prick aren't you? Unless I've given it to you, and it's all part of my big genius plan.

My Babycham.

Hey, that rhymed.

Listen up, this is DJ Cal, bringing you the truth about Glesga.

And it's expensive, so I hope you're paying me a bundle for it, aye?

See. I know a secret. And it's a big wan. There's this lassie. She's been working in the gangs an' that. But she's here on a super-secret mission, like. But her boss is dead, and it looks like naebody else knows about it.

She's got naebody to turn to.

But here, I'll let her tell the story. See, I got her stoned, and she started telling me all aboot it, and I've got it all on tape, haven't I?

So hang on, let's get her filling you in on it all.

>click<

>click<

Aye. Well. Okay. Cal's Log, stardate whatever, like, a few seconds after the last wan. What is it they call that on the TV? 'Cal's Log, suppository.'

So. Well, I've been a bit of a fud, and I taped my log over the top of Paula's confession. So I'm back at the start.

But, if you're listening to this, then that means I found extra proof anyway, and I've sent it to you.

I can't wait to find out what it is.

PART THREE
June 7th

'I'm a part-time private detective. I'm paid to have trust issues.'

—Sam

TWENTY-EIGHT
SAM
07:08

I got to the office later than usual.

Normally I'm there by half-six, loading up my messenger bag with a couple of water bottles, brewing a coffee and checking my emails and tyres before getting the early shift in.

Orders for the courier service came in around seven-thirty. Those runs, along with regular slots we had booked with law firms and surveyors, gave us a busy period that lasted from eight until ten. Our crew was made of young guys and old punks. They liked to sleep in, and start work just before the second rush at lunchtime.

It worked out fine. I liked to do the morning work myself, and it meant they all understood if I took time off later in the day to focus on investigation work. I liked the mornings. I used to be a runner, before a string of thigh injuries made me switch to the saddle, and I'd always enjoyed getting out into the morning air. Added to that was the buzz of being timed, of having deadlines to deliver the packages.

It was a fun game.

Usually.

Trouble was, I'd stayed up too late listening to the tapes and drinking wine. Cal seemed to be saying Paula was an undercover cop. But for what? Was this why the feds had taken the case so quickly? The second tape was more difficult to listen to. It was a mostly sex noises, with two men talking cryptically beforehand about a meeting set for the ninth. They mentioned the words 'takeover' and 'the cartel'. They meant nothing to me, out of context. Had they meant something to Paula? Was that what she'd died for?

The third tape was a mix tape. Nineties' pop music.

I'd tried to find Paula Lucas on social media. I'd tried all the usual sites, then a births, marriages and deaths database that I had access to as a private investigator. The name got plenty of hits, but none of the profile pictures matched the woman I'd seen, and the database wasn't going to be much help without more data to narrow the search.

Wait—

If she was undercover, she'd probably use a different name.

I remembered that the delivery had been paid for by debit card through our app. I logged in to check the details. The card was in the name of Paula Lafferty. I texted the name to Hanya, along with *Cop?* I didn't get an immediate response. She'd still been at the bar when I left; maybe it had turned into a good night.

I searched for Paula Lafferty on the same social media sites, but still didn't find anything that looked like the right match.

It hadn't stopped me sitting up most of the night and trying, though.

And keeping me company, each step of the way, had been Fergus. There hadn't been any small talk. There hadn't really been any big talk, either. Just *talk*. I was sure they hadn't intended it, but Paula Lucas and Fergus Fletcher had combined to make it very difficult for me to get up and make the morning deliveries.

I pulled off the main road and skidded my bike to a childish, tyre-balding stop in front of the office. I wheeled the bike past a parked car, a blue Ford. The driver was sat behind the wheel reading a book. I recognised the cover but not the reader. *Girl Meets Boy on a Crime Spree.* Everyone in the world seemed to have it. I had a copy in my bag, but I'd never cracked the spine.

The PI business operated out of the backroom of the courier depot, in a small Gorbals unit. Most of the space was taken up by spare bikes, tyres, tubes and other equipment. We had a selection of second-hand sofas arranged around an Xbox and a cheap TV. We had two desks in the office. One was filled with paperwork, comics and the computers that Phil used to run both companies. The other was arranged with chairs on both sides, and lined with empty coffee cups.

As I turned the coffee percolator on, I heard a car door shut outside. The guy who'd been sat in the blue Ford stuck his head in around the entrance. 'You open?'

Technically no. We didn't open the door to customers until around seven-thirty, but I'd be out on my bike by then and Phil wouldn't roll in until later, so I started seeing people as soon as they turned up. You don't make money by turning it away.

'Hiya.' I walked forward and waved for him to come on in. 'How can I help?'

'Are you Sam Ireland?'

'Yup.'

I took his hand in a shake. He had the grip of someone who'd never been told not to do it so hard. He was a little taller than me, but on the short side for a man. He had broad shoulders, and his body stretched out in all directions from there, with belly fat, back fat, man boobs and thick arms.

He didn't look unfit, despite the flab. He was strong, and looked like he worked out with the same vigour that he ate cheeseburgers.

'Mike Gibson,' he said, and everything made sense.

I knew who Gibson was.

'You know me?' My reaction had given it away, but he smiled. 'Don't worry, hen, most of it's made up. I read about the work you did with the arson case last year. That was good stuff.'

'Thanks.'

He looked around at the bike equipment. 'This your office?'

I led him through to the back and waved for him to take a seat at the desk. I walked round the other side and settled in. It's a clichéd bit of theatrics, but it serves a good purpose. Clients tend to think they can treat you like crap when you're freelance, but if you put them in their place right at the start, and establish a little control, you'll get treated better.

'How can I help?'

'You know I have properties in town, aye?' I nodded. 'Right, well, one of them burned down last night.'

I had an idea where this was going. Ever since I'd solved a big case last year that involved a string of arson attacks, people thought that was my *thing*. I was a pop band, and fire was my hit single.

'I don't really work arson cases, Mr Gibson—'

'Mike—'

'Sure, okay. Mike. I don't really work them. And yours was last night?' His turn to nod. 'Well, see, the polis will still be investigating it. And the water fairies.'

'Water fairies?'

I smiled. 'Sorry. Cops and paramedics hate the fire service. I don't know why, really, but I've picked up the slang.'

He laughed. A little too much. It was polite of him, but the joke hadn't been that good. 'Well, see, I'm not bothered about the building. The insurance'll pick that up. And I already know who's done it.'

'You do?'

'Aye. My shite of a son. Callum. He's been trying to piss me off for ages and, bully for him, he's finally done it. Done a fucking runner, though, hasn't he? I want you to find him, let me know where he is.'

Callum?

As in *Cal*?

It couldn't be, could it?

Glasgow is a big city, but it gets very small when there's trouble. Everybody knows each other. Especially in Gibson's world. If his *Callum* and my *Cal* were the same, then this was all linked to my dead undercover cop. Why not let Mike Gibson pay me to work it from both sides?

TWENTY-NINE
FERGUS
10:00

Man, I'm having fun.

Sam and me stay up way too late messaging each either. She's full of good chat, and not afraid to get in digs at me. I like that. No standing on ceremony. No pretending. Just straight to taking the mick.

I sleep in later than usual and get up at 10 a.m. I like to get a run in around nine, but I don't have anything on this morning so I can afford to take it easy. I take a cold shower to get my senses awake, and drink a pint of water before getting into my running gear. Usually when I go outside I try to appear nondescript. On the job I want to blend into the crowd, pass by unnoticed, and when I'm off the clock I still find myself wanting to be unmemorable. I don't want to stop and chat. I don't want to be spotted by old school friends.

When I first decided to leave New York and move back to Glasgow, a lot of people on the circuit assumed it was some kind of crisis. They said that everyone gets it, around 28–30, and we all feel the need to go home and reconnect with old friends, or our first loves, or compare our new lives to our old ones. And what other reason would I have for leaving the busiest city in the world for paid assassins, and moving to the west of Scotland? To them, I was an artist choosing to become wilfully obscure. It *had* to be the third-life crisis, right?

Nope.

Since moving back, I've made no effort to reconnect with old friends. And I'm still pretty much the same idiot now as I was at seventeen, so why would I want to meet up with old flames and assume things would be any different?

I haven't really made any new friends in Glasgow, either. This isn't a very sociable line of work. Some people choose it for that very reason. Others, like me, simply end up that way. It becomes difficult to form any lasting bonds with people who aren't in the life. What do we have in common?

And if all of this sounds dangerously like I'm going on an introspective philosophical ramble, don't worry. It's for a purpose. What I'm winding up to here is a punch line that says I'm a wee dick.

Because, for all that I like to blend in, and wander around unnoticed, I can't help that I'm a runner. And like everyone else cursed with that affliction, I need to buy the latest gear. So when I'm out for my daily spot of long-distance self-punishment, I'm very noticeable. And proud of it.

So I get decked out in:

Gore Air Shirt.

Gore 2-in-1 Shorts.

Asics Metarun Trainers.

And—

Most important—

My Garmen Fenix Sapphire GPS Watch.

I don't listen to music. That's really only for amateurs, people who don't want to listen to their own bodies and the world around them. But I still need to be contactable, so I strap my phone to the inside of my right forearm, and run with a Bluetooth headset in my ear.

I head out at a steady pace, and pretty soon I'm running alongside the Clyde. Some days, this river looks like absolute shite. Catch it on a good day, though, and it's stunning. I'm focusing on the way the sun bounces off the calm surface of the water when my phone rings. I tap the screen, and Stan's voice fills my ear.

'Hey,' he says.

He's out of breath again. It sounds like he's running, but I can't quite tell over the sounds of my own feet.

'Are you running again?' I say.

'Yep. I'm at the gym.'

'Stan, it's five in the fucking morning where you are.'

'Best time for it.'

His actual words. Manhattan is a wonderful place, but it's fucking crazy. I only lived there for two years, but even at that, it had started to do strange things to me. I would go out for my morning run every day along the East River Promenade, but I swear, right before I left I found myself doing it at six. And enjoying being up at that time. That's when I knew it was time to come home.

'You're running, too, it sounds like?'

'Yeah,' I say. The two of us on the phone, running at each other across thousands of miles. 'At a normal time. When sane people do it.'

'You've got all that deep fried food to work off.'

Ah yes. Deep fried food. The one thing people from outside of Scotland are guaranteed to bring up in every conversation. Along with rain. Well, I don't eat chocolate bars that have been stuck in hot oil, and it's the middle of a heatwave.

'I've got something for you, something you could do tonight. Client doesn't care what happens to the body, so you'd be able to use it afterwards for whatever. There's one catch with the job.'

'Okay?'

'It's pro bono.'

'So now I need to kill someone for free, in order to pretend to kill someone for money?'

'Right. It's for some local sex workers. They can't afford to pay, but there's a guy who keeps hurting them. They hired a PI to find his address, but that used up all of their money.'

'They can't wait a few nights and earn some?'

'He's left them in bad shape. They can't work right now, and they're worried he'll hurt someone else if he's left to it. It's been sitting in the queue for two weeks and nobody's been willing to do it.'

'Now you're *guilting* me into killing someone?'

'Hey, you said—'

'Aye, I'm just being a dick with you. I'll take it. Send me the details. Before your third run of the day. Oh, and, Stan? I'm a little rusty on explosives. I'm thinking car bomb, but I haven't blown anything up in a while. Could you send me the manual?'

Stan laughs and hangs up.

I stop running. There's something eating at the back of my mind. I want to check my messages, just like when I got my first phone and I kept texting Sandra Carter. I would stare at the phone, willing it to beep response.

Well, I'd play Snake, too.

That was fun.

I've downloaded the dating app to my phone. I know, right? My rules lasted right up until I finally started talking to a woman. I'm a dick.

I load up the messenger screen from the night before and type a message.

FergusSingsTheBlues – Ooooft. We were up late.

FergusSingsTheBlues – What you up to? I'm going for a gun.

Shit. That's not what I meant. This thing keeps trying to correct what I say. I think it's predictive, based on words I've used the most. That's not a good sign.

FergusSingsTheBlues – RUN. Bloody auto correct.

Her icon pops up, along with some dots that tell me she's already typing a response.

My stomach—

turns—

over.

THIRTY
SAM
10:00

Once work drops off around ten, I always have a late breakfast with Phil, who would be just starting for the day. We both used the excuse that it was a business meeting, because it gave us a chance to plan the rota for the day ahead, and talk about any problems that needed to be sorted. But all of that was just a cover; we just wanted to hang out.

Phil is not a morning person by nature. And he barely counts as one now, clocking in after ten in the morning. But he's improving. The extra responsibility of running both companies has made him step up. He's a big guy, but he's been losing weight recently. He didn't talk about it, but I knew he'd started cycling to and from the office, a couple of miles each way. As the fat was going from his face, he was starting to look more like our father.

Naturally, I never mentioned any of this to him. Come on. He's my *brother*, I can only be nice to him up to a point.

We meet at a coffee shop round the corner from the office. They keep a tab for us, and usually write some of it off in exchange for us running a few deliveries for them.

'Wakey wakey,' Phil said. He set his coffee down on the table. 'I've been thinking.'

I knew the look in his eyes. It said he was about to go on a tangent.

'Is this going to relate to the job?' I said.

'Maybe.' Phil put up a hand. 'Bear with me on this. See The Batman?'

'We're talking about Batman now?'

'*The* Batman, Sam. It's important. Same as the hyphen in Spider-Man – gotta be there, otherwise you sound like a bam.'

'Well, I wouldn't want to sound like a bam while discussing Batman.'

'*The*. Anyway. See how he keeps fighting all these villains, and they keep losing, aye? I mean every single time. They break out, they try to take over the city. The Batman shows up. He broods at them until they surrender, then he goes back to his cave to play video games.'

'I don't think he—'

'Have you read the comics?'

'No.'

'Okay, shush then. See the other thing is, loads of the baddies know who he is by this point, right? Ra's Al Ghul knows. Talia knows. I think Riddler knows. Bane knows, for sure. Bane had this whole crazy thing where he tried to send The Batman insane by breaking out all the villains at once.'

'Good plan.'

Phil sighed and shook his head, like I'd just disappointed him, then waved his croissant at me. 'You're not going to be in charge of the plan when we try to take over the city, okay? It was a rubbish plan. The logistics alone. No way. Or Talia, that time she wanted to blow up Gotham, but instead of building a bomb, she funnelled billions into building some cold fusion machine, that she then *converted* into a bomb. You and Talia, you'd get on. Rubbish at plans. My point is, there are a lot of people who know who he is at this point, Bruce Wayne, I mean. And a lot of them want to defeat him, aye?'

'As you pointed out, I'm not really up to date with the literature.'

My phone buzzed. It was a message from Fergus.

FergusSingsTheBlues – Ooooft. We were up late.

FergusSingsTheBlues – What you up to? I'm going for a gun.

FergusSingsTheBlues – RUN. Bloody auto correct.

I wrote back.

TheSamIreland – My brother is telling me about Batman.

FergusSingsTheBlues – He knows about The Batman? I thought it was a secret.

I snorted. Phil was pretending not to notice. 'Well,' he continued. 'What I think they should do is, see, he's grieving, aye? The whole dead parents thing. Why don't a bunch of the villains all club together and hire the best therapist they can afford. Then lure Bats into a trap. When he thinks he's got them cornered, they whip out a sofa, sit him down, and let the therapist work his magic.'

'You want them to give Batman counselling sessions?'

'It's genius. Just make Bruce Wayne get over his shit, then, presto, no more Batman. The baddies win by default.'

'So, when I asked if this was going to have anything to do with the job?'

'I was maybe being a bit cunning.' He gave me a look. He wanted me to think on the hidden meaning, but it was too obvious. No thought required.

'So I'm Batman now? Because usually you—'

'Just this once.'

'I'm fine,' I said. 'I don't need to see a therapist.'

Phil's concern for me was sweet, but bordered on annoying. Sure, I'd had a tough year. My ex-boyfriend had turned out to be a killer. I'd seen someone get hit by a train. And, before I'd had time to deal with any of that, our father had passed away. I still hadn't cried. Phil and Hanya both insisted that I was storing things up, letting everything change me.

I just told them the truth: I've been keeping busy.

'I'm fine. Seriously, you and Hanya should hook up. You act like an old married couple – you may as well be one.'

'Well, if she had a brother who looked enough like her—'

'Anyway.' I took a sip on my own coffee. Still too hot. 'Getting back to the work you're being paid for?'

I checked my phone while he talked. Hanya hadn't texted me back yet. I sent her a follow-up message that was just a row of question marks.

'I planted the trackers,' Phil said. 'One on each car. The job we're being paid for, and the job you've invented for yourself. Sammy, do you remember back when you used to trust people?'

'I'm a private detective.'

'Part time.'

'Okay, I'm a *part-time* private detective. I'm paid to have trust issues.'

THIRTY-ONE
ALEX
11:00

Alex's PA, Emma, buzzed him on the intercom.

'Asma Khan's here,' she said.

Alex grunted. He'd been staring at the same document for twenty minutes. The lines kept blurring on the page, and rubbing the bridge of his nose was doing nothing to fine tune his eyesight.

He hadn't meant to hit it so hard last night. The combination of whisky and beer had given him a killer headache, and to top it off he'd had bad dreams when he finally drifted off. He didn't remember what they were now, but he'd been restless with them all night, and woken up a number of times feeling scared.

Kara hadn't stirred at all.

'You have an appointment with her for two o'clock,' Emma said.

'Wait, come in here. I can't hear you on this bloody thing.'

Emma let him wait just long enough to play with his patience. Her desk was in the next room, but she liked to move slowly when Alex was being rude, to remind him to play nice. She walked in carrying a mug of coffee and a stack of papers.

'Two o'clock,' she repeated. 'With Joe Pepper. The file's on your desk just there.'

MHW used files and paperwork more than most companies these days. Even at Alex's previous job, which had been a smaller firm, all the information was shuttled about electronically. But for MHW, half of the job was choosing which information to have on the computer, and which to have on paper. The art was in shuffling the two around, hiding things in plain sight.

'Sorry.' Alex squinted at the document she was pointing to. 'I must have lost track of it.'

With anybody else he would have covered for the hangover, pretended to be ill and maybe asked for some Lemsip to lay it on thick. But Emma knew him too well. He could never slip anything past her. In fact, he wouldn't be surprised if she'd figured out he was up to something dodgy, but she was too loyal to say anything.

She smiled and set the mug down in front of him.

'It's been in the book all week.'

Alex knew she was right. He couldn't afford to act the fool on this one, not even to try and bluff his way through a headache. Khan was Emma's boss just as much as his, and he needed to appear on the ball at all times.

Khan and Joe were booked in to discuss the big takeover. Alex and Emma had lined up all of the deals. The gangs, the businesses, the lawyers, everything. All of the last round of buyouts were due to go through at 1 p.m. on the same day.

It had been Emma's idea, actually. A brilliant way to broker the peace between all sides. If some of the deals had gone through before others, people might have got antsy, suspected double crosses. If they were all done at exactly the same time, nobody would feel left behind.

It would be a bloodless coup.

The deal was going through in two days, and that's why Alex wanted his own project with Fergus to go through *now*. People were distracted. They were busy. This was his one chance to slip away.

Emma had proved invaluable to Alex since he had joined the firm. To begin with, she would do the honest work. The legitimate customers and the clean accounts. She would set up meetings, deals, paperwork, and then pass them off to Alex at the last moment to rubber stamp. This left Alex free to be more hands-on with the other side of the business, the list of clients euphemistically titled 'Friends of MHW'.

Over the past few months, since Khan's big project was put on the table, Emma had stepped in to help with the *friends*, too, and she was a natural. She was also good at running interference with Khan. Alex could handle Joe. They got on well enough, and Joe was a skilled people person – he could make you feel valued even if he hated your guts.

But Khan? That was different.

She was ridiculously young, for one thing. Her family had sent her to study in America, and she'd gone native. She came to high-powered business meetings in jeans and a hoodie, or a retro band T-shirt. Usually, her hair would be styled and coloured. It was blue the last time he'd seen her.

Alex's career was being controlled by some dot-com brat, and he hated it.

He blinked, put his professional mask back in place. 'Of course. What time did you say the appointment was? Two o'clock?' He checked his watch. 'But it's only eleven. You said she's here now?'

Alex noticed for the first time that Emma was wearing her jacket, and her handbag was slung over her shoulder. 'Well,' she said. 'Ms Khan is here early, but not to see you.'

Alex shook his head, his mouth forming an O in question.

'She's hot, she's single and she's asked me to lunch.'

'It's *eleven.*'

'It's going to be a long lunch.'

'And you're telling me all of this now because?'

'Well, you've got one of the worst hangovers I've seen in a long time. I thought you needed time to prepare yourself.'

'I sense an "*and*".'

'And a hot woman wants to take me out, for a very long lunch, and I think everyone should know.'

Emma smiled and left. Alex rubbed his face and opened the file. Emma had typed out the whole brief for him. He started to read, and his eyes drifted out of focus after three sentences. He couldn't concentrate on work.

He opened a desk drawer and pulled out holiday brochures.

THIRTY-TWO
SAM
10:48

I asked Phil to start running background checks on both Mike and Callum Gibson. Three jobs was too many to have going at one time, but I could get away with it if I delegated. Phil could get a head start for me on the Gibson case.

I headed out to my bike from the coffee shop, and loaded up the GPS app on my phone. It was linked to the two devices Phil had planted, and showed me two dots: a blue and a red. We used similar technology for the courier firm. Clients could log onto the app and track our phones to see how close we were to making the delivery, and what route we'd chosen.

I'd say we were Uber for parcels and mysteries, but I've already cracked that joke, haven't I?

Phil hadn't bothered to label the trackers with each of the Pennans' names, so all I had were the dots on the screen. If I pressed one of the dots, I'd be taken to another page, full of information about where the tracker had been, and how long it had stopped at each location.

I wasn't going to need that to figure it all out, though. The red dot was located near to where Alex Pennan worked, in the city. The blue dot was at Firhill. So, unless the Pennans had decided to swap jobs for the day, I could tell which was which.

I took a chance to fire off a quick reply to Fergus.

TheSamIreland – I used to run. Cycle now.

I crossed the river and headed into the city.

There's an area to the west of Central Station that the council have been trying to rebrand as the 'financial district'. For over a year, signs and billboards had been up over empty land and derelict buildings, each depicting a photoshopped vision of the future, with tall buildings of metal and gleaming glass. Some of the older buildings that stood in the way of progress had managed to burn down, but I wasn't going to look too closely into that. The area was also home to two of the most popular brothels in the city centre. They'd clubbed together to hire me a few weeks back. There was a guy who was making a habit of roughing up the women. I tracked down his home address, but there wasn't much they could do. Reporting him to the cops wasn't an option. It would be impossible to prosecute the case when the victims had to lie about how they'd met the attacker.

The *financial district* idea was starting to take hold, and developers were throwing up tall structures, wrapped in glass and steel. They were being filled by banking firms, call centres and pension companies.

MHW was based in a three-sided building, halfway down York Street. I'd delivered packages to this place a few times. I locked my bike up to the stand outside the building, and then logged on my phone that I was starting surveillance. I'd stand there for a couple of minutes while our detective agency app recorded my GPS data. Phil had built a small cheat into the software, so I could pause the GPS, effectively stalling it in one spot while I moved to another. It came in handy on days like this, when I could go and work a personal case while I charged a client. Leaving it there meant that the tracker on our app would show Kara I was doing her work.

Of course, I don't put that kind of behaviour in my adverts.

My phone buzzed in my hand.

FergusSingsTheBlues – Oh god. Cyclist? You're one of THEM ;)

Fergus, you don't know the half of it.

Before I left York Street, I called the number of my own solicitor, Fran Montgomery at Crowther & Co. He'd been my father's lawyer before I took over the business, and we'd pretty much inherited each other when everything was passed to me.

The call was answered quickly by the Ukrainian receptionist, Alexei. He was big on self-improvement, and had spent his first couple of years in Glasgow trying to master the language. He spoke it fluently now, but he still liked to show off by using a different word for *hello* every time he greeted someone. 'Howdy, Crowther & Co, how may I direct your query?'

'Hiya, Alexei,' I grinned at the sound of his voice. He was a loveable big bear of a man, and even hearing him made me feel happy. 'That's a pretty formal greeting there, dude.'

He laughed. We had a running joke to use the word *greet* as often as we could slip into conversation. It started back when he got confused over something I'd said, because he'd only just learned that *greeting* meant to say hello, when I'd used it in the Glasgow form, to mean crying.

'Aye, I've been working on it.' It was strange listening to Alexei talk. He still had most of his original accent, but with the occasional Glaswegian edge to it, and he dropped in Scots dialect. 'You're wanting a blether with the boss?'

'Please. Is he around?'

'Haud on.'

The line beeped a few times while I was on hold. Then, Fran's voice boomed down the line. 'Samantha, how are you?' Considering he had two degrees, I didn't want to be the one to condescend to him by pointing out the handset had a microphone, and he didn't need to shout.

'I'm fine, Uncle Fran. You?'

'Aye, crackin',' he said. 'Especially now I've heard your voice. What favour is it you'd like from me this time, my dear?'

'Am I that obvious?'

He chuckled but didn't answer.

'Okay, you got me,' I said. 'Couple of things. First, do you know who represents Mike Gibson?'

Fran had been working in the town for fifty years. He knew all the old names, and their connections. He always managed to give me information without breaching any confidentiality; he stayed on the right side of the line.

'Dave Lockhart,' he said. 'Shady bugger. Works all of those old lot.'

'Do you know if he looks after Callum, too?'

'I don't, no. Not sure. Maybe, but I think they had a falling out. I can ask around for you?'

'That'd be great, Uncle Fran. Could you ask if he has a money man, too?'

'Aye. As long as the answer doesn't involve anyone I work with, you know.'

'Of course. Hey, listen, I want to sound you out here. A wife hires me. She says her husband is cheating, and she wants proof.'

'The wife?'

'Yeah. But I reckon she might be up to something. Would there be a way to find out if they had a pre-nup?'

'No. A prenuptial agreement doesn't really exist in Scots or English law. But if there is a pre-written agreement, it would be a private contract – it wouldn't need to be publicly posted.'

'Crap. Okay.'

'Sam, no good marriage ends in divorce. Your dad told me that. Even one that starts out good, it's in a bad place by the time they end it. It could just be she wants help ending it.'

Maybe it was that straightforward.

When did I start seeing lies in everything I was told?

THIRTY-THREE
FERGUS
11:50

I get a call from my dad.

Can I go pick up Zoe? Sure. It beats sitting here and thinking of other ways to pretend to kill someone.

I don't say that to him, of course. My parents think the same thing the taxman does: I run a small security consultation firm. Stan and my sister are named with me on the board of directors, and we each draw nominal salaries. My real income comes through the dark web, and never shows up on my tax returns.

Oh aye, you're judging me right now, right?

Look at him. Dodging tax.

Playing a little fast and loose with the amount I owe to the government is probably the least of my offences. But I don't mention that to my dad, either. He's Mr Left Wing. Shop steward wherever he worked. Our family pet when I was a wee boy, a cute little terrier, was named Trotsky. When I was working for the government, I found out our family had been on a watch list in the eighties, with my parents suspected of being in league with the communists. Our phones were tapped and some of our mail was intercepted.

And yet, somehow, despite being from a family of alleged commie spies, I was still able to land work in both the military and British Intelligence.

Kind of shows you how seriously they take their records, aye?

But, anyway. I don't tell my dad that I'm fiddling my taxes. I suspect he'd be more upset over that than at the thought of what the money had been paid to me for originally. But I didn't want to put that theory to the test.

The income Zoe gets from my fake company covers a lot of her living costs. She gets money from the state, too. Disability benefits. But the government keeps messing with her entitlement, and I think having income of her own is good for her independence and self-esteem.

Zoe also has a part-time job at a school in Shawlands. She works mornings in the office, answering phones and sorting paperwork. She designed a new filing system for them, updating the attendance register onto a spreadsheet that automatically sends out alerts based on lateness or absence, and generates an email telling the relevant department heads to contact the parents.

She talks me through all of the things she does to improve how the school functions, and I marvel at all of it.

I don't tell her that, though. Because she's my sister.

Zoe would be well capable of driving if she took the test and got a specially adapted car. I've even offered to buy one for her, and pay for the test. She tells me she wouldn't feel confident, and that her attention span is too shitty to drive. Secretly, I think she just likes being chauffeured about.

On the way there I get a call from Joe Pepper. I take it on the hands-free.

He gets right to it. 'So I tried booking a job, but your agent says you're on holiday?'

'Yeah.'

'What kind of bullshit is that?'

'Serious, Joe,' I say. 'I'm taking a break.'

Maybe forever, I don't say.

'Aye, mebbe. Well, look, I know you lied to me about the last job. That girl you didn't mention? She had something I need. So I think you owe me a going away present.'

You fucked up, so do this, or else. Maybe. I'm starting to hear threats in everything he says, so maybe it's just me being nuts.

'You want me to do the woman?'

'No. That's been sorted. But I want you for something that's more up your street. I'll need someone to vanish afterwards. Keep the rest of your day free.'

Zoe's already waiting for me at the kerb when I get there. We play the usual game of me offering to help her into the car, and Zoe insisting she's fine to do it herself. We can't break out of these roles. I always offer way more support than she needs, and she always insists on needing less aid than she does. I fold down her chair and put it in the boot, while she settles into the passenger seat and starts fiddling with the radio.

She's switched it over to a sports phone-in show by the time I sit in the driver's seat. She shares our dad's passion for the game where they pointlessly kick a ball around a field. We sit in silence at first while she listens to the opinions on the radio. She disagrees with almost all of them with quiet scoffing and tutting sounds.

She turns to me. 'You coming for barbecue tonight?'

'They had barbecue last night.'

'So? Sun's out. They'll have another.'

This is true. They almost certainly will. 'We'll see. I might be working, depends how late it goes.'

'All work and no play.' She pulls out her phone and starts pressing the screen. I figure we're about to sit in silence again when she says, 'Hey, she's cute.'

'Who?'

I take my eyes off the road for a few seconds to look at her phone as she holds the screen up to me. She has the app loaded for the dating website, signed into my account. She's looking at Sam's profile. I should have guessed Zoe's keeping tabs on me.

Zoe presses play.

Hi. My name's . . . Okay, I'm Sam . . .

'Turn it off,' I say. I can hear the embarrassment in my own voice, so I know for a fact that Zoe will have picked up on it.

She presses a button, and the messenger app loads up.

'You two have really been getting on.'

'Stop.' Even I can tell I don't really mean it. I want to talk about Sam, but I want it to sound like I don't. You know, proper teenage stuff.

'Have you asked her out yet?' Zoe says.

'No, 'course not. Barely know her.'

'Huh.' She sounds like she doesn't believe me. I look over to see her flicking the screen down to show how many messages Sam and I have sent each other. 'Looks like you two have been talking loads.'

'On a website. Doesn't mean she wants to meet me.'

'See lassies that you've asked out before, in pubs or clubs or wherever?' She seems to be under the impression this is something I've done a lot. Fine. I'll go with it. 'How many of them had you talked to as much as you've talked to this Sam?'

'None. Okay, I get the message.'

She's right. Maybe I need to ask Sam out. For a coffee, at least. At least. Doesn't need to be a big thing, just to hang out.

I kill people for a living, how scary can this be?

THIRTY-FOUR
SAM
12:00

I walked round to Virginia Street.

Hanya had mentioned that the police had found eye-witnesses. Touching an open police investigation was risky. It could get a private investigator burned. The worst-case scenario was usually that I could be arrested. This felt different. Paula was undercover, and I didn't know why. She'd felt the information on the tapes was worth dying for, and it had been me she'd handed them to, not the police. I wanted to see it through.

I had an advantage over the feds. I'd been at the scene before the cops arrived.

Virginia Street doesn't get much footfall during the day. It's just off Argyle Street, one of the city's busiest shopping areas, but it's not a useful shortcut to anywhere. There hadn't been anyone else on the scene in the moments before the attack, because I would have seen them.

Sure, someone could have walked into the street after I left. But there was also a good chance that whoever had described me to the cops had been inside one of the buildings overlooking the exchange.

And if they saw me, they may also have seen the attacker. Even if they didn't realise it.

The road was open to the public again. The spot where Paula had died was taped off. The entrance to the garage was closed, with a phone number written on a piece of paper and taped to the door.

I stood in the same spot I'd been when I'd stopped my bike the day before, in the seconds before Paula had stepped out of the entrance. Immediately opposite the closed garage was the side wall of another high street shop. There were closed fire exits on the ground floor. The windows on the first and second floors were black, reflecting the opposite side of the street. I couldn't tell whether they were painted black or if it was just dark glass. It was possible someone had seen something from there, though would anyone in a busy high street shop be stood staring out of the window?

The next building over was the hotel I'd noticed the day before.

It had stuck in my mind straight away when I was looking for my pickup. Had there been something about it? I took a few steps closer, and then it hit me. The reception had a window that faced out onto the street.

Had I seen someone in the window?

Or maybe seen something that suggested there was somebody there?

I walked over to the window and looked back in the direction of where the attack had happened. The angle was tight. I doubted anyone inside would have had a direct line of sight, unless they pressed up against the glass. They would have seen people coming and going, though. Including me.

I pushed in through the door and smiled at the short man behind the desk. He looked friendly and round. Maybe the faintest whiff of ex-cop, but not enough for me to be sure. There are a lot of different types of authority figures in Glasgow. Some smell completely of being polis, but anyone from a Mason down to a schoolteacher gives off signs in a city that doesn't trust someone in authority unless they support the right football team.

'Hiya,' I said.

'Hulloo.' His accent had a lilt of one of the northern islands. Lewis, maybe. 'How can I help?'

I wanted to gauge his personality before I went for the real information. Some people need to be lied to or tricked, spun a sob story. I preferred to smile and tell the truth, and it usually worked in this city. People liked to tell stories. If he *was* ex-cop, he wouldn't give anything up. If he wasn't, he'd be as happy to gossip over a police case as anyone else.

'Are you the owner?' I said. I smiled along with it, made the question good natured rather than confrontational. To seal the deal I followed with, 'Because it's a nice place.'

He grinned. 'Great, isn't it? No. I just work here. During the summer, you know.'

'Oh? Lazy the rest of the year?'

'I wish. I work in the café at the university, but they've started closing it down over the summer. Cuts an' that.'

Bingo. Perfect. He wasn't a cop. He worked in a job that got messed around by people higher up the ladder. That was ideal. He'd want to feel like he was part of something.

I leaned on the desk in front of him. 'I'm a PI,' I said.

His eyes widened. 'Aye? That's amazing. I've never met one of those.'

'Oh, it's fun,' I said. 'Car chases. Scandals.' I leaned in a little closer and lowered my voice. 'And I get all the cool gossip.'

'I bet.'

'Actually, I'm looking into the attack that happened out there yesterday.'

His face fell. Real emotion. This guy would be a terrible poker player. 'That was so sad,' he said. 'I heard the lassie died.'

'Did you see anything?'

'No. Not really. I told the cops the same, like. I saw some lassie on a pushbike a few minutes earlier, and I saw the cops, but I didn't see anything else. Didn't hear nothing, either. Real shame.' His voice dropped lower. 'Real shame.'

'This lass on the bike, what did she look like?'

He shook his head. 'Couldn't really see her face, she had a helmet on. She was dressed a bit like you, but she whizzed by quick on the bike, so I didn't get that much of a look.'

My helmet was hanging off my messenger bag. It was down below the line of the desk, so he couldn't see it.

'Okay.' I handed him one of my business cards. 'Anything comes up, give me a call?'

'Sure,' he said. ''Course.'

I turned and left, swinging my bag round as I moved, to keep the helmet out of sight from where he sat.

THIRTY-FIVE
ALEX
12:00

Alex had been staring at the brochures for at least twenty minutes when his office door opened again. He looked up, ready to snap something at Emma, but Joe Pepper was framed in the doorway. He was holding a takeaway coffee cup in one hand, and a bagel wrapped in a napkin in the other.

'Hey, Joe, come on in.'

Alex didn't know if his greeting had sounded genuine. He bloody hoped so.

'I know I'm here early,' he said. 'But I wanted a word before the meeting.'

'Sure, have a seat. You're sorted for coffee?'

Joe held up the cup in answer and nodded. Alex was glad of that, because he made terrible coffee and Emma was away on lunch. She always saved his arse on things like that.

Joe sat down and took a bite out of the bagel. He looked around the room and made Alex wait, chewing on his food and nodding to himself about something. As he swallowed, he fixed his eyes on

Alex and did that thing where he cocked his head slightly to the side and smiled.

'That was good work you did on the Mitchell thing.'

The Mitchell thing. Alex had noticed irregularities in a number of accounts. None of the main political parties used MHW, but Alex still saw pretty much everything they did financially, because enough of their members were on his books with other companies and fronts.

Marxist Martin Mitchell had been siphoning money from the party. Some of it had been easy to miss. A few grand here, a couple hundred there, moved through registered charities and then into payments to himself for services rendered. Well, they all did that, so Alex didn't think much of it. There was something else. Something bigger. Alex had found a trail. Some money was transferred from a tanning salon, which worked with MHW, into an events planning company, also with MHW, and then into a political party who didn't have any ties to Alex's firm. The political party was small, a group of local campaigners who had been active during the referendum a couple of years back. To the outside world, it looked like the events company were simply making donations to a cause they supported.

But Alex had access to the accounts of the companies sending the money to them. All of the payments were made to the party via Paypal, and they were going to a private bank account belonging to Martin Mitchell. So, not only were these hidden payments going directly to him, but *any* donation made to the group from the public would be slipping straight into his bank. And the Labour Party had been on the opposite side of the referendum to this party. Martin was donating money, significant sums, to a cause his party didn't believe in, and then pocketing the proceeds.

The most brazen thing was how blatantly he was doing it, almost like he felt he was invincible.

That was a scandal just waiting to explode.

Alex had thought long and hard about handing this informa-tion over to the press in exchange for a finder's fee. Ultimately he'd done the right thing. He'd picked up the phone to Joe Pepper, and told him about a mess that needed to be fixed.

'Good work,' Joe said again. 'I've managed to sort it. But, what I'm wondering, was there anyone else at it? Aside from Martin? Is there someone I need to speak to?'

Alex played this one carefully. Like a hand of poker. Truth was, there were a lot of people at it. Pretty much everyone. On all sides. On his way to seeing what Marxist Martin was doing, he'd turned a blind eye to the many small fingers in the till along the way. If he started naming one person, he would need to name them all.

But he didn't think that was what Joe was asking. He wanted to know if anyone else was involved in the same scam as Martin, or one that could be equally explosive. It was almost as if he was fish-ing. Did he already have someone in mind?

'I don't know,' Alex said. 'You have anyone in mind?'

Joe took another bite of his bagel and chewed on it. He kept his eyes on Alex. He didn't blink. 'How about Dominic Porter? The Nationalist?' Joe spoke in a pause between chewing. 'I hear rumours he's up to something.'

Dominic Porter was one of the few names that never came up in Alex's work. He wasn't implicated in any paper trail, and wasn't listed as a real or fake board member of any of the companies who worked with MHW. As far as Alex knew, he was the rarest of beasts: an honest politician.

He was also on the other side to Joe and Martin. The opposi-tion party. Why was Joe fishing for info on Dominic? Was it insur-ance in case Martin's dirt was ever made public, someone from the other side who could be smeared in retaliation?

'Sorry Joe,' Alex said. 'I've got nothing on him.'

Joe sighed. 'Worth a shot,' he said. Then, almost as an after-thought he got to the real reason for his visit. 'So, the meeting with Asma later. We need everything to be smooth, okay? You confident?'

'Yeah,' Alex nodded, overly eager. 'No worries. No surprises. It's all ready to go.'

Joe tilted his head again. 'Aye. Well. I hope so. Can't have any-thing big change before that.'

Alex knew he shouldn't care. He was close to being free and clear. Soon he'd be flying off into the sunset with Kara. He already had fifteen million, plus whatever Kara would pocket from their various life and health insurances – he didn't need more money.

But something was tickling him.

Joe had wanted this conversation without Khan here. He'd wanted to ask about Dominic Porter, about Marxist Mitchell, and to check how the project was going. And he hadn't wanted Khan to hear any of it.

Joe had his own angle on this. He was up to something.

If Alex could figure out what it was, maybe there would be another payday?

Alex heard a buzzing phone. Joe put his hand up with his fore-finger extended, both an apology and a *Hang on a minute*. He put the phone to his ear. 'She's where? Right now? Okay, thanks.'

Joe killed the call and climbed to his feet.

'Something's come up,' he said. The political smile slipped back into place. 'Good talk. See you a little later, Alex.'

THIRTY-SIX
SAM
12:32

I walked round to the front of the shop with the painted windows overlooking the garage.

I noticed the security guard clock me the minute I walked in. I've started to feel like I'm a superhero with a secret identity. By day, I'm a bike messenger, by night I'm *Detective Woman*. Each persona dresses differently, and it's given me a chance to see how much women are judged on our clothes.

If I walked in dressed in one of my blazers or business suits, nobody would bat an eye. But when I was dressed down, as I was now, in Vans, cargo shorts and a hoodie, I was an instant target.

The windows I wanted to check out were on the next floor up. I paused at the foot of the escalator and pretended to be reading the directory while I scanned the space at the top of the magical moving staircase. That's where the window was. It was going to be hard to take a look without standing out, now that the guard's eyes were on me.

I should have come as *Detective Woman*.

I stepped onto the escalator and let it take me up, marvelling at the wonders of modern technology. Or moving slow enough to try and show the guard I wasn't being suspicious. I'm not sure which was the most believable.

At the top, I walked over to the window and looked down.

The street was visible through the tinted glass, as was the garage. It took a little effort, though. I had the advantage of knowing what I was looking for, but would a casual passer-by have paused at the top of the escalator and strained to look down into the street, at just the right moment to witness anything? The sun was directly overhead, which threw a glare down onto the window. It wouldn't have been quite so harsh when the attack took place, in late afternoon.

As I watched, two suited men walked into Virginia Street and paused in front of the garage. I didn't recognise them, but they had *the* look. Not just authority figures, but the real deal. These guys were definitely cops. One of them was inspecting the garage door, and the other was talking on his phone. They turned and looked up in my direction, which creeped me out for a second, but neither of them registered anything in their faces to suggest they could see me. I was hidden by the tint.

So it was possible that somebody could have been stood on this spot during the attack, but it didn't feel likely to me. It would have been too much of a coincidence, and I've already mentioned I don't believe in those.

I turned to see the security guard was now on the escalator, rising up toward me. He was speaking into his radio.

Oh come on.

As he got within hearing range I said, 'Hiya,' and walked toward the back of the store, where the magical moving staircase moved in the opposite direction. He reached out and put his hand on my arm, pulling me back.

I turned round and gave him my full 'Excuse me?'

Every woman on the floor knew that tone. They all turned to look. The guard let go and stepped back, awkwardly. 'I, uh, are you looking for something?' he said.

'Well, not *now* I'm not.'

I looked down at my arm, then at his hand. I was wearing my mask of full offence. I turned and stalked toward the back of the store, feeling quite proud of my performance.

Back down on the ground floor, I walked to the exit and headed back out into the sunshine. I turned toward Virginia Street, and saw the two cops rounding the corner. One of them was thin and blond, with large sunglasses. The other had broad shoulders and a beard. Both suits were expensive, but the blond guy wore his like he'd had lessons, and the bearded guy wore a shirt and tie like he was preparing for a fight.

'Pardon me,' the blond guy said. He had clipped, East Coast accent. 'We noticed you went into the hotel a few minutes ago?'

My first reaction was another shot of, *Oh, come on.*

I followed that up with wondering how they'd noticed me. I'd been alone in the street. Unless they'd been in one of the other buildings, watching to see who came snooping around.

'ID, fellas?'

They both reached for their warrant cards and flashed them. The blond said, 'I'm DI Alan Dasho. This is DI Todd Robinson.'

I nodded an acknowledgement.

'And you are?' Robinson said.

Dasho was the one who approached his job by being patient and polite. Robinson was clearly the other guy.

'Can I help you, detectives?' I skipped past giving my name.

'Why were you looking around a crime scene?' Robinson said.

'I wasn't aware that it was,' I said. Did they buy it? Probably not, but I'd learned that the trick was to keep talking. 'I was interested in booking the hotel.'

'The police tape back there was a clue,' Robinson said.

There was something off about this. First I find out an undercover cop is dead, then two detectives I've never met turn up at the scene right after me. My gut was telling me to hold back. I'd learned to trust it.

'I'm sorry if we're being rude.' Dasho played nice. 'See, a woman was killed there yesterday, and we're still looking for witnesses to come forward. You match a description we've received.' His eyes went down to the cycling helmet hanging from my bag. 'Quite closely.'

I smiled. 'I always say, coincidence can be a cruel thing.'

I needed to change my approach.

They already had enough to question me further, and wisecracking was only going to make it more likely that they'd decide to act on it.

'Sorry,' I said. I hoped I looked suitably contrite. 'I'm an investigator.'

I fished another business card from my pocket and handed it to Dasho. He scanned it quickly, then passed it to Robinson.

'I was fishing around to see if there's a case there. Times are tight, you know?'

'You'd need a client to have a case,' Robinson said.

'I'd need to find one first.'

'Fucking ambulance chaser,' Robinson said. He glared at me for a second before saying, 'Clear off.'

I nodded and headed back toward York Street.

I'd come back and try again later, dressed as *Detective Woman*. I was more likely to slip by unnoticed and get more answers. I paused to look in a shop window and take a chance to see if the cops were following me. They were both still standing where I'd left them. Robinson was talking into his phone, and Dasho was chatting with the security guard from the shop.

I was outside the Radisson Hotel, only a block away from my bike, when my phone rang.

'Excuse me, Ms Ireland?'

The party never stops on Sam Ireland's phone.

'My name's Joe Pepper. I think we should talk,' he said.

THIRTY-SEVEN
FERGUS
13:10

Stan sends me the details on the pro bono job.

The target's name is Scott Christopher. He's the manager of a bar on Bath Street: FuBar. I've been in there a few times; they do good burgers and pizza. He's never put 'sexual assault' on the menu, because I suppose that would be considered something of a clue.

As far as I can tell, The FuBar is usually full of off-duty coppers and lawyers. Other professional types. I don't really understand how a cop bar works. I mean, surely the quickest way to guarantee a drugs bust is to have bartenders and cops in the same place?

Scott Christopher lives in a ground-floor flat on Gardner Street, in the West End. I sit outside in the car until I see him leave. Skinny guy, his forearms are coated in tattoos and he wears a flannel shirt and a beanie. I watch as he turns the corner at the end of the street, and then give it a few extra beats. People can often turn back. If you've forgotten something, there tends to be a zone of a few hundred yards in which you'll turn around. Up to around half a mile. If you're past that point when you realise, you'll say, Fuck it, I can get by without.

Once I'm comfortable that he's not coming back, I let myself into his building. It looks like an old tenement apartment that's been divided into two. Where the central hallway to the older, much larger apartment would have been, there's a wall running down the middle. And the rooms on either side have been converted, with a small toilet and shower installed in what was probably once a closet.

The kitchen unit is pressed up against that new wall, and the fridge is stocked with a mix of health food and beer.

Gotta love this guy's self-delusion, aye?

In the small living room there's a TV unit, some musical instruments, and a black leather sofa. The place has clothes lying around in stupid places. I mean, next to the TV? Come on, who does that?

Close inspection shows the sofa's not really leather.

Up above the furniture, about six feet off the floor, I find what I'm looking for. There's a white closet door set into the wall. Before this floor was converted into two separate apartments, there would have been a closet off the living room, backing onto the wall of the old kitchen. When it was all changed, they must have used that closet space for a new smaller kitchen in the flat behind the new dividing wall. And above that kitchen, in a space that's now useless, is a small closet. The only reason to have a door so high in the wall is for a conversation piece.

I climb onto the arm of the sofa and take a look behind the door. As I expected, there are a few cardboard boxes in there, and a plastic Christmas tree. I push the boxes over to one side, and lift the tree on top of them. There will be just enough room for me to fit in there, if I need to.

I'm still working out the details, but I know I'll want to fake Alex's death in the morning, before he leaves for work. And I'll need the replacement body to be fresh enough to fool a casual examination.

I sit on the sofa for a second and think about what Zoe said.

I know she's right. I know I need to build up the guts to ask Sam out for a coffee. I don't want to keep this thing going on too long if it's not going to work, because that'll just set me up for disappointment. And, if she's not interested in meeting me, I may as well know now rather than wait until I'm too attached.

I write her a message saying all of this.

Or, I start to, because I keep deleting it.

Then I chicken out, and send the blandest bit of useless chat in history.

FergusSingsTheBlues – At work. Bored.

FergusSingsTheBlues – Know any good jobs?

Fucking auto correct again.

FergusSingsTheBlues – JOKES. Good JOKES.

Fergus, sunshine, yer patter will never win any awards.

Okay. I know where Scott lives, and I think I know the best time to take him out. I know how I'm going to fake things for Alex. I'm back on form.

THIRTY-EIGHT

SAM

13:10

I knew who Joe Pepper was. Both versions of him.

Publicly, he was a solicitor who'd left a lucrative career as a prosecutor to start taking mostly pro bono cases in the East End. He was a big figure behind the scenes in the local Labour Party, known to be the pit bull who fixed everything in private but one of the party's most effective councillors in public.

Behind all of that, and most relevant to the way my gut was trying to climb out through the soles of my feet, was the other side of Joe. The orphan who had been raised by Mike Gibson. Linked to a number of crime families, and one of the most feared men in the East End.

So of course I knew who he was.

But I wasn't going to let him know that.

'How can I help Mr, uh, Pepper, was it?'

He laughed. Maybe he was used to people pretending not to know who he was. 'There's a café on Argyle Street. Laurie's. Nice place. Decent coffee. It's a lovely day and I'm sitting out front. I'd like to talk to you, and it's a nice public space, so if you're worried, you know you can walk away anytime.'

Oh, thanks. I like having someone mansplain to me about the safety of public places. The only thing I find creepier than men who assume I never need to think about my personal safety are men who assume they need to think about it on my behalf. First thing I do when I walk in a room is check out all of the ways *out* of it. I know why I do it, but I worry about men who do it. Why do they need to? What are they hiding?

I'd already talked to Mike Gibson today. And stared down a couple of feds. Talking to Joe Pepper – a bigger fish than both – felt like a hat-trick I didn't want to go for.

'No thanks.'

'Okay,' he said. 'No foul. I'll just have that drink, and when I'm finished, I'll probably call the polis and let them know about the package you picked up off a dead woman yesterday.'

Crap.

He killed the call before I could say anything. Smart move. It put all the pressure onto me to make the decision.

I headed to the café.

Laurie's faced right out onto the street. It had wide windows, with the front door in the centre. The windows were partially obscured by the café's name, painted across them in frosted letters. The paint around the windows was black, and there was a dark awning that came out a few feet, casting a slight protective cover down onto the silver metal tables and chairs on the pavement. The pavement on Argyle Street wasn't very wide, so our conversation would be overhead by any of the few passers-by.

How did he get my number?

Well, that's easy. I have a website. Anyone can make a booking for my services. I've delivered parcels for all kinds of people, and done investigation work for some high-profile clients. It's not hard to find me.

But why?

And how did he know I had the parcel?

By the time I reached the café, he was already sat at a table, giving an order to a waitress who looked young enough to have been conceived in her parents' celebration shag after Blur vs Oasis. Joe ordered a coffee and mentioned his tab. I asked for a glass of water and sat down across the table from him.

He was waiting until the waitress was out of the way before speaking to me. I decided to take the opportunity to take control and rattle him. 'How did you know to call me?' I said.

The waitress looked down at me, startled, before realising I wasn't speaking to her. Joe simply smiled. He continued to stay silent until the waitress had gone, like he'd intended, then started. 'You know who I am.' He said it matter-of-factly, dismissing the game I'd played before.

'Yes.'

'And what I do.'

'Yes.'

'I have a package I need to find. A woman stole it from me yesterday, and then she was, unfortunately, murdered. I'd like you to find it for me, urgently.'

He was watching me as he spoke. Was he gauging my reaction, waiting to see if I connected what he was saying to what had happened to me yesterday? I'd be an idiot not to. I was determined to hold back, but I've never been a poker player. He smiled, and I got the impression he'd seen whatever he was looking for.

He continued. 'Let's say I pay you to find it for me.'

'What if I'm fully booked?' I said, pushing as much ice into my veins as I could. 'I might not have the time to take on the work, but I could recommend another good detective to you.'

Joe nodded, but it was sideways, with his head bobbing a little on his neck. It was a move I'd seen George Clooney do in films, and it looked cute as *hell* when he did it. On Joe, it just looked like an act.

He slipped a phone out from inside his jacket and swiped at the screen a few times. He put it on the table between us and nodded for me to take a look. I picked it up. There was a picture of me, talking to Paula yesterday as I took the package. The quality was a little off, and it looked like a video still. The angle was pointing downwards, from farther up the street. A security camera.

'There are others,' he said, nodding at the phone with his chin.

I pushed onto the next image, then the one after that. And again. Each of them showed me, from different cameras, talking to Paula, and then pushing off on my bike.

How did he have these images? I was pretty sure the cops still didn't have them. If they did, Alan Dasho and Todd Robinson would have arrested me. I felt my own phone buzzing in my pocket. It kept going. An incoming call. I ignored it. Now wasn't the time.

The drinks arrived and he nodded thanks at the waitress. He lifted his cup and held it in front of his face, blowing at the surface but not putting the coffee to his lips. I didn't touch my glass of water. I knew my hand would shake, and I didn't want Joe Pepper to see it.

'I always like to sort things out the easy way,' he said. 'I think all problems can be dealt with reasonably, by throwing cash at them. That said,' he set the cup down and leaned forward for effect, 'I am under a lot of pressure lately, and I can't afford to be as patient as I would like.'

I felt three shorter buzzes on my phone. Messages.

Joe placed a bound bundle of twenty-pound notes on the table, and said, 'What do you say? Can you find the package for me?'

I was rattled, and stuck between a rock and a scary place. Because even if I took the bung and handed over the tapes, I'd then have to explain to the cops why it was I didn't have—

Wait.

Wait.

Wait.

Joe kept saying *package*. He hadn't mentioned *tapes*. He hadn't said 'them' or 'those' or anything that suggested he had an idea of what had been handed to me the day before.

He didn't have a clue what was in the package.

'I need a few hours,' I said. 'It's in a safe place.'

'Of course.' He stood up and handed me a business card. 'Meet me back here at four. And please, let's just do it the easy way. Better for both of us.'

He smiled as if he'd just delivered a warm farewell rather than a threat. I watched him walk away. The bastard had a spring in his step.

I headed back down the block toward my bike. I pulled out my phone to switch the GPS back on. The messages were all from Fergus. Straight away, I wanted to reply to the messages. But I knew I needed to get the phone call out of the way. She was off the case, but maybe it was in relation to the investigation. She could be trying to warn me of something.

I dialled the number.

'Hiya, Han. I know, they need me to come—'

'No,' she cut right in. Her voice sounded as rattled as I felt. 'Where are you? I need to talk. Out of the office.'

'What's up?'

'Paula Lafferty? You were right. Looks like she was a cop.'

Here we go.

THIRTY-NINE
ALEX
13:55

Holy shit.

Alex had it. Joe's big plan. He could see the edges of it. The trail of numbers wasn't conclusive, but he could see what Joe was up to. It was just a matter of taking a step back, and looking at things from a distance. Usually, he had to get up close to follow a trail. Look for all the tiny footprints, all the tracks that have been covered. It was a job of remembering dates and numbers, and seeing the incremental steps that added up to one big leap.

This time it was more about taking a wider view and seeing the pattern. He would never have noticed it if he wasn't already looking.

Joe was going to try and pull a fast one.

Asma Khan wasn't going to see this coming.

More important, was this something Alex could use? He saw three different options. First, he could try and cut in on the deal. Take some of the cash. Second, he could use it to blackmail Joe if things went bad. If Joe discovered what Alex was up to. Third, he could hand the info over to Khan, make himself bulletproof.

He was trying to figure out his angle when Emma knocked on the door. She walked in without waiting for a response.

'Why do you knock?' Alex said.

Emma shrugged. 'Politeness, I suppose.'

'So you knock to be polite, but don't wait for me to respond?'

'Were you going to tell me not to come in?'

'No.'

'Have you ever told me not to come in?'

'No.'

'Well, then.'

She smiled and waited him out. Alex laughed. He could never stay mad at Emma, she had something about her. Even when she was being rude, it was with a sparkle. Everyone who met Emma fell for her, just a little. Never all the way, but just enough to enjoy being around her.

'How was lunch?' Alex said.

Usually he didn't care about the sex lives of his co-workers. He'd never had a personal conversation with anyone else in the building. Truth be told, he didn't know who was married, who was single, who had kids and who was shagging each other in the toilets.

Didn't know.

Didn't care.

But Emma was different. She was gay. Woman on woman? Yeah, he could talk about that. Showing an interest in the details of her love life did two things: it got him excited, and it let him appear to be supportive and modern. Fake feminism was where it was at. Plus, it involved his boss. The only person in the world he answered to.

Emma sat on the edge of the desk and waggled her eyebrows. 'It was great. We're doing it again tomorrow.'

'It?' He leaned forward a little.

'Coffee and pasta.' Emma smiled. 'Maybe even some red wine, if my boss doesn't mind.'

'Just one glass is fine,' Alex said.

'A bottle is just one glass.' Emma gave a fake-innocent look. 'A big one, mind. I think my boss's boss will be okay with it.' She gave him a small grin just to let him know she was playing around. 'Which is why I'm in here. Asma's waiting outside, but Joe's running late. Should I stall?'

Alex looked at the screen on his computer. The clock told him it was time for the meeting. An hour ago, he'd been dreading it. Now? He was looking forward to it. He could sit there, listening to the two of them being all cool and smug, and he would know something they didn't. He'd be the only person in the room with *all* of the information.

He liked the thought of that.

FORTY
SAM
13:55

I found Hanya sitting in the back corner of FuBar. She was nursing a vodka, which was a bad sign for that early in the afternoon. I asked for a glass of water from the bar and joined her at the table.

'What's going on, Han?'

She snorted, petulant like a teenager. 'You tell me.'

Okay. Did I deserve that? Had I read her signal wrong the night before? I didn't think so, and I was the one who'd fed her Paula's real name. I waited her out. After a moment she nodded, deciding to start again.

'Sorry. This thing's got me in a weird mood. I have *no* idea what's going on.'

'I'll start,' I said. 'So, I got her real name off our app. She'd booked the pickup using a card as Lafferty.'

'That's odd.' Hanya's eyes screwed tight with confusion. 'She didn't have a debit card in her purse. Maybe she knew the numbers off by heart?'

'Maybe.'

'So what made you think she was a cop?'

I put a hand up. 'In a minute. First I want to know where you got with that. You said she was?'

'Took some digging, but yeah. She was. Or, she used to be, back in Belfast. She worked undercover over there, helped to bring a few gangs down. But then, about two years ago, she quit.'

'Why?'

'Well, it gets weird. See, I called a guy she used to work with, a detective called Brennan.'

'Did he know why you were calling?'

Hanya gave her head one quick shake. 'Nope. I said I'd arrested someone who was claiming to be her, then described someone completely different to him, he said, no, doesn't sound like her. Then I got him talking.'

'So nobody over there knows she's dead?'

'Not as far as I know.'

'She have any family, anyone who'll miss her?'

'I didn't look at that.' Hanya looked pissed off, but it was at herself, not me. Sometimes it was easy for cops to forget the human aspect of their job, the emotions of the victims and their loved ones. 'Brennan said she left suddenly, never said goodbye to anybody. But Paula's boss did the same thing, at the same time. They both just vanished.'

'Either of them married?'

Hanya waved that line of thought away. 'He was gay. Brennan was very clear on that. He'd tried to raise the whole thing with his bosses. He said, with all the undercover work they'd done, he was worried that maybe someone had killed them, a revenge thing, and he wanted to investigate. But his bosses shut that down, said they were both fine.'

'That's fishy, yeah. Would you be able to speak to his boss? Find an excuse?'

She shook her head. 'Heart attack twelve months ago.'

Ouch.

'And it gets better. I'd been off the phone to Brennan for ten minutes when one of the feds asked to talk to me in private. Took me out to the car park and warned me off it.'

'Seriously? Like in a movie?'

'Exactly.'

'This fed who warned you off, wouldn't happen to be either Alan Dasho or Todd Robinson, would it?'

Hanya's eyes narrowed at me. 'How'd you know?'

'In a sec. Did you get a name for the guy? The one who left with Paula?'

'Robert Butler.'

Holy crap.

I pulled the package out of my messenger bag and showed the name to Hanya. Robert Butler. Hanya's mouth dropped open like in a cartoon as she read it.

I put my hands out in a wide *Tell me about it* gesture. 'I know, aye? So she gave me this in the street. Sent me to an address that doesn't exist. Well, the address exists, but you know what I mean, there's no Robert Butler there.'

I handed the package to her. Hanya opened it up and looked at the tapes inside. She pulled them out and read the labels, then cocked an eyebrow at me. 'Have you listened to them?'

'Yeah. There's not much on there, but the first one makes it pretty clear Paula was here undercover. Second one is like a sex tape, practically, but there are mentions for the ninth—'

'That's in two days.'

'Yeah, and also two guys on it mention a *takeover* and a *cartel*. Mean anything?' Hanya gave me another *What the fuck* look and shook her head. 'The third is just a mix tape.'

'Good music?'

I shrugged. 'So-so. But read the labels again.' I watched as she scanned across them. 'The arson job you've been assigned to, know who the building belongs to? Because I'll bet it's Mike Gibson. And you know his son's name?'

'Sure,' she nodded. Callum Gib— I could see in her eyes the exact second she connected *Cal's Log* with Callum Gibson. 'He's one of our suspects.'

'It gets better,' I said. 'See, this is how I know the fed names. I was just down on Virginia Street asking around, looking for the witnesses who described me—'

'Sam—'

'Hang on. I figured, since I was in that alley, I could ask the right questions. So, then Dasho and Robinson stop me in the street. Out of nowhere, they just turn up and start asking me questions. Then, I'm just done with them, and I get a call from Joe Pepper.'

'Joe Pepper?'

Hanya knew the same things about Joe as I did. The police knew just how dodgy he was, but this is Glasgow, knowing about a problem doesn't mean fixing it. Joe knew the right kind of handshake, and that was what mattered most around here.

'Yeah. He has pictures from CCTV showing me picking it up from Paula and riding off, just like you predicted. And he wants to pay me to hand it over to him. He's told me to meet him at four. The only thing I've got going for me right now is I don't think he knows what's in it.'

'Maybe Gartcosh were running Paula?' Hanya said. 'She found out something, and then she was killed. Maybe Cal killed her and did a runner? But then, what's Joe's part in it?'

A dead undercover cop.

A crooked politician.

A missing criminal.

'I don't know,' I said. 'And how does the fire tie in? I can't get a feel for it. But I don't trust Dasho or Robinson any more than you seem to.' She nodded agreement as I spoke. 'So we keep it to ourselves for now. I just don't know what to do about Joe and these tapes.'

Hanya sat in silence for a moment. She was staring down at the table, but her eyes were moving from side to side, like she was reading off a page. I knew she was thinking things over, and I gave her the space to do it.

I remembered the messages from Fergus. I hadn't checked them.

FergusSingsTheBlues – At work. Bored.

FergusSingsTheBlues – Know any good jobs?

FergusSingsTheBlues – JOKES. Good JOKES.

I didn't have time for this. Even still, I found myself making the time. I left Hanya to her thoughts while I typed a response back.

TheSamIreland – TBH I'm starting to think my job IS a joke.

'Okay,' she said. 'The biggest problem is that he's set the time for the meeting. That means he could be setting you up. But you reckon he doesn't know what's in the package?'

'Right.'

She smiled. 'Then we give him what he wants.'

FORTY-ONE
FERGUS
15:20

I walk with Alex through Central Station. You'd be amazed at the meetings and deals that are conducted on the concourse here, beneath the large glass roof. When I worked for the government, I saw a report about how a Russian spy defected to MI6 underneath the clock.

I called Alex at work and asked to speak with him urgently.

He's all nervous and shifty when he turns up.

'I left in a hurry,' he says. 'And this wasn't in the appointment book. It *looks* like something strange. Emma, my secretary, she'll think something's strange.'

'I'm counting on it,' I say.

That throws him for a loop. His poor wee face gets all confused and he opens his mouth, like, *What?*

'You've told me you don't want the details,' I say.

'Okay. Okay. But I want the details on this bit. Just enough to know it's going to work.'

'Aye, okay. Well, you strike me as a guy who's watched a few crime movies. I bet you love you some Scorsese, right? So you'll know the scenes where the guy who is in trouble starts acting all weird?'

'Yeah.'

'Well, your secretary will know them, too. *And* when you die under mysterious circumstances, and you want the police to think it was anybody other than you or your wife that arranged it, Emma will be remembering that you were acting all nervous the day before.'

'I didn't act ner—'

'You're a natural, don't worry about it. Anyway. So it all adds to the illusion.'

'But that's just complicating things, making people more suspicious, not less. That's not what I want. I want it simple. Quick.'

I stop walking and look back up at the big clock. It's almost time to head to a job. Joe's sent me details of a possible hit. He wants me to sit in a coffee shop and watch a meeting he's got with some PI. If I see him raise his hand and scratch the back of his head, I'm to follow the PI after the meeting, take her out, and make her vanish. If he scratches his chin, I'm off the hook.

I really don't want to do it.

For the first time, I'm getting antsy at the thought of killing. It's bad enough I've got to do Scott Fucking Christopher for Alex, but at least I know Scott is a sex pest.

Joe's threatening me, though. He knows I lied to him. He knows I fucked up. And he also knows someone else who could take me out if I refuse.

Stan's right, I need a holiday.

I turn my attention back to Alex. 'For someone who doesn't want to know the details, you're asking a lot of questions.'

'Okay.' He puts his hands up, *You got me*. 'I need to know this is a good plan. How are you going to convince people? Why are we making people at my office more suspicious?'

'Here's how it's going to work. You know who you work for. I know who you work for. They're not people who want too much media attention. They like things done quickly and quietly. If you die in a very public, very media-friendly way, they're going to want the investigation over with quickly, to make sure their names stop coming up in the news.'

'Probably, yeah.'

'And we both know Joe Pepper will be asked to fix the mess. So, it helps that I know how he works. There's no way to fool a medical examiner if he or she does the job properly, but if there's a distraction, if someone is leaning on them to get it all over and done with—'

'Like a magic trick.'

'Right. There's hope for you yet, big man. Distraction. Your death slips through unnoticed, by being the most noticed thing in town.'

He smiles. Nods. He's bought it.

Truth is, it's a plan that sounds better in theory than practice. There are any number of things that could go wrong. And it almost certainly means I'll need to lie to Joe at some point, because I'm the first person he's going to ask after it's done.

But all that matters right now is that Alex believes me. He's onside. So now I can get some information.

'You've got somewhere to go, afterwards?'

'Yeah, yeah.' He nods. He wants to show off now. Make me see he's as good at cool plans as I am. 'Yeah. Got a flat leased in town. Under a different name, you know?'

'And you've got some walking around money? You've got enough to last if you need to stay hidden for a few weeks.'

His grin would put the Cheshire cat to shame. 'Walking around? Yes, if you want to walk round Vegas. I've got bags full of cash at the flat.'

I hand him a fresh burner. When he gives me a blank look I say, 'You'll need to leave your main one in your car tonight. If I need to contact you, I'll use this.' He nods, looks a little confused. I give him a smile. 'Relax. You'll be fine. Dying's going to be easy.'

FORTY-TWO
SAM
15:48

We got to the café early. On the way down, Hanya had stopped at a bar on Bothwell Street and told me to wait outside. She came back out a few minutes later with three bags of cocaine.

(Well, I assume it was cocaine, I'm not an expert.)

We took the first two cassettes out of the package, leaving the mix tape, and replaced them with the drugs.

At the café, Hanya sat out front and I took a spot inside, at one of the high tables near the door. I could see Hanya, but the frosted lettering on the outside of the glass would keep me hidden.

I put my earphones in and pulled out a book. *Girl Meets Boy on a Crime Spree.* I had no intention of ever reading it, but I still picked up a copy at the supermarket. Impulse buy. They had it on the till, and it was either that or chocolate. The book was cheaper. Phil uses computer software to call friends in America. He had opened a conference call from his computer and called both me and Hanya. I'd muted my own phone, so I could listen in without my noises interfering with the recording. Hanya gave her order to the young waitress who had served me earlier.

Joe walked across the front of the café. He scanned the tables, looking for me, then took a seat in front of me, just the other side of the frosted letters painted onto the window. Hanya waited until the waitress carried her drink out, then stood up and walked over to where Joe was sat. She was carrying my messenger bag.

I pressed a finger to my right earphone, making sure it was in place.

'Mr Pepper,' I heard Hanya say. 'Nice to see you.'

I saw Joe look up, but my view was of the bald spot at the back of his head, and I couldn't see his facial expression. 'Er, you too, Miss—?'

'*Detective Inspector*,' Hanya corrected. 'Hanya Perera.'

'Oh, of course.' If Joe was lying, he was polished enough to get away with it. 'How are you?'

I saw Hanya smile, then point at the empty seat across the table from Joe. She didn't wait for him to say *No*. 'I'm good, thanks. I'm here on behalf of a mutual friend. Ms Ireland.'

There was a long pause. I watched as Joe tilted his head to one side. I could imagine his smile as he tried to act cool about the surprise. 'Okay,' he said, finally.

I watched Hanya fish the phone from her jacket pocket, and then heard the clank in my ear as she set it down on the table. 'She's here in spirit,' she said. 'But I'm sure you can understand she's nervous to meet you under the circumstances.'

'Okay,' Joe said again.

'And this conversation is being recorded, naturally.'

'Unusual job for a police officer, Detective.'

'Unusual job for a politician.'

There was silence again. Hanya reached into my bag and pulled out the padded envelope. She placed it on the table and slid it across. Joe picked it up slowly, and opened the flaps to look inside.

'This is it?' he said.

'That was all she was given,' Hanya said. Her voice was level. Her eyes never flickered. I made a note never to play poker with her. 'I have to say, I'm curious as to why you are interested in the contents of that package.'

What was she doing? Why rattle his cage?

When Joe answered, I understood her game. She'd put him on the defensive, and he wanted the conversation over. 'Personal business.'

'But you understand why Ms Ireland was cautious about meeting you here?'

'Of course.' He sounded irritated, but like he was going to play along, let it go.

'I understand you've got images that place her at the scene?' Hanya waited until Joe acknowledged that with a tilt of his head. 'That's going to cause her some problems if my colleagues get hold of them.'

'She doesn't need to worry about that,' he said.

Hanya thought that over for a second. I didn't doubt that Joe had the pull to make that problem go away, and I doubted she did, either. 'Okay,' she said. 'So, it's in your hands. It's not in Sam's interest to take this issue any further. She knows that. And, given what I've just handed over, you and I both could get in trouble if any of us made it public.'

'Sure,' Joe said.

Hanya picked up the messenger bag and put it over her shoulder, signalling she was ready to leave. 'So we've all got insurance. We're all protected. I think the best thing is if we all just agree to play nice and forget about this.'

'I agree,' Joe said. 'Ms Ireland won't have any problems from me.'

Someone tapped me on the shoulder.

What now?

FORTY-THREE
FERGUS
15:55

I get in line at the café. Nice place. Never been here before. Joe has already sat down out front, and it looks like there's table service out there, but inside there's a small queue at the till.

There's air conditioning in here, making it much more comfortable inside than out in the sun. Behind me, in a cooler, is a selection of sandwiches and cakes. My stomach tells me it wants one of them. Maybe all of them. I ignore the rumble, because I'm working.

Never mix food and killing. It leads to some very strange dreams.

I grab a black filter coffee and find a table in the corner at the back. It gives me a clear view of Joe through the front window, but it also lets me keep an eye on everyone else in the room, too.

I don't like having my back to anyone.

Looking around, all I can see are people on breaks from their offices, or holding meetings. Men in suit trousers and rolled up shirt sleeves, looking uncomfortable in the heat. Women in bright summer dresses, looking far more chilled.

Hang on.

That young woman, sat by the window—

Is that Sam?

She looks like Sam. But all I've seen is her photo and the video. You can't always tell from just that. She's looking out the window, with a paperback novel on the table. It's the same one my mum's reading. I get the feeling I'm the only person not interested in what *the girl* is up to. She's got earphones in, too, so she might not want to be disturbed.

Her hair's a brighter colour than on the website; a kind of coppery shine that can only come from a bottle. And her legs, hey, if all cyclists have pins like those, I'll never talk shite about them again.

But now I feel a bit creepy. I'm checking her out, and I'm sure it's Sam, but she hasn't spotted me. I don't know why, but I start to feel like I'm cheating on Sam *with* Sam, because I know her as the funny lass on my phone.

I should just go over and talk to her, but I'm working. I can't get distracted right now. What if Joe gives me the signal and I miss it, because I'm chatting up Sam?

And now I'm feeling creepy again, because I'm deciding not to talk to her. Which is worse, to go and interrupt her now, and fuck up my job, or to concentrate on my job but feel like I'm being a creep to Sam?

I get the luxury of pushing all of that out of my mind when I see movement outside. An Asian woman in a business suit stands up from her own table and walks to where Joe is sat.

Game on.

FORTY-FOUR
ALEX
15:50

Alex was bored.

More than bored. He was a caged animal. Waiting. Restless. This was his last afternoon at work. His last moments in his old skin. He'd never do any of this bullshit again, and any work he did now was a total waste.

In all of his jobs, Alex had always had fantasies about his last day at work. Based on the day he won the lottery, or received an inheritance from some rich uncle he'd never heard of. He'd pictured all the ways he could walk out, swear at his bosses, become an office legend.

At MHW, he didn't really have anyone he could swear at. Sure, he could call Khan and be a dick to her, but that would only increase the risk of things going wrong. Emma would be the only person who would really notice his dramatic flounce out the door, and she would probably just laugh at him.

He couldn't take the chance of making a big scene. Everything needed to seem completely normal. He needed to file paperwork for clients he no longer cared about, and ask Emma to set up meetings he'd never attend.

By four it was all too much. He needed air.

He headed out. He spoke to Emma on the way, saying, 'I'm going for coffee.'

'No, I'm fine,' she said with a slight smile, pointing out his lack of a question.

Out on the street he turned right, and walked to the café. The place was usually quiet at this time, just a few people from the offices, probably some from the same building. He saw Joe Pepper sitting out front, but the man was deep in conversation with a woman. They were both dressed for business, and Alex knew well enough to leave him alone.

Things got even worse inside. He saw Fergus sitting in the back, and immediately averted his eyes. He didn't know much about the etiquette of hiring a hit man, but he was pretty sure that nodding at him in public would be breaking the rules. Already, he'd had to avoid looking in two directions. Now he could see the girl behind the counter staring at him as he swivelled around on the spot, and he felt like a prick.

The ground never really opens up and swallows you at the right moment.

Then he saw someone else he recognised. The young PI that Kara had been speaking to. She didn't look like she wanted to be bothered, but that was tough luck. Alex needed a way out, someone to focus on.

He stepped over and introduced himself.

FORTY-FIVE
FERGUS
16:04

I see Joe raise his hand. I lean forward a little, just to get a better view.

He scratches his chin.

The game is off.

I relax back in my seat. Looks like Joe maybe doesn't need me. If I'm off the hook, I can focus on whether or not to go talk to Sam.

But now Alex Pennan walks in, and things start turning into a fucking farce.

He makes a comedy show of turning his face away from Joe Pepper as he comes in through the door. Then he looks over and clocks me, and does the same. He swivels on his feet to face the till. His shoes squeak on the floor as he does it.

I realise he thinks this is subtle.

In his head, he's just being really cool about the whole thing.

My biggest problem right now is that I can't sit back and laugh at what a prat he's being.

Then he turns to Sam and taps her on the shoulder. She looks pissed off to be bothered, which makes me glad I didn't try it. But how the hell does he know her? I mean, Glasgow can feel like a small city sometimes. Six degrees of separation is a pointless game here, because most people can be connected within three moves.

Maybe that's all it is.

Outside, the PI gets up and walks away. Joe hasn't given the signal. He gets up and goes the other way.

Sam's said something to Pennan, brushed him off maybe, and then she's standing up. Shite, the dumb wee bastard has annoyed her.

But maybe that's good. If she leaves, I can end this guessing game that I'm playing, and go back to wondering how to ask her out for real. Online, where things are a wee bit less scary.

Then she turns and sees me.

I think she recognises me, too.

Oh shit, decision made.

Fergus, you gotta go for it now.

Girl meets boy . . .

FORTY-SIX
SAM
16:07

Alex Pennan couldn't have picked a worse moment if he'd tried. Hanya and Joe were wrapping up. This was the key moment. He'd agree with what she was saying, and I'd be in the clear, or he'd want to kick up a fuss, and I'd be in trouble.

Before I could hear what he said, Alex tapped me on the shoulder.

'Hey,' he said. He sounded nervous. Jumpy. I don't know why, because I'm not that impressive. 'It's Sam, right? We met yesterday.'

'Mr Pennan, hi.' I smiled, but it was a rigid, perfunctory gesture. I hoped he read it. I also didn't add, *I've been paid to follow you.*

On that score, he was making things ridiculously easy for me.

'Good to see you,' he said.

Neither of us really believed that. There's a feeling you get. You know when someone is stalling. They've picked you as the random distraction from something else. Maybe I'm more attuned to it, because I've had to do it myself plenty of times while tailing people.

I just didn't know why Alex Pennan was doing it to me.

I caught movement outside in the corner of my eye. Hanya was standing up. I'd missed the end of the conversation. Crap. I picked up my book and smiled again at Pennan, a *Well, thanks for chatting* gesture.

Then Joe got up and walked away. The meeting was definitely over.

'Good to see you, Mr Pennan.' I nodded and took a step away.

Pennan took the hint. He looked at the table that Joe had just vacated and nodded to himself. He stepped out toward the empty seat, putting his hand on the back of the chair before anybody else could take it.

I didn't want to follow him straight away. There was always the chance he might try to restart the conversation. I gave him a few seconds, and took a look around the room.

I locked eyes with Fergus Fletcher.

There's usually doubt when you meet someone that you've only known online. Profile pictures don't always look the same as the person you'll see in front of you. Even the honest photos will look a little different.

But I had no doubt about this one. I knew straight away that it was Fergus. He looked good, too. Annoyingly. In his video I'd seen someone who looked a little vulnerable, hiding something beneath the surface. I still saw that in his smile as he walked toward me, but it was buried beneath a confidence, a cool.

It was a good mix.

'Sam,' he said.

I gave him a smile, and hoped it looked as genuine as I wanted it to. 'Hiya.'

Not now. Please. This is the exact wrong moment for this.

'I was just looking up,' he said. His Scottish accent was less pronounced than I'd assumed from the video and messages. He sounded almost trans-Atlantic. 'And I thought, that's Sam.'

We both stood there for a second, and an awkwardness crept it. I didn't know what the right response was to this. Should we shake hands? Hug? We'd only been talking for a day, but we'd been doing it a *lot.*

'What's the right thing here?' he said it with an easy grin. 'Do we shake hands? Are we hugging people?'

How did he read my mind like that?

I needed to leave. I didn't want to. It caught me by surprise, but what I really wanted to do was stay right there and wait for him to smile again. I hoped he could read my mind about that, too, because I was going to have to cut this short.

'I, um, I'm sorry, but I need to go.'

I turned and walked out the door, fast, before my common sense lost control of the rest of me.

FORTY-SEVEN
FERGUS
16:10

She hates me.

Shit.

Shite.

Shiteybaws.

She couldn't leave any quicker if she tried. Practically has a jet pack on. It must have been my joke about hugging. It came off as creepy, aye? Baws. I tell myself it doesn't matter. I've not even been talking to her for a full day. But I know it's a lie. I've been getting my hopes up.

And just for a second there, when we were both smiling, I was sure there'd been . . . I don't know. *Something.*

Fuck it.

Note to self, don't mention hugging a lassie within the first sixty seconds of meeting her.

Well. I'll back off. Can't stand those guys who think it's fun to keep pushing. I mean, I don't believe the bullshit about *plenty more fish in the sea,* either, because I've seen too many fishermen who come back at the end of the day without a catch. But if a woman isn't interested, it's time to move on.

You have a job to do tonight, Fergus.

And first, you need to finish this one.

I call Joe's mobile, and he answers pretty quickly. 'No, you didn't miss it,' he says. 'Calling it off. She's no problem.'

'Looked hot,' I say. 'The PIs in New York were all cheap and old.'

I'd been friends with a PI, in Astoria. He'd been the exception to half of the rule; he was the same age as me, but still cheap.

'That wasn't her,' he says. 'They were being clever. That was a cop, sent in her place to make peace.' His tone changed a little, tired, shrugging it all off. 'And it worked. What the hell? Now's not the right time to be dropping any more bodies.'

He says he'll send me some money as payment for backing him up, then hangs up.

Right.

I've got the whole evening to kill before I head back to Scott's place.

I feel like shit.

FORTY-EIGHT
SAM
16:40

I met Hanya back at FuBar as we'd arranged. Pennan and Fergus had slowed me down, so Hanya had two gin and tonics lined up at the table by the time I got to the bar.

'I missed the end,' I said. 'How did it go?'

She took a sip at her drink and nodded as she set it back down. 'He's going to leave you alone.'

'Now the real question,' I said. I still hadn't touched my drink. It felt a little early. 'Are we going to leave him alone?'

'I think *you* should. We don't know what's going on yet but if it involves him, then I don't think you should pull the thread.'

Hanya was right, of course. The year before, I'd linked a series of arson attacks and a decades-old murder, and along the way I'd walked right up to the edge of something big. Hanya had talked me out of taking it any further. She said the same thing she was telling me now, *This is a thread, and if you pull on it, you don't know how high it goes.*

I'd got justice for a dead woman, and exposed the people behind the fires. I'd left the rest of it alone. But now, this was another mystery, and there was another thread dangling in front of me. I've said it before: I'm the queen of stupid decisions. I'd made the right choice once; asking me to do it twice was expecting a miracle.

No way was I leaving this alone.

'You're right.' I took a sip of the drink, a prop to cover for my lie. 'I'll leave it alone.'

'Cheers.' Hanya waved at the air with her glass. It was a distraction; she was playing the same game as me. I looked at her eyes and could see she was trying to read me. 'So, why were you late?'

Oh, that.

She didn't know I was lying about the case.

Hang on. *The case.* Pennan. He'd left the office. I checked the trackers on the phone. Both his and Kara's cars were still where they had been earlier. Alex Pennan was out and about, but I was sure that if he was on his way to an affair, he wouldn't have been stopping to talk to me.

Kara could wait.

'There was this, a, there was a guy.' Crap. I could feel my cheeks reddening. It wasn't the alcohol. 'I was talking to someone.'

'*Someone?*'

'Remember the one guy I liked? The video? Well, we've been sending each other messages all day. I like him, he's funny.'

Hanya made a high-pitched noise somewhere between a squeal and a giggle. 'You've met someone?'

'No. Well, yes. But not now. I messed it up. He was at the café, wanted to talk, but I brushed him off because of our thing. I was pretty rude.' I sighed. 'I blew that one.'

'But you like him?'

'I think so? I mean, how would I know? All we've been doing is messaging. I've only spoken to him for about a minute, and I was crap to him. It's not like I really know.'

'Rubbish. You know. Online is like the best way to know, these days. You talk to people in advance, get a feel for whether you'll get on. What did you feel like when you met him?'

The good news was I couldn't blush as I answered.

The bad news was that the only reason I didn't go red was I was still flushed from a few seconds before.

'I liked him,' I said.

'Well then.' She drained her glass and stood up to get another. 'You like him, you know he's in town. Ask him if he wants a drink. Now.'

'Now? While I'm dressed as Messenger McMessengerson?'

'Okay. Maybe after you've changed.'

FORTY-NINE
SAM
19:15

I met Fergus outside a Mexican restaurant on Candleriggs, a street in the Merchant City. I was fifteen minutes late, and he was polite enough to tell me he hadn't been waiting long. I hadn't earned it. First I'd been rude to him at the coffee shop, then I'd texted him, out of the blue, asking if he wanted to meet up. He'd rolled with it each time. That felt too good to be true.

I'd taken an hour deciding what to wear.

An hour.

I'm not sure why. I didn't really have any intention of anything happening after the date. Sure, with the messenger boys we jumped in bed straight away. And Milo had wanted sex from the minute we were introduced. But this felt different. I wanted to be a grown up about it.

I just wasn't sure what that actually meant.

I looked at the clothes I was wearing when I got home. Cargo shorts and a hoodie. It was a practiced look, and it said, *Don't date me, I'm too much of a fixer-upper.*

I knew Hanya was at least right about that. I'd spent the past year seeking out the men least likely to be a long-term proposition. That's why Milo managed to hurt me. I was used to being with guys who *I* could finish with. Walk away just as I see them turning the sex and the laughs into something deeper, when their eyes go all puppy dog.

But Milo finished with me.

And right after I'd bought him a load of Star Wars toys.

Growing up with Phil had made me think all geeks were nice. Milo taught me a lesson; I should probably thank him.

In the end I went with the basics. A black pencil skirt, tight but not *too* tight, and a matching blouse. Battered biker jacket over the top. That was just the right mix. It was like, *Hey there, I want to look cute for you, but I'm still wearing a dead cow as armour, don't get ideas.*

The waiter sat us at a table for two out front, in an area cut off from the street by a small canvas barrier that bore the logo of a Mexican beer.

He'd dressed simply in dark blue jeans and a thin jumper that clung in just the right places, showing a little bone on his shoulders that ran into the strong definition of lean muscle. I recognised a runner's build. I thought for a few seconds about what it would feel like running my hand along the lines that showed through his clothes, then reminded myself to take several steps back along that board.

'Hey,' Fergus said as we looked down the menu. 'I know I'm meant to be making a good impression, but you don't mind if I eat the biggest bowl of chilli you've ever seen, do you?'

'Hell no,' I said. 'After the impression I made this afternoon? Go for it. You don't mind if I laugh when you make a mess?'

He smiled at that. It was an easy smile.

Fergus was hard to read, but not in a bad way. On the video he'd looked vulnerable. When I'd met him in the café, he'd seemed tougher. More sure of himself. He kept shifting between the two, but he didn't seem to be trying to hide either of them from me.

There was an honesty to it that made me far more comfortable than any of the immature guys I'd been with in the past year. They were always working so hard to show me something. It got exhausting just watching them.

'I want to eat a burrito,' I said. 'But I might make a mess.'

'Go for it. Food of the gods. I'd usually be having one, too, but I had one earlier.'

'This is your second Mexican of the day?'

'I don't mean to brag, but sometimes I can fit in three.'

We both ordered the beer that was advertised on the barrier. It seemed only polite. When it came, the drink was sweet but heavy. I was going to need to sip it. Fergus put the drink to his lips and I saw him calculating for the first time. Should he sip? Swig? How fast was it okay to drink in front of me on a date?

'If it makes you feel any better,' I said. 'If I let you buy me a gin later, I'll be downing it like an alchy.'

He laughed and took a long pull on the beer.

'So how has your day been?'

I played offended. 'Oh, we're at the "how was your day" chat already? Have we got that bored of each other so soon?'

'Okay, let's talk about something else.'

'No.' I grinned. Let him see I was joking. 'I'm kidding on. How *was* your day?'

I wasn't completely joking. I'd been dreading this part of the conversation. I was interested as hell to find out more about him, but I wanted to hold off on telling him about my detective work. Once someone found out I was a PI, they would either drift away from me, or they'd draw in closer but only want to talk about the job. So far all he knew about me was that I was a bike messenger.

FIFTY
FERGUS
19:32

I tell Sam about my weird day. Not all of it. Well, not *any* of it, really. I tell her I'm self-employed, and I do security consultant work. I also tell her I've not been enjoying it lately, and that I'm thinking of getting out.

She gets right to the point. 'What do you want to do?'

Damn. I have no idea.

'No idea. I'm thirty, I thought I'd have figured out what I wanted to do by now.'

She raises her drink. 'To never growing up.'

'How about you. Figured out what you want to do?'

'What I'm doing now,' she said.

Sam must really like riding that bike. I mean, I get it. I love running. But winter in Glasgow can last for whole decades, and I'm not sure I'd want to be a cyclist in all that rain.

The food comes. It looks *amazing*. I'm glad we've set the ground rules on embarrassing ourselves, because we both make an arse of it while eating. I get full halfway through. Sam's burrito comes on a plate and coated in sauce. I go on a playful rant about how burritos should be eaten by hand, wrapped in tin foil. Sam tries to play along by picking it up, but then the bottom falls out and she's basically eating a plate of something that looks like paella.

She keeps getting some on her chin. The first couple of times I find a polite way to do it; I touch my own chin and she gets the message. The third time I just go for the funny, 'God's sake, lass, do you need a bib?'

She laughs, which is good, because the alternative would have been the end of the date.

There's this weird energy between us.

I mean good, but weird.

Like, suddenly I want to tell her the truth. I know she'll walk away the minute I say it, but I want to be honest.

And that scares the crap out of me.

I change the subject from relationships by talking about relationships. See, I'm a clever guy like that.

Master tactician.

King of all logic.

'Okay,' I say, draining the last of the beer. 'You can sleep with any man you want, from any time in history—'

Sam makes a show of looking around the restaurant. 'What, right now? In here?'

I smile at that. 'But in order to qualify for this magic spell, you need to sleep with one woman first.'

She gives me a well-judged comedy side-eye. 'Is this really where you're going with your attempts to impress me?'

'Come on.' I feel myself blush. Does she notice it? 'Play along.'

She nods. 'Okay, but first, you need to buy me that gin. And I need time to think about it.'

As I wave the waiter over I catch Sam shiver a little, and, because I'm such a super guy, I ask the waiter if we can move inside to the bar. He says no problem, and so Sam and I hike up onto stools inside while they get us two fresh drinks. A gin for her, and a second beer for me.

I want to stay here.

I want to get drunk, and flirt like hell.

But that voice at the back of my head is saying, *Remember you've got a job later. Make this your last beer.*

Spoilsport.

FIFTY-ONE
SAM
20:12

'Okay,' he said, after I'd sipped my gin. 'Let's get to it. People need to know.'

'People?'

'Well, okay, me.'

He was persisting with this game of his. I didn't mind it, really. It was fun, and it replaced all the stupid small talk of a date. We weren't trying to size each other up while pretending to talk about politics, we were getting straight down to the important stuff. Which movie stars we'd have sex with.

But I wasn't going to make it easy.

'This is really just an attempt for you to decide I'm gay, isn't it? You want me to name a woman I'd sleep with, so you can go bank that image, and then laugh and call me gay.'

He put his hands out palm up. 'Hey, if you want to name the man first, that would be fine.'

'Any man?'

'Any.'

That was easy, I didn't even need to think.

'Paul Newman.'

'When?'

'Anytime, doesn't matter. But I'd probably say from around *Cool Hand Luke*. He was pretty.'

'Okay, and the woman?'

I grinned at this. I had a way out.

'Jessica Rabbit.'

'That's pure cheating,' Fergus said straight away. He became more Glaswegian with a beer in him. 'Cannae have a cartoon. That's just a way of not having to name a name.'

'Okay. Lemme think. You go first, who would yours be?'

'Right. Well, the woman is easy. You ever see *Bound*?'

I nodded. It had been one of those *cool* films at university, the one every girl in my class had a copy of.

'Okay,' Fergus said. 'Well, Gina Gershon from around then.'

'Then and not now?'

'Don't know what she's aged like, do I?'

I gave him a sly look, teasing him. 'Sexist.'

'And the man? Let's see.'

'Sounds like there are a lot of men you want to sleep with.'

'Hey, maybe there are. But from the list? I'd say Brad Pitt from around the time of *Fight Club*. Not his character, mind. But him.'

I was glad he'd clarified that. I wasn't really sure I'd want to hang out with a man who idolised Tyler Durden. I'd made that mistake in the past. Never again.

'Okay, my woman?' I said. 'I'd probably say Cameron Diaz, but specifically from *A Life Less Ordinary.*'

'Why that film?'

'A,' I held up one finger, 'it's brilliant. B,' I held up another, 'she's hawt in it.'

'But only that film?'

'Yeah, there's something about it. Anyway, is there a point to this game? You're not Brad Pitt and I'm not Cameron Diaz, so I think we're not helping each other here.'

'Ah, well, see. I have a theory. I think the actor a straight person picks in these games is actually a giveaway of how they wish they saw themselves.'

'So, you think I want to be Cameron Diaz in *A Life Less Ordinary*?'

'Do you?'

'Maybe. But you are *definitely* not Brad Pitt.'

We stick around for one more drink. He hesitates before we order, and I wonder if maybe he's worried about having a third beer on our first date, but then he takes one and sips his way through it.

Once we head out into the evening air, the booze hits me.

Three drinks, and I'm feeling drunk.

I can usually take more than that. It must be the date, the mood, the *everything*. I turn to face Fergus and look up into his eyes. I picture us, and I picture my hands running across the lines of his shoulders and chest.

Crap.

No way, Sam.

Grown up, remember?

It looks like he's trying to figure out what to do next, too. I step closer. I go up on my toes and kiss him. Our lips are warm together, and I press further. He matches me. My breathing picks up and I can feel myself getting warm, getting into it.

I pull back and give him *what I hope* is an enigmatic smile.

'We should do this again,' I say.

I turn and walk away without looking back. *Grown up.*

FIFTY-TWO
FERGUS
June 8th
02:00

I might be lying in among the plastic Christmas tree and the boxes full of shitey decorations in Scott's apartment, but my mind is still back on the date. The kiss.

I made Sam laugh about five different times.

I say 'about' as if I'm guessing.

I counted each one.

I went back to my place for some supplies, then drove out to Rob's, armed with a can of petrol and a rag. They're going to be key props in faking Alex's death.

I hear Scott come in. He's shuffling, and it sounds like he walks into the wall at one point. He must have hit it hard in FuBar. He rattles around in the kitchen for a while, and it sounds like the oven is being put on. Then the television hums into life.

I don't know what he's doing, but I can hear a regular electronic 'click' followed by a running commentary of Scott saying, 'No, nah, hmmmm, no. Seen it.'

Shite, he's going through Netflix, isn't he?

He clearly settles on something. Lots of explosions and running. Some lines that are probably supposed to be jokes. I've never seen whatever it is. He could have at least had the decency to put on something we'd both enjoy. I mean, does he not have any Roddy Piper movies?

Half an hour goes by. I can smell burning, and hear snoring.

He's fallen asleep with the oven on.

If he has a smoke alarm, my whole plan is going to be ruined within seconds, because it'll draw attention. Not to mention the can of petrol that I left in the kitchen. If any actual flames get to that, well, I won't be happy when I meet my maker.

I ease the door open and look out. He's beneath me, sprawled on the sofa. Great. That wasn't the plan. He was supposed to go to fucking bed like a normal. I ease myself down onto the arm of the sofa. If I move too quickly, he'll wake up. If I move too slowly, I won't get to the oven in time to stop the alarm going off.

I step off the sofa, putting my weight onto the leading leg to take the pressure off where he is sprawled.

He snorts, clicks his tongue and then sighs.

He doesn't wake up.

I walk through to the small kitchen and turn off the oven. I bend down and look inside. There's something in there that was once probably a pizza. Now it's a black disk. If I open the door, the smoke will definitely give the game away.

As I'm down looking at the casualty of cooking, my phone buzzes. I forgot to turn it off, like an idiot.

It's Sam.

TheSamIreland – What you up to?

TheSamIreland – I'm watching a crap film.

I listen to the sounds of whatever pile of crap Scott had selected.

FergusSingsTheBlues – Me too.

I hear Scott sit up.

Baws.

I pocket the phone.

Scott talks to himself. Mutters something I can't make out. He grunts something that sounds like 'Nah.' Then silence. Within a few seconds, he snores again.

The sleep force is strong with this one.

I pick up the petrol from the corner where I'd left it, and tiptoe through to the living room. There's a cushion on the floor that Scott probably knocked off the sofa when he stirred.

I douse one side of the cushion with petrol. Then I pull the tea towel out of my pocket and do the same with that.

If this goes well, he stays asleep. He can just go out, never waking up. Even asshole rapists probably deserve not to die scared. Truth is, though, that rarely happens. When people say someone *died peacefully in their sleep?* Think about all those times you've woken up suddenly because you think your heart has stopped, or because you've stopped breathing. They're all false alarms, right? Well, then think about the day it actually happens, and your brain screams to you, *Wake up, fix this.* Except you can't fix it. And you die knowing that.

Wow, I'm cheery tonight.

I didn't used to get so morbid.

I lean over him, ready to put my weight down when he stirs.

My gloved hands start to shake. I tense my arms to try and stop them. His mouth is half open, which helps. I fold the tea towel over, and start shoving it into his mouth. This wakes him up. I was hoping he'd stay asleep. It's rare, but it has happened. So, his eyes open and he starts to panic. I drop onto him, knees first, crushing the air out of his lungs, then pick up the cushion and press it down over his face, petrol-side down.

For a few minutes I'm sitting on a bucking bronco ride, and a strong one. He almost throws me. But I hang in there, and his movements start to fade. Each time he's sucking in for air, he's taking in petrol fumes. It's going to make him choke, so if the suffocation doesn't get to him, his own throat will. If the medical examiner decides to start looking any closer into the stiff on his slab, there will be signs of petrol inhalation. The fumes will back up Alex's fake cause of death.

Scott's arms go limp, and I feel his body relax.

I lift off the cushion and look into dead eyes.

Then I feel something new.

Puke.

It's rising in my throat. I get to the toilet just in time to empty out into the white bowl. I clean up my face in the sink, then stare at myself in the mirror.

That's never happened before.

Who are you?

My hands start to shake again.

This is my last one. I can't do this anymore.

FIFTY-THREE
ALEX
June 8th
08:12

Alex Pennan overslept on the day he died.

He had intended to get up early, take a long shower. He'd loaded up a laptop with the data he'd stolen from MHW and put it, along with the keys to his new flat and paperwork for his secret bank accounts, in a small leather bag by the front door. He'd make his wife a full breakfast and then see if maybe she was in the mood. Fool around before it became illegal. After all, the next time they did it, she'd be fucking a dead guy.

But then, he'd thought, he shouldn't do any of that. Nothing out of the ordinary. Okay, he'd get Kara breakfast in bed on her birthday. And, ever since a miscarriage a couple of years before, he'd make a fuss of her on Mother's Day. But he hadn't tried morning sex since the honeymoon. Kara couldn't stand his morning breath, and Alex felt that brushing his teeth in preparation took any spontaneity out of the matter.

Maybe just a longer kiss, and some toast.

Would a rose raise suspicions?

It was all academic. His mind had been too full to go to sleep. He finally drifted off a couple hours before the sun came up. He slept through his first alarm. And his second. Kara was already in the shower when he finally stirred.

Shit, he didn't want her to leave the house before he did, or to be downstairs at the same time. She might see something fishy if she was there to witness it. He grabbed the clothes he'd laid out in advance, and headed downstairs to the smaller bathroom they had at the back of the house. There he took a quick shower, dried off and dressed. Upstairs he could hear the shower had stopped, and Kara was moving around the bedroom, humming.

He moved to the bottom of the stairs and called up, 'Bye, babe.' Kara murmured something in return.

Alex pressed his back to the front door and breathed in deeply. This was it. Once he was outside, there was no going back. Last chance to change his mind. Last chance to be a chicken. Last chance to be a loser.

Nope.

Sod that.

He opened the door and stepped out. Pulling it closed behind him with a bang loud enough to make sure Kara heard it.

His car was on the drive, exactly as he'd left it. He didn't pause to look at it, because Fergus had said he would only have ninety seconds once he left the house. Even still, in his peripheral vision he could see there was somebody sitting behind the wheel.

Crap. He was an accomplice now, right?

What if this didn't work?

What if the medical examiner looked at the body?

What if the guy had people who missed him?

What if—?

What if—?

Move.

He ran round the side of the house, and pushed his way into the hedge. There was a gap there that he was hoping that damn navvy gardener wouldn't have fixed. He hadn't. On the other side of the hedge was a small lane that led to a small wooded area behind the house. It would lead him across the top of the hill and down to the main road on the other side.

Alex was hunched down in the bushes when he heard the car explode.

SECOND INTERMISSION

Sexy Time Mix Tape 1999

Side One

Lovefool – The Cardigans – 3:18
That Don't Impress Me Much – Shania Twain – 3:56
Something for the Weekend – The Divine Comedy – 4:20
Mambo No.5 (A Little Bit Of . . .) – Lou Bega – 3:40
Scooby Snacks – Fun Lovin' Criminals – 3:03
My Favourite Mistake – Sheryl Crow – 4:08
She's the One – Robbie Williams – 4:18
Burning Down the House – Tom Jones, The Cardigans – 3:39

Side Two

Torn – Natalie Imbruglia – 4:05
Pick a Part That's New – Stereophonics – 3:34
Right Here, Right Now – Fatboy Slim – 6:28
Fly Away – Lenny Kravitz – 3:41
Sonnet – The Verve – 4:21
Mulder and Scully – Catatonia – 4:11
Mama Told Me Not to Come – Tom Jones, Stereophonics – 3:01

PART FOUR
June 8th

'Clearly, you're the brains of the operation.'

—Hanya

FIFTY-FOUR
SAM
09:30

The morning run was quiet. Aside from our scheduled deliveries, there wasn't much in the way of fresh work. It was good to get that kind of morning occasionally, because it gave me time to stop and talk to the receptionists at each client.

I liked building up relationships with them. Getting to see who they were. It gave me an advantage over almost everyone else who walked through the lobby, because none of them took the time to be friendly.

I was delivering a bunch of legal documents to Nicolay & Turner when Tina on the desk mentioned an explosion. She said it was all over the news. I headed back out to my bike to ride to the office, but then I thought again about what she'd said.

I was curious.

Cars don't just blow up in Glasgow.

When did that become a thing?

I searched for the news on my phone and read enough for my gut to start tingling. The report didn't mention any names, but it did give away the location. Henderland Road, Westerton.

That's where Alex and Kara Pennan live.

And I still didn't believe in coincidences.

The GPS tracker app on my phone now only showed one dot at their house. The red one. Alex's blue dot had vanished.

I sent Hanya a text: *Explosion, Pennan?*

She replied straight away with, *Husband.*

Holy crap.

A woman hires me to prove her husband is cheating.

The husband blows up.

Yeah, right.

The whole thing smelled of fish. Very bad, rotten fish. Did Kara have the means to get Alex killed? Had my investigation just been a backup, in case she couldn't make it work?

And, first things first, what would be the social etiquette on me invoicing her for the hours Phil and I had logged on the case? How long should we leave it?

I cycled back to the office in a half daze. I was switched on enough to be safe on the road, but I couldn't swear that my mind was entirely there. When I pulled up outside I saw Mike Gibson sat in his car.

There was a baseball bat displayed prominently on the passenger seat beside him. It was stood on end, with a seat belt strapped across, holding it in place. Bats were a large part of the Gibson legend. Cricket, baseball, vampire, didn't matter. The exact details of the stories would change, but the damage he did stayed the same.

He got up out of the car and walked toward me. His legs rotated outwards as he walked, probably a habit picked up from trying to stop his thighs rubbing together.

'How you getting on with looking for Cal, hen?'

Neither of the first two answers that popped into my head were good choices.

Well, the good news is, the other person I was investigating just blew up in his car, so now I'm all yours.

Or:

Well, actually, there's a chance your son killed a woman I've been investigating, and he's done a runner after trying to blackmail some really bad people.

Instead I went with a handshake and said, 'Nothing solid yet, but I've got a couple of leads I'm following up this morning.'

'Ah, that right, aye?' He looked me up and down for a long time. I was used to it. 'Okay. I'll stop back a bit later, then. Just taking my pal out fer a drive.'

My pal.

How lonely do you have to be, that a piece of wood becomes your best friend?

He headed back to his car and I wheeled my bike into the office. A couple of the other messengers were in early, playing computer games and downing cans of energy drinks. I walked through to the back where Phil was checking messages and orders that were coming in via the app.

'How's it looking?'

'Lunchtime's going to be busy.' He looked up from the screen for a second. 'Uncle Fran called. He couldn't find your mobile number, so he called here.'

I took my seat at the desk and dialled Fran's office.

'Salut, Crowther & Co, Alexi speaking. How may I be of service?'

'Hola, Lex.'

'Sam. *Вітаю*. Hello. Hang on, I'll see if the gaffer's finished on the crapper.'

After the line beeped a few times, Fran picked up and greeted me. 'Right, Sam, straight to it. Callum Gibson doesn't have any legal representation that I could find. Davey Lockhart confirmed for me that he doesn't do it, because Cal and his old da don't get on anymore, but he wasn't going to tell me any more than that.'

'Thanks for checking, Uncle Fran.'

'On the other hand, I did manage to get a name for you. Because I'm that good, aye.' He chuckled. 'Cal's money man is Gary Fraser.'

Gary Fraser, I knew him.

'That's fantastic, thank you.'

Gary used a bar as his office. Lebowskis on Argyle Street. If I was going to find Cal, his money man would be a great place to start. Lebowskis wouldn't be open until eleven, so that gave me time for breakfast with Phil.

My phone buzzed.

FergusSingsTheBlues – Can we do that again tonight?

FIFTY-FIVE
ALEX
08:30

Alex caught the bus a couple of miles away from the house. After hearing the explosion, he had walked on farther, putting more distance between him and the inevitable cops. He hadn't caught a bus since they moved to Glasgow. Almost didn't remember how it worked. Were they the same up here?

It pulled to a stop in front of him, and the door opened. He stepped on and stared at the driver in his plastic enclosure. Then he noticed the metal coin machine.

He dropped money into the slot. 'Uh, a pound please.'

The driver looked from the machine to Alex. 'Where you wanting, pal?'

'Into town.'

'Glesga?'

'Yeah.'

'Two pound, pal.'

Alex dug the extra coin out of his pocket and dropped it into the slot. The driver pressed a couple of buttons, and a ticket printed out. Alex tore it loose with some effort, then started to shuffle down the aisle of the busy bus as it pulled away into traffic.

It was peak travelling time. Commuters were packed in tight, already sweating in the morning heat. All of the seats were taken and most of the standing spots were claimed, too. Alex managed to find a place in the section that was reserved for pushchairs and the disabled, and clung onto a metal rail that hung from the ceiling.

Alex knew rationally that nobody was paying him any attention. Half the passengers were deep into *Girl Meets Boy on a Crime Spree.* That didn't stop the creeping feeling that he was being stared at. Fergus had given him advice on how to blend in for his maiden voyage on public transport.

'Wear a hat.'

'But that'll mean everyone will look at me,' Alex had protested.

'No. It means everyone will look at your hat. Then they'll look away, not wanting to seem like they're staring. Later on, they won't even remember you. If they do, it'll only be the hat. They won't be able to describe you.'

So Alex was wearing a fedora.

And feeling like a prick.

But on the plus side, he was a prick who was on his way to a brand new flat, in which he had five million in cash.

So he could put up with feeling like an idiot for a wee while.

He got off the bus in Glasgow city centre. It felt odd. Nobody around him was acting like the world had changed. Nobody seemed to care that he was dead, or about all the money he had.

It was just rude, frankly.

The apartment was on the third floor of a renovated building on Albion Street. It overlooked Merchant Square, and was the only part of the city Alex could really stand. It would have made a great bachelor pad. In fact, for the next week or so, it was going to be just that. He had Netflix set up. He'd got a few books to read, and there was some exercise equipment in there. He could hide away for a week and think of it as a holiday. A break from everything, even Kara.

He would need to stay locked up in there until the heat died down. There was a chance his face might be on local news, or on the front of the newspapers. If he ventured out of the flat, or ordered a takeaway to be delivered, he would create chances to be seen by people, and any of them might recognise him. The kitchen was stocked with meat, bread, pasta, and all kinds of sauces and spices he didn't understand. The real question had been, how much booze would he need?

He'd gone with *lots*.

The apartment had two levels, with the main living area and kitchen sitting below a small mezzanine that held the bed. There were large windows across the front wall, which threw the sun onto both levels.

The redevelopment had replaced the entire inside of the old structure, with the outer walls and the roof being the only thing left. Alex had paid for his in cash. It was an off-the-books arrangement that had suited both him and the seller, Mike Gibson.

Mike had no love for Joe Pepper. He'd refused to take his business to MHW because of Joe's links to the company, so Alex had known this deal would stay secret. He got to the main entrance, a secured glass door off Albion Street, and made to get his keys out of the bag.

Shit.

The bag.

In all the rush of oversleeping and getting out the house, he'd left the bag by the door. It held his keys. More than that, his laptop. Loaded with data of criminal activity, and Joe's big plan.

He couldn't just leave it there and hope for the best. The house was going to be crawling with cops. All it would take is one of them to open the bag, to get even a wee bit curious, and this whole thing was over.

Shit.

Shit.

Shit.

He needed to go back to the house.

FIFTY-SIX
FERGUS
08:56

Tracking Alex down is simple.

He's wearing the hat I told him to. That makes him pretty easy to follow. He doesn't know, of course. It would blow the whole point of *secretly tailing him* if I told Alex I was going to keep tabs on him this morning.

I just don't trust him to get it right.

Alex's weird job was supposed to be my big goodbye. The stylish full stop to my career. But, as I watch Alex get off the bus looking like an idiot, I realise this is just one more thing I need to keep from going off the rails. Another in my career-ending line of fuck-ups.

I wasn't thinking straight when I said yes. He had me rattled, bringing my family into it at the same time as challenging my ego, giving me something interesting to take on.

But Alex is a big liability. He thinks he's getting away with something huge, but he's going to want to brag. He'll do stupid things, take risks. Act the big criminal billybaws. I tested him yesterday, seeing how tight-lipped he would be, and he basically spilled everything. He told me about his secret apartment, and the bags of cash.

I'm retired now.

I don't want to kill anymore.

No, wait, that sounds wrong.

I never sat around *wanting* to kill. What I mean is, this is the first time I'm not wondering when my next job will come in. I'm no longer reserving a place in my thoughts for all the ways to end someone's life.

I think I've decided, deep down, that killing people just isn't really a fun job.

High five?

Problem is, Joe's got some big deal going through, and the last thing I need is to give him a reason to turn on me. I've got plenty of money tied up in investments and saving schemes, but it's going to take a while to divest them. Until then, I'm vulnerable, and so is my family.

If Joe, or the people behind him, got any wind of this little job, I'd be in shite so deep that I'd be washing the smell out of my nose hairs for a month. I want to make sure Alex gets to the flat, and then I'm going to impress upon him, in the nicest and most semi-threatening way I can manage, that he is going to play this one absolutely by the rules.

My rules.

Stay in that flat.

Don't call anyone.

Don't email anyone.

No takeaways.

For the next two weeks, he's going to call me anytime he needs anything. Food? Fine, I'll get it. Drugs? Sure, I can do that. Sex? Well, I'll remind him he's married, and that the internet is a magical thing.

I'll be his delivery boy, keeping him safe, and my own ass covered. And he can pay me for the service, from his small amount of savings. Not much, I won't be greedy. My rates as a guardian angel will be competitive.

A thousand a day?

Seems fair to me.

Alex has told me he's getting the bus, and I checked to see there's only one that goes near his place. I'm waiting by the bus stop when he gets off, and I follow him down through the town. He never even pauses to check if he's being tailed.

Sometimes I have to remind myself that not everybody has lived the same life as me. Other people haven't been trained to be suspicious. Still, you'd think that a guy who is about to steal from the mob, and is walking through town dressed like Indiana Fucking Jones, would know to check if someone was following him.

I almost get too complacent because of how easy he's making it. A couple of times, I drift off into thinking about the date last night. The kiss. Sam.

Oh shit, you bloody schoolboy.

Man up and send her a message.

FergusSingsTheBlues – Can we do that again tonight?

Straight away her image starts to flash, telling me she's responding.

TheSamIreland – Yes. Yes we can.

While I'm off in dreamland, I lose sight of Alex.

I step faster, pushing past people. This is a total no-no when tailing someone, because it's nothing but noise and attention, but I've fucked up. Again. It's becoming my leitmotif.

Yes, I know a clever word, don't fall over in shock.

Just as I'm starting to worry that I've lost him, I spot the hat. He's walking through Royal Exchange Square.

Thank fuck for that.

He walks straight to the Merchant City.

Of course.

That's exactly the kind of guy he is.

Alex leads me straight to his front door, but then it looks like he's forgot his keys. He goes reaching to his side like a bag should be there. Then he makes a big comedy show of patting down his pockets and turning around in a circle.

I get a sense of what he's about to do, and duck out of sight just as he turns back this way.

The wee bam is going back to the house. You believe that? See, when I talked about him doing something to mess it all up, that's *exactly* what I was talking about. I start to go after him, but my phone buzzes an incoming call.

What now?

I have a call from Joe Pepper.

'I need to see you,' he says. 'Now.'

FIFTY-SEVEN
SAM
10:00

Hanya joined us for breakfast.

She'd come straight from the scene of the explosion, and carried the smell of petrol and fumes. She'd asked if she smelled bad when she sat down with us. I'd said, *No, of course not.* Phil had said, *Yeah, totally.*

See that?

Teamwork.

'Gartcosh is taking the case,' she'd said as she sat down.

'Different team?'

'Nope.' She stretched away the morning's work. 'Same guys. Starting to wonder if they're cloned. Maybe everyone there is a duplicate of Dasho and Robinson, and they just send out a new one for each case.'

'But you're still on the arson?'

She took a sip of coffee. 'Yup. Though that's more my case in name only, it seems. I'm getting pressure to close it. The insurance company is ready to sign off and pay, and the water fairies want to call it, too.' I sensed a *but*, and left her to keep going. 'There's a couple things that don't stack up. An old lady who lived up on the top floor said some guy saved her cats, she described him.'

'So? Maybe a visitor?'

'Where she says she met him was right by the apartment that the fire started in. And guess who leased that one?'

Phil said, 'Michael Keaton?'

Hanya laughed. She looked tired, and the laughter came out wrapped in a sigh. 'No, Martin Mitchell.'

'Marxist Martin?' I said.

Phil said, 'I liked mine better.'

'The voices on the second tape,' Hanya said. 'I listened back to them on the drive over. One of them sounds a lot like Martin.'

'The recording is in that room?' My mouth flapped a little. That made enough sense as to feel blindingly obvious. 'Whatever Paula got, thought she got, was in the building that got torched.'

'Right.' Hanya added one more thing before tucking into a bacon sandwich. 'And one of our uniformed guys outside took possession of the cats. He was teased for it at the time, because he put the lady and the cats in his car and drove them out to one of her relatives. The guys said he was on the pull. But he caught a look at the guy who carried them down, and it sounds nothing like Cal Gibson.'

Who was it?

Each time I thought I could see how the jigsaw fitted together, someone threw in another piece.

'I've got a lead on Cal,' I said. 'I know who his banker is. I'll let you know if I find something.'

With Hanya munching through her food and thinking over what I'd said, Phil took the chance to fill the silence. 'I've been thinking,' he said. 'About Superman.'

Oh god.

'So, here's the thing, right? Krypton is going to explode.'

'Do planets really explode?' I said, hoping to sidetrack him.

'What?'

'Well, they heat up and cool down. They die. They get wiped out by expanding suns. But do planets actually explode, or is that just in the films?'

Phil gave me look. Picking plot holes with comic book characters was his shtick, not mine. I was treading on his toes. I smiled. 'Sorry.'

'Anyway. So, the possible inaccuracies of explodey science aside, Kal-El's home planet goes boom, right?'

'No idea,' Hanya said through a mouthful of bacon.

I doubted she'd ever touched a comic book in her life, and superhero movies weren't really her style. I once found out she didn't even know who Obi-Wan Kenobi was.

'Yeah, it does. Now, Kal-El's dad is this super genius scientist. Cleverest man on the planet. He's like Super Boffin. He's been trying to tell people that the planet was going to explode, but everyone ignored him.'

'Like climate change,' Hanya said.

'Exactly, grasshopper.' Phil turned in his seat to face Hanya. 'Are you sure you don't have a cute brother?' Hanya laughed and shook her head. Phil continued. 'But because he's Super Boffin Man, he builds a spaceship, to escape from the planet before it all pops. But,' he held up his forefinger, emphasising the point, 'he's got a wife and a baby, and he only builds a ship big enough for the baby.'

'Yeah, I've seen the films,' I said. 'That's how he gets here.'

'Well, yeah. But my point is, this guy is a super genius. He's clever enough to build a rocket, all on his own. And he knows they're going to need it, to escape. And yet, still, he just makes one big enough for the wean?'

I decided to play along. It was easier that way. 'I get you. It's pretty mean. He could at least have made it big enough that his wife could fit in, too.'

'Exactly. See what I mean? How would that conversation go? "Honey, good news, I've built a rocket ship to escape." "Great, I'll go pack a bag." "Ah, well, there won't be room for a bag." "How no?" "Well, actually, there won't be room for both of us, either." "You expect me to leave you behind?" "Well, no. What I'm meaning is—" '

Hanya joined in. That surprised me. '"What I'm meaning is, we're going to take this wee boy here, and throw him out into space, in a tube, on his own." I hope she gave him a good kicking.'

'That bit seems to be missing from the literature,' Phil said.

'Men,' I said.

I sat and waited. I was sure Phil was going to follow up his speech, like he usually did, but he stayed quiet.

'And?' I said.

He looked at me. 'What?'

'No deeper meaning for me to take from this? No big moral lesson?'

He pretended not to know what I was talking about, but I could see from the slight smile in his eyes that he understood. 'Just that Superman's ol' da was a bit of a fud,' he said.

'You're not trying to say that I need to build a bigger rocket? That I need to let more people in on my journey and start to trust a wee bit more again?'

Phil blinked. He turned to Hanya and made a show of being confused, sticking out his bottom lip and shaking his head.

'I don't know, Sam,' he said. 'I was just talking shite about comic books. You got something you want to say?'

'Men,' I said, pushing back hard into my seat with a sigh.

Hanya chuckled beside me.

'But really, though,' Phil said. 'He had all that technology. I mean, how come nobody else on Krypton had a rocket? Nobody else had a way to get off the planet? He had the knowledge, and chose not to share it with anybody.'

'What a dick,' Hanya said.

'Maybe the planet didn't actually explode,' I said. 'Has he ever checked? Maybe he was just a whiny brat who wouldn't shut up about stupid things, so they fired him off into space, and they just told him the planet was doomed to get rid of him.'

Phil thought about that. 'No, we see it explode, too, in the stories, aye? It happens.'

I checked the time.

Lebowskis would be open by the time I cycled there. Time to trigger the ejector seat on this geeky conversation. I needed to go see Gary Fraser.

FIFTY-EIGHT
ALEX
10:52

Alex walked home.

It was five miles, and he covered it in just over an hour and a half. He'd decided that one bus journey was a calculated risk. Two was pushing it. He could tell from checking the internet on his burner that the news of the explosion was already the main feature of the Scottish section of the BBC site.

He hadn't been named yet. His own image wasn't splashed across the news. But it wouldn't be long before that changed. Walking allowed him to take shortcuts and alleys, to change directions if there was a crowd and to stay off the beaten path. He took the long way round to his house. He circled the base of the hill at Westerton, and then walked up through the woods, coming to the back wall of the property.

He could hear chatter and radio squawk. The police were at the front of the house, and he could tell people were also moving around in the small lane beside the property, the one he'd used earlier. He crouched behind the bushes and moved a few inches to his right, to take a look.

At the end of the lane he could see a large flatbed truck, with the burned-out shell of his car strapped down on the back.

Between the truck and Alex were three people he assumed to be cops. They were wearing the white overalls that covered their whole bodies, with blue mouth guards pulled down around their necks. They were smoking and chatting.

'Too soon?' One of them said, holding her cigarette in the air.

One of the others turned to look toward Alex's car. 'I don't think he'll mind,' the guy said.

All three of them laughed. Then the third one, shorter and rounder than the others, said, 'Now *that* is too soon.'

As Alex watched, the three of them reacted to something he couldn't see, maybe a signal from the front. They dropped their smokes to the dirt and rubbed them out. A man in a jumpsuit, maybe a fireman, walked past them and climbed up into the cab of the truck. The engine rumbled into life and the large vehicle started to pull away.

'Now would be the wrong time to start a bush fire,' the woman said.

'Eh,' the taller guy said. 'What damage can it do at this point? The vic already has a tan.'

They walked around to the front of the house laughing. Alex listened as the doors to another vehicle opened and closed a few times, then another engine started. They were leaving.

Alex climbed to take a look over the wall. He could see Kara through the back patio window. She was talking to two cops. Or rather, they were *trying* to talk to her. Following Kara around the room as she pushed away, and shouted.

One of them reached out and put a hand on Kara's shoulder, but she turned and lashed out. Even at this distance, Alex could hear her screaming for them to leave her alone.

Both cops nodded. They looked at each other for a few seconds, and walked out of sight toward the front door. Kara turned to stare out the patio window, and Alex dropped down out of sight. There was a click as the glass door was opened, and then a few soft footfalls as Kara stepped into the yard.

Alex heard her sniff a few times, but couldn't tell if she was working through full-blown tears. Then the sounds receded. She was gone when he looked again.

He eased over the wall and lowered himself onto the large mound of dirt that the builder had left there. Finally, there was some use to the idiot's laziness. The patio door was still open. Alex stepped into the living room quietly. He heard the sound of Kara going up the stairs.

Singing?

She was singing?

Grief did strange things to people.

He took a look out the front window. There was a car parked across the street. It was unmarked, but the two people sitting in front were clearly police. Alex pulled away from the window to avoid being noticed.

He walked to the front door quietly, conscious that he was the only other person there, and eased the bag up slowly off the floor. He slipped it over his shoulder and headed back to the rear of the house.

The doorbell rang.

Alex froze.

He crouched down below the kitchen counter and waited. The doorbell chimed a second time. Kara called from upstairs, *Just a minute.* After the bell went a third time, Kara ran down the stairs and answered.

'Hey, babe,' a male voice said. Young. Alex half recognised it. 'Permission to come aboard?'

'You shouldn't be here,' Kara said.

'It's cool,' the guy said. 'I told the polis out there that I'm here to see if you're okay.'

'Hang on. I'll get them to go farther down the street, put on my crying face and ask for some privacy.'

The door closed. The stranger was still inside, Alex could hear him breathing a little heavily. The door opened again, and Kara stepped back in. She shut the door, and there was a loud thud, as if she'd been pushed into it.

Was she being attacked?

Alex stood up, ready to charge. Then he heard something else. A kiss.

Soon they were fumbling about on the stairs.

'Not down here,' Kara said, squealing a little at whatever the kid was doing. 'Someone might see.'

Alex heard a second kiss.

FIFTY-NINE
FERGUS
10:00

Joe tells me to meet him at the Carlton Place suspension bridge. It's a thin, pedestrian-only job, stretching across the Clyde. It's a great spot for controlled meetings. You have a view of who is coming at you at all times, and it's public enough that nobody ever wants to try anything funny.

It's never a good sign to be asked to a meeting on that bridge. It means the other person wants to be able to see you coming. They can spring a trap at any point by closing off the ends. If the call had been from anyone else, I would have ignored it. But as long as I'm in town, I play by Joe's rules.

He's already on the bridge by the time I get there. Walking onto it from the Clyde Street side, I see a big bearded guy in a suit. Looks like a bouncer or barman, but smells like a cop. He's trying not to look like he's eying me, but I'm too experienced to fall for it. On the far side I can see another guard. A slender blond guy, also trying not to be obvious.

Joe is in the middle, leaning against the railings and looking out west toward the tall buildings and the old shipyard crane. I join him, leaning with my back to the same railing and looking in the other direction, toward Glasgow Green.

'The city pretty much raised me,' Joe says. 'Never knew my parents. Mike Gibson was the closest thing I had. And Cal, I spent half my life keeping him out of trouble.'

Well, at least he wasn't going to have that problem anymore . . .

'I'm taking over,' Joe continues. 'Glasgow is the family business, and it's my turn. And if I'm willing to kill the closest thing I ever had to a *brother*, you can imagine how I'll feel about anyone else.' He looks at me. 'Did you do the Pennan job?'

I've been expecting this question.

'The thing on the news? Car explosion? I didn't kill that guy.'

See what I did there?

Didn't even need to lie. No way can he tell that I'm bluffing, because I'm not.

'Any ideas who it might be?'

I make a show of thinking about it. Breathe in deep. Sigh. Total Academy Award stuff. 'To be honest, the only person I know who can pull of a job like that is me. So if it's not me who killed him, I really don't know.'

He rubs his face. I watch in profile. He's not looking good. Tired. Worn down. Joe makes a job out of always looking in control and on top, but right now he's looking like his battery needs recharging.

'Are you okay, Joe? I mean, no offence, but you look, well, you know.'

'Aye.' His voice changes a little. Exhaustion creeps in at the edges. 'It's this thing I've got tomorrow. I'm not going to get much sleep until it's finished.'

He reaches into his jacket pocket and pulls out a small plastic bottle. He pops the child-proof lid and dry swallows two small pills.

'Got a fucking ulcer,' he says. 'Doctor says it's stress, like that's a new thing. He says I need to do more to relax, lighten my workload. I didn't know my GP was a comedian. Anyway. This thing with the explosion. Could you ask around? See if any of your, uh, colleagues did it?'

'I gotta be honest with you, Joe. This isn't a really social job. We don't talk to each other much. We tried it once. A bunch of us all got together to have a party, maybe get to know each other better.'

'What happened?'

I pause. Think how best to put it. 'We accidentally triggered a civil war in Cambodia.'

That kills the conversation for a second.

'I might need you for something else,' he says.

I push off from the railing, ready to walk away. I don't want to raise suspicions. If I tell Joe I'm *retired*, he'll start asking questions about the timing. It'll look like I'm up to something. So instead, I go with, 'I'm not taking any jobs right now. I need a break.'

'You fucked this up,' he says. 'And you lied to me. I had eyes on Martin's building. Backup. I knew you'd let the lass go, and I knew you lied about it. The only reason you're up here, and not down there,' he nods at the water, 'is I managed to clean it all up. I got my boys to kill her.'

'The two trying not to look like cops at the ends of this bridge?'

He smiles. 'That's them.'

Okay. So now he has cops killing people. What does he need me for?

He looks back down at the water. 'Cal came looking for her. I think they'd caught wind of what we were up to, wanted to try and get proof. I'm not sure what he thought he was going to do with it – I've got the papers onside, nobody would take the details.'

For all Joe's big thinking, he suffers from the same blind spot as most of the top names in Glasgow. He forgets this city isn't the world. My years away, especially living in New York, had given me a perspective that these guys lack. Joe has the local media on a leash, and that means he's got control over what slips out in Scotland. But down south? He has no power. If someone has proof of what he's up to, all they'd need to do is take it down to one of the editors in England.

Or put it on the internet, and let it grow from there.

But Joe, like everyone else around here, forgets that Glasgow is in a bubble, and the rest of the world isn't in it with us.

'Seems to me, you've got a leak problem,' I say. 'If this lass knew, and Cal knew. And clearly, Martin or Dominic Porter knew, otherwise why would the whole thing be happening. You've got a leaky pipe somewhere.'

He hands me a piece of paper. A list of names.

'Those are Cal's friends,' he says. There's a sadness in his voice. If they were tight with Cal, that means this is a list of his old friends, too. 'Cal's never had a thought in his life without someone giving it to him. One of these guys will know where the information came from. Find out who.' He leans in close. 'Find it, and then you can take as much time off as you need.'

I point to the big guy at the end of the bridge. 'Joe, you've got actual detectives on your payroll. Can't you get them to do it?'

'They've got other problems to deal with.' He smirks. 'And so have you.'

Now what does that mean?

He pulls out his phone and swipes through to a photo. A CCTV still of me handing the cat baskets over to the old lady.

Shit.

'There's a cop on the lookout for these,' he says, showing a second picture. 'If she places you at the scene, you'll end up in cuffs. By 1 p.m. tomorrow I'll be calling all the shots. It'll be me that decides what happens to you.'

A rock and a hard place. Like one of those old cartoons, where Daffy Duck has an angel on one shoulder, and a devil on the other. Except I have a devil on both sides. Joe on my right, threatening to turn me over to the cops, and Alex on the left, ready to mess up his whole plan at any moment.

Okay, Fergie.

You've been in worse scrapes.

I just need to do this thing for Joe. Find Alex.

Keep everything from exploding.

Simple, aye?

SIXTY

SAM

11:04

Criminals in Glasgow tend not to trust banks, or bankers. Polis could gain access to bank accounts, and, even worse, so could HMRC. The bigger fish use companies to manage their assets and massage the figures.

People on Cal's level use *money men.* They're walking savings accounts, and a place to go when people like Cal need some cash to walk around with.

If you need to find someone who has gone to ground, always start with the money.

When I'd first met Gary Fraser, he'd been a dealer. He could get you pot, weed, coke. Maybe at a push he could get guns. But dealers were also a good source for cash, so people had started hitting him up for loans.

The city's most established money man, Gilbert Neil, had been killed and Gary had switched careers. He was now a walking bank, with the added bonus that he could get his customers high if they needed to relax.

I locked my bike up outside Lebowskis and walked in. Even at 11 a.m., the lighting inside kept the room at a permanent dusk. It was the right level of illumination to make all the spirits behind the bar look perfect.

Gary was sat at the bar.

I wondered if the staff kept that seat for him when he was away, because I'd never seen anybody else sat there. Gary was about the same height as me, and the kind of skinny that pisses most men off. He'd gone through a few looks in the time I'd known him, but now he was trying to look respectable and made of money. He'd grown a beard that he kept well groomed, and he was wearing a shirt and tie.

He nodded his chin upwards in greeting as I walked toward him. ''Right?'

'Hiya.'

I pulled up a stool and asked the barman for a glass of water. Gary frowned at me. When your office is a bar, there's no such thing as 'too early to drink'. If the doors are open, it's the right time.

'Listen, Sam, you know my heart will always be yours, but I cannae talk about any kinky stuff. I'm a married man now.'

'I heard.'

'But seriously.' He leaned in close. 'Maybe if we're quiet about it. You free tonight?'

'Cal Gibson.'

'Aww shite.' He leaned back with a heavy sigh. 'That fud's always ruining the mood. What's he done this time?'

'You bank for him, aye?'

'You know I can't—'

'Gaz, let's skip the data protection stuff. You're not a real bank. I'm not a polis. Let's just be real and talk about what I need to know.'

Gary looked impressed. He pursed his lips together and nodded. His expression said, *Way to go.* 'You've toughened up,' he said. 'So, about tonight. Are you a fan of toys?'

'Has Cal contacted you in the last day or so?'

'Okay, we're really doing this? Nah. I haven't seen Cal in a couple days. He came by the day before yesterday, Monday? He was needing some money in his pocket. He had some big deal lined up, and had that Paula with him.'

They were here together?

I tried something. 'I didn't think Paula liked Cal.'

Total stab in the dark. I didn't know either of them, and had no idea what kind of relationship they'd had. But if Cal was blackmailing her, then it seemed a good guess that they weren't exactly friends.

'Nobody really likes Cal,' Gary said. 'But she was in on whatever scam it was he was working on.'

'Did he say what it was?'

'Nope. See, when it's Cal? I don't bother asking. That only goes two ways. He tells me, and then I get in trouble later for knowing it, or tells me, and it's so stupid that I have to laugh in his face. You know he keeps talking about how he's going to pull a Babycham.'

'A what?'

Gary shrugged with his hands. 'It's what he calls a big crime. A masterwork.'

'That's the stupidest thing I ever heard.'

'Oh, talk to Cal more, there's plenty where that came from.'

I waved at the barman then asked him to pour whatever Gary was drinking. It wasn't a drink that needed pouring. He placed a bottled drink on the counter in front of us, one of those flavoured cider things.

'So he was planning something big, and he hasn't been in touch since?'

'Nope. You're thinking he burned down his old man's place, aren't you?'

When I didn't answer he just smiled, like, *I hear everything.* Then he picked up the bottled cider off the counter and raised it in a toast to me. 'Cheers.'

Hang on.

Wait.

Back up.

If Gary knew Paula, maybe there was a chance here to get something the cops hadn't been able to find. 'Did Paula bank with you?' I said.

'I gave her a couple loans.'

My heart picked up speed. 'Do you know her address?'

SIXTY-ONE
ALEX
11:00

Alex had been given a set of high-quality golf clubs once, by a footballer client.

He didn't play golf. Didn't care about golf. Didn't even know how to tell the top of the range clubs from the cheap ones.

Weren't they all just bits of metal, really? With round bits on the end, and flat bits, and hooked bits. Just tools for hitting things. Like expensive hammers that came in a big leather bag.

But Alex was terrible at throwing stuff away. And he was obsessed with his own status. When a rich client gave him something, he would treasure it like an Academy Award. In the case of the golf clubs, they had travelled with him on the move to Scotland, before being abandoned in the garage, never to be seen or touched.

Until now.

This seemed like the perfect time to practise his swing.

Alex lifted a club out of the bag. One with a big round end. He climbed the stairs and pressed his ear to the bedroom door. There was some serious kissing going on.

He lifted the club and kicked open the door.

Kara was lying on top of the kid on the bed. Her tongue was down his throat and she held his dick in her right hand like a joystick. All things considered, Alex had to admit, it was a pretty impressive piece of equipment. When he finally got a look at the guy's face, he recognised him.

Milo something-or-other.

The cocky kid from Kara's football team.

Of all the—

—Wait, was that a Yoda tattoo?

Milo reacted first. His eyes widened and his mouth dropped open. He started to crawl backward across the bed, and let out a comical high-pitched yelping sound. Kara turned to look up at Alex. Her face ran through a range of emotions in the span of just a few seconds. Alex saw surprise, then shock, and maybe a little fear.

The final expression was one he'd seen every time he'd said something she didn't like.

'Seriously?' she said.

That wasn't what Alex would have expected.

He stepped forward and swung the club at Milo. He connected with the footballer's shin, and felt the solid thud vibrate back up his arm. Milo screamed and pulled his leg up toward his chest, and rolled backward off the bed in the process. He landed with a thud.

Alex turned to glare at Kara.

'You couldn't even wait until my corpse was cold?'

'Well,' she stuttered a little. Alex was glad to see that there was at least some fear under the calm front. 'You're not . . . dead?'

'That's a technicality.' Alex's voice was wounded and desperate, even to his own ears. 'You didn't know that.'

'My leg,' Milo wailed, out of sight down below the other side of the bed.

That reminds me, Alex thought.

He ran around the bed and lifted the club high, holding it half-way down the shaft to get the weight right. He swung for another shot. This one made a solid impact on Milo's shoulder, and the noise the little prick made was most pleasant.

He lifted the club again, but Kara climbed across the bed and made a grab for it. 'Wait,' she said. 'Wait.'

'I've *been* waiting,' Alex shouted. Spit flecked his words. 'Waiting to surprise you.'

'I'm surprised,' Kara said, with the hint of a smile.

'I think I need an ambulance,' Milo said. His voice was as thin as his frame.

'Honey.' Kara moved closer to Alex. She started rubbing his legs, running her hands up his belly and chest. 'Baby. I thought you were *dead*. I thought, I don't know what I thought. I just needed—'

'999,' Milo said. 'Please.'

'I mean.' Kara was massaging Alex's shoulders now. 'What happened?'

'I had a plan.' Alex could feel himself growing hard and soft in all the right places as she pressed into his body and kneaded his muscles. 'You and me, we're supposed to go away.'

'But why, baby?' Alex was surprised how well she was taking his resurrection. She'd skipped right past his whole *not being dead* thing, and moved on to the details of his plan. 'Why do all this?'

'I'm really hurt,' Milo said. 'Anyone?'

'Not in front of this shit,' Alex said. 'I'll tell you the details later.'

He was too busy trying to decide what they should actually *do* with Milo. He could blow the whole thing. The stupid kid knew Alex wasn't dead, and he wouldn't be in a mood amenable to staying silent.

Fergus. He'd call in Fergus. Offer him more money to deal with Milo. One last job before Alex and Kara could fly off into the sunset. And yeah, okay, so she was cheating on him a bit. But she'd thought he was dead. He couldn't really—

Kara grabbed the club before Alex could tighten his grip again, and she thrust it forward, driving the handle into Alex's abdomen. He hit the wall and slid down a little, his knees buckling as he fought for air.

Kara swung the club in the air above her head, and hit Alex hard to the temple. His world flashed white and yellow, and he fell onto his side.

'I can't be done for killing you,' he heard Kara say, from far away. 'If you're already dead.'

SIXTY-TWO
FERGUS
11:00

The first name on the list is 'Nazi Steve'.

There's an address but no surname. Great. I hope he's not a real Nazi. The house is on Brisbane Lane. I'm not familiar with the area, but I can guess where it is. There was a brand new housing estate built to accommodate the athletes for the Commonwealth Games. After the show was all finished, the place was turned into a mix of social and private housing, and the streets were all named after cities that had hosted the Games previously.

I pull up at the end of Brisbane Lane, but it's paved – there's nowhere to park. I leave my car on Sunnybank Street, which I remember from the old days, before they demolished a whole community.

I walk along the path. All of the houses here look the same. Reddish brown bricks and black wooden cladding. Not bad. I could see myself living somewhere like this. I ring the buzzer at the right house, and hear a woman shouting on the other side. A few seconds later I'm greeted by a stressed-out looking bird with fizzy red hair and a fresh stain on her T-shirt. I can hear kids running around and screaming behind her.

She looks both happy to have adult contact and annoyed that I've intruded.

'Aye?' she says, no messing about.

'I'm looking for Na-uh-Steve.'

'Oh, you an' aw?' She looks me up and down. 'You're no' polis. Money, is it?' It's a pointless question, because she doesn't give me time to answer. 'Well, he hasnae got any, but yer welcome to try an' find him.'

'He's not here?'

'No shit, Sherlock. No. I papped him oot.'

'Do you know where he'll be?'

'Prably with Cal or Baz.'

She shuts the door in my face.

Right-o.

Well, I know Nazi Steve isn't with Cal. He might be at Cal's place, but that's not on the list. The next name is Baz Monroe. He lives to the south, across the river in Cessnock. I'm more familiar with that address. It's on Govan Road, near The Cess Pit, a pub I've been in a few times.

I ring the buzzer to the tenement's main door, and it buzzes open without Baz using the intercom to see who I am. Great. This guy doesn't seem to give a shit about security. Makes it all the easier for me.

I climb the stone steps to the top floor. A fat guy is waiting for me. He's got black hair in an afro, and hairy legs stick out beneath cargo shorts. He looks like a hobbit. Smells like one, too, with the skunk coming off him.

'Aw shite,' he says. 'Thought you was my dealer, man.'

I've been trying to think how best to handle this on the drive over. I've decided to go with being up front.

I pull out my gun. I don't aim it at him, I just want him to see it. To know it's a possibility. But I can feel my hand shake. I rest the gun against the side of my leg to mask the movement.

What, I can't even *threaten* to kill someone now?

'Joe sent me,' I say.

He doesn't look me in the eyes. He's too busy staring at the gun. Shite, this is easy. Maybe I can be a private detective for my new job.

I wave the gun toward him, and he steps back into the flat. I follow. The smell of weed is even stronger in the hallway, and there's a cloud hanging at head-height. I can feel it getting to me a little. Easing the tension that's been building in my gut. I almost smile.

Almost.

'You Baz?'

He nods. 'Uh, yeah.'

'Is Nazi Steve with you?'

He waves his hand toward a door to the right. I nod for him to go on through it, and we walk into the living room. Futons are arranged in a loose semi-circle around a huge TV. Ashtrays are scattered around the floor, though people's aim seems to be off.

A skinny guy lazes on the futon nearest to me. He has black hair and a thick Che Guevara beard. Baz nudges his foot, and he looks up at me through sleepy eyelids.

'Nazi Steve?' I say.

He nods.

I wave the gun so he can see it. 'Joe sent me.'

'Oh right?' he says. 'Cool.'

'*Not* cool, you fucking idiot,' Baz says. 'He's got a gun.'

Nazi Steve looks again at the object in my hand. I can see the effort it takes him to focus. 'Aw shite, I thought that was, 'hingmy, a lighter.'

They're scared to see me, and dropping Joe's name clearly has an effect. One thing they're not, though, is *surprised.*

They've been expecting a visitor.

SIXTY-THREE
SAM
11:55

I called Hanya next, and cut straight to the chase. 'How would you like to see Paula Lafferty's flat?'

Hanya met me twenty minutes later outside Paula's address. It was a tenement building on Bunesan Street, a few miles south across the river, backing onto the motorway. Hanya parked one street over. I needed to change my clothes, and we couldn't be seen doing that right out front of the place we wanted to visit. I chained my bike to a lamppost next to Hanya's car, then climbed into the backseat. She kept a spare suit in the boot, in case her clothes got dirty on the job. It was better than the creased clothes I had in my bag. Hanya stood and watched for passers-by while I got changed.

It wasn't a perfect fit, but it would do for now.

Round on Bunesan Street, the buzzer had the surnames of everyone in the building; all eight apartments had a listing. None of them mentioned either *Lucas* or *Lafferty*. The number we'd been given for Paula was 0/1 on the ground floor. The name on the card read *Monroe*.

I shrugged and pressed the button. When a small electric voice spoke, Hanya took the lead. 'Police, ma'am. We're here about Paula.'

There was a muted buzz and the lock clicked open on the entrance. We stepped into the hall and knocked on the entrance to flat 0/1. A chain rattled on the other side, and an elderly woman opened the door. Her hair was black gone to grey, and she stood with a stoop in her shoulders, hunched forward.

'Hi there, Ms Monroe?' Hanya produced her ID. 'I'm DI Hanya Perera. This is my colleague Sam Ireland.' She left a pause. Time for Ms Monroe to assume I was a cop, too. 'May we come in for a minute?'

The old lady stepped back to open the door. 'Please, call me Sarah, officer. I'll put the kettle on.'

She walked away from us down a short and narrow hallway and turned left through a door. We followed her into a large kitchen. The floor was covered in red tiles; half of them were cracked and in need of replacing. The fitted cupboards looked like they'd been put up in the seventies, but gleamed damp. The smell of disinfectant hung in the air.

'Ignore the smell,' Sarah said. 'I was just cleaning. Tea or coffee?'

'I'm good, thanks,' I said.

Hanya gave me a look that said, *Take the drink,* and asked for a black coffee.

'Actually, I'll take a glass of water,' I said. 'If it's no trouble.'

Hanya gave me another look. I'd gone from refusing Sarah's hospitality to choosing something that wasn't on the menu. Sarah picked a glass off the draining board next to the sink and poured me a drink from the tap. I took it with a nod. Hanya's coffee was going to take longer, as Sarah filled the kettle and switched it on.

Win for me.

'How can I help, officers?' Sarah said, busying herself by wiping down the counter with a damp towel.

The surface was already shining wet with the same disinfectant as the rest of the kitchen. I wondered if she would spend her whole day doing this, over and over. The hallway had been spotless.

'We'd just like to ask a few questions about Paula. She lives here with you?'

'Oh aye. Rents a room. It's been so quiet since my Charlie died, you know, I like to have another voice in the place.'

'Charlie your husband?' I asked.

The look she gave me said I should leave the questions to Hanya. 'Och no, he was my dug. When your dug passes away, first thing everyone asks is, when are you getting another one? Like they're just things on one of they, whatya call them, factory belts?'

'Conveyor belt.' Hanya nodded along. 'Sure. They're family.'

'Too right,' Sarah said. 'I couldn't replace my Charlie, so I got a human in instead.' Her eyes twinkled as she smiled, showing she was in on the joke of it all. 'Paula's a nice lass. Friend o' my grandson. She's not in any trouble, is she? Not seen her for a couple days.'

'Does that happen often?' Hanya avoided answering Sarah's question like a boss.

'Young lassies. Like yourselves, I bet you know how it is. Off chasing the men, going to the dancing. Sometimes we're like ships in the night, me and Paula. Other times I don't see her for a week. I know she comes in, because she cooks and cleans up.' She dropped her voice, conspiratorial. 'I always have to clean again after she's finished – she never gets it all out.'

'Could we take a quick look?' Hanya said.

Sarah paused. She was thinking it over. Should she ask for any paperwork? Was Paula in trouble? Was it okay to let strangers into Paula's room?

I decided to go onto the front foot, ease her decision. 'It's nothing serious. She's made a few bad friends, and we're trying to help her out, make the problem go away before she gets hurt.'

Sarah sucked on her lips then nodded. 'On you go.'

Bingo.

SIXTY-FOUR
FERGUS
11:42

I should go easy on these guys. Getting information out of a couple of stoners isn't going to be simple. I'll just guide them along.

'I think you know why I'm here,' I say. Giving it a try.

'Well, if Joe sent you, it's gonnae be about the Babycham, aye?' Nazi Steve says.

The what?

I don't say that. I just nod. Wait them out. The more they assume I already know, the more I'll be able to get them to tell me.

'It's about that 'hing he wanted recorded, innit?' Baz says. He turns to Nazi Steve. 'Remember how he got us going to the Barras to buy him a new tape recorder, replace that one you broke.'

'Oh, *I* broke it, did I?' Nazi Steve sits up, showing emotion for the first time. 'Cal puts it through the dishwasher, but I'm the one who broke it?'

'Well, he only put it in to get rid of all the shit left over from those old batteries, the wans you'd left in there too lang.'

Nazi Steve looks at me smiling. He shakes his head like, *You believe this?*

'Okay, guys,' I say. 'Sounds to me like it was Cal who broke it. So why did he need a new one, what was he recording?'

'Okay, well, see—' Baz pauses, looks at me with some serious side-eye. Maybe he's wondering why I'm asking this. Don't I already know? But he's high, so he presses on with the talking. 'So Paula had started hanging out with us, aye? Fucking hot, that lass. I think she wanted me.'

'Nah,' Nazi Steve says. 'She wanted me.'

'Thing is, Cal wanted her, so I couldn't make a move—'

'Fuck oaff, man.' Nazi Steve slapped his groin. 'It was me she wanted, I telt ye. But I'm a married man. Well, mostly.'

'So she'd hang out here, and we'd all get stoned. Then one day she goes on a weird trip, starts telling this story, says she's an undercover cop, but her mission was abandoned and nobody seems to remember she's here.'

'Just sounded like the story to *ET* to me,' Nazi Steve laughs.

'Aye,' Baz continues. 'But Cal believed it, didn't he? So he keeps asking questions, and she keeps spinning this story. Like, she says that the polis in Glesga are corrupt as fuck, and they're helping to control the drugs an' that. But that's fucking bullshit, by the way, because the cops did all that big reorganisation, didn't they? Changed every'hin'.'

'And I didn't leave the batteries in the fucking tape player, did I?' Nazi Steve turns on Baz. 'The thing was working fine first time around. It was when the batteries were running oot and Cal says he can get more juice out of 'em by sticking it in the microwave for a few minutes, that's when it got messy.'

'Oh aye, aye,' Baz says. 'Right an' all. It was all Cal.'

Nazi Steve throws his hands out to me to say, *Finally*. He settles back into his seat.

'So this story she's telling?' I prompt them to get back on track.

'Aye, well. That's it, mostly. She says the cops used to be one of the biggest gangs in Glasgow, but now there's this new lot, some rich banker wankers.' He sniggered at his own rhyme. 'And that they're aw trying to work out a new deal. It's aw baws, you ask me. Think we'd live here our whole lives and not hear any of this, till some lassie fae Belfast starts talking?'

'So what did Cal do?' I ask.

'Well, he thinks this is good information, like. He thinks he can blackmail Paula, because she's been working in the drugs and all that carry on, so if she was an undercover cop, all them gangs would want to kill her.'

'And what's he blackmailing her for?'

'To try and get his hole, probably, what else? He'd been crackin' onto her for ages.'

'And how does the tape fit into all of this?'

'Aye, well. We recorded what she was sayin', didn't we? Stevie here likes to record people when they're high, because it's pissin' funny to listen back to it all after.'

'It's great.' Nazi Steve nods. 'People come out with some daft shite.'

'So,' Baz keeps going. 'Cal has all o' this on tape. But then he gets the idea of getting more. He wants Paula to record a conversation with those guys.'

'What guys?'

Nazi Steve slaps Baz. 'You've missed the best bit.' He turns to me. 'She says that some of the cops are working with two guys, Joe and, whassissname, the commie wan.'

'Martin Mitchell?'

'*Aye.* That fuck. So, Paula says she's heard rumours that Joe and Martin are going to try and fuck everyone over, and work with some of the cops to take control of every'hin' theyselves.'

273

My gut tightens. They might think this is all bullshit, but I saw that bedroom. This is all making too much sense. Joe and Martin working together. Joe decides Martin is drawing too much attention, and orders me to take him out. And he wanted the body to be found to send a message to everyone else, *Don't fuck this up, or else . . .*

'So Cal says he can set up a meeting,' Baz continues. 'She can pretend to be a hooker or something, and he can be her pimp, and then blackmail her into getting them to talk about it on tape.'

'That's horrible,' I say. 'For her.'

'Oh, aye, I suppose.'

I'm buying this. All of it.

So that puts Paula in the room with Dominic Porter and Martin Mitchell. It doesn't explain who Dominic was trying to call when I killed him, but that's the least important detail in all of this.

'Do you know where Paula lives?' I ask.

'Sure. With my nana,' Baz says.

He reels off the address with no thought to the fact he might be landing his grandmother in trouble. Skunk and a gun will do powerful things to a person's conscience.

I slip my gun into the harness stitched into my jacket. My hand stops shaking straight away. I bow a little at the guys and say, 'Thanks.' Then add, 'Might be best if you lay low for a few days. Joe is pissed off.'

I walk out and leave them to their cloud of imagination fuel. On my way down the stairs I call Joe.

'The leak is already dead,' I say when he picks up. I give him a quick rundown of what they said. I only do the edited version, saying Paula was an undercover cop who'd lost touch with her people, and that she'd been claiming the cops were corrupt, and a foreign gang were buying out Glasgow. When I mention the bit about

Paula's boss being killed, he makes a grunting noise that tells me he already knew that part of the story.

'I didn't know he had someone working with him,' he says. 'Butler never gave anyone else up. Good for him, I guess. We worked him hard.'

'I have Paula's address,' I say. 'Want me to head round and see if she has any proof hidden away that might burn you?'

'No,' he says. 'I'll deal with that.'

I give him the address through a grin. I've left out the parts about him scheming to take over the city, and the real reason I was hired to kill Martin. Joe has no idea *I* know about that, and he wants to keep me in the dark.

He'll send one of his dirty cops round to Paula's address.

'Are we clear?' I say.

After a long pause he says, 'Yes. Enjoy your holiday, bawbag.'

I know what you're up to, Joe.

That might come in handy.

One problem down. One to go.

Time to get back to Alex. I try dialling his burner, but it rings out. Baws.

I'll head round to his building again, try and figure out which flat is his.

SIXTY-FIVE
SAM
12:32

The room was small.

The old tenements had huge rooms. In poorer times, each room would have housed two or three families. Now, many of the buildings had been renovated, and the rooms divided up to create private spaces. The wall to the right looked like it was original. It had older wallpaper, and there was a fireplace in the middle.

The wall to the left was thin and new.

There was a single bed pressed against the new wall, neatly made with a cushion on top of the duvet. The disinfectant smell was in the air, and the window had been opened to let it dissipate.

This didn't strike me as how Paula would have left it.

'Sarah,' Hanya called out. 'Have you tidied in here since Paula went out?'

'Oh yes. Always do. She never makes the bed. Gives me something to do.'

There were no bookshelves, DVDs, not even a TV. There was a dressing table underneath the window, and a chest of drawers near the fireplace. A wooden kitchen chair was next to the bed. I started going through the dressing table, and Hanya took the drawers.

I found a small ashtray on the windowsill, with a few half-used joints stacked neatly. There was a plate on the dressing table that had been used as a dumping ground for loose change, hair pins and assorted business cards. One of them was mine.

I raised it up for Hanya to see, then slipped it into my pocket. Best not to have anything in here with my name on.

'If you were an undercover cop,' I said to her quietly, 'where would you hide things?'

'If I were an undercover cop, why would I be here?' she said. 'And why would I be undercover in the first place?'

Well, sure, those were better questions.

I got down on my knees and started looking under the furniture. Under the bed I found a small notebook and a purse. The latter held a few bank cards in Paula's real name, and fifty pounds in notes. I opened the notebook on the mattress. A few other business cards fell out. Journalists, a couple of other private investigators. The first few pages were covered with dates and names. The last one with anything written on just contained three words in big black ink, *Who is clean??*

The rest of the pages were blank.

'Wait a minute,' I said.

I looked down again at the words. I thought back to the guy on the reception desk at the hotel.

'I saw some lassie on a pushbike a few minutes earlier, and I saw the cops, but I didn't see anything else.'

I hadn't really listened to what he said. Or rather, I had, but I'd let what I knew about the events taint what I heard. He'd only seen me and the cops. He wouldn't have connected a timeline, because he didn't know when the attack took place. I'd added that on afterwards. *Of course he'd seen the cops,* I'd assumed, *they turned up after the attack.*

What if they'd turned up before?

Then Joe Pepper had called me *after* I'd handed my business card to Dasho and Robinson. I'd watched Robinson talking into his phone seconds before mine rang. Had it been Joe on the other end? This all fit together too neatly.

'Han, I've got a very bad feeling. You know those loose threads you're always telling me not to pull on?'

She nodded. 'I'm getting it, too.'

'Paula is an undercover cop. She's investigating a conspiracy. She's killed in the street, and the only people my witness can remember seeing are me and the cops.'

'Yeah.'

'And everywhere we go in this, we're running into Joe, Robinson and Dasho.'

'Yeah.'

'And the CCTV footage seems to have gone missing.'

'Yeah.'

'And Joe Pepper is able to make CCTV footage vanish.'

'Yeah.'

Hanya pulled her jacket off and rolled up her shirt sleeve, then leaned into the fireplace and started feeling around. She grunted as she found something. She slipped on a pair of plastic gloves from her pocket, and reached back inside, producing a gun. I don't know the first thing about weapons, but Hanya is an expert. She ran her hands over it, wiped some dust away, and smoothly clicked a button that released the clip.

'Glock,' she said. 'Fully loaded.'

She slammed the clip back in.

The door buzzer rang. We both froze as we listened to Sarah shuffle down the hallway. She held a brief conversation with a muffled electronic voice, then called out for us to hear.

'It's more of your polis.'

Hanya slipped the gun into the waist of her trousers, at the small of her back. She shrugged her jacket back on to cover it. Neither of us could be found there. Hanya wasn't on official business, and she'd helped me impersonate a police officer.

We heard the front door open, and Sarah said, 'Oh, hello, come on in. I was just talking to some friends of yours.'

Then we heard Alan Dasho say, 'Really?'

SIXTY-SIX
ALEX
12:38

Alex opened his eyes.

He regretted it straight away.

The room was spinning, and his skull was buzzing beneath the skin. There was a red stain creeping across the vision in his right eye. Alex closed his eyes again and willed the room to stop moving.

There was a copper taste in his mouth. Running his tongue across his teeth, he felt some of them coming loose.

Okay.

Let's take this slow.

Test it out. One eye at a time.

He eased his right eyelid up. The red mist still tinted the room. His skull was still hurting, but a little less so. Either the pain had faded, or he'd got used to it. He opened his left eye slowly, then tried blinking a few times.

There was a delay with his right eyelid. It was running a few seconds behind.

Alex tried to stand. No dice. He was tied to a chair in the living room. He felt a cramp in his right leg and rotated his ankle to ease off on it, getting some blood flowing.

That was the first time he really noticed that he couldn't feel anything at all in the other leg. He strained against the rope to lean forward and look down. A piece of pale bone was sticking out from his shin, and his ankle was on its side, at a right angle to the rest of his leg. A belt had been fastened tight around his thigh as a tourniquet.

Alex threw up and passed out.

When he came to, he had to go through the whole thing again, closing his eyes and then gradually opening them when the pain faded.

Kara and Milo were standing over him.

Alex couldn't help but notice that Kara had changed her clothes. Even in his present situation, he let his mind wander through all of the dirty and insulting reasons she might have needed to get changed.

'I'm sorry about the leg, honey,' she said. 'But we dropped you coming down the stairs.'

Milo put his hand up like a schoolboy. 'I'm not actually sorry.'

'What do you want?' Alex said. Well, he tried to. He found that his mouth wasn't working all that well. His jaw was slow to respond, and a tooth came loose as he spoke, sending pain across the side of his face in waves. The words came out as, 'Wha woo woo wan?'

'You mentioned money,' Kara said.

Alex didn't respond. Partly out of contempt, but mostly because it was going to hurt too much to try.

'Was that your plan?' Kara spoke again. 'Put away some cash, then fake your death. What came next, were you planning to run away somewhere? Were you even going to tell me?' She took a step forward and slapped him across the cheek, the one that was already hurting. Alex felt something damp on his lips. 'You let me think you were dead.'

'Wnu womb weme wo wave ween whab wubseb,' Alex said.

'What?' Kara leaned in closer. 'Speak up. You sound drunk.'

You don't seem to have been that upset, Alex wanted to scream at her. *You've been fucking this kid behind my back, and you want to make out like I'm the bad guy here?*

The anger was followed straight away by a deeper hurt.

This was for us. I wanted you to come with me. I was making us rich.

'He's speaking Wookie. I think we broke his jaw last time,' Milo said.

'Wast wimb?'

Kara looked into Alex's eyes, one after another. 'Oh shit,' she said. 'I think we've concussed him.' Then to Alex. 'You don't remember, do you?'

'Why wou woin wis?'

'Oh honey.' Kara stroked his cheek. It was a tender touch that only highlighted how violent everything else had been. 'You ask me that? You, who faked his own death and didn't even tell me? Who let me believe you were toast, and was going to let me cry, and grieve, and hurt?'

'Wo won't wook wad.'

'I, what? Oh, *sad?* Well, okay. You got me there. Look, Alex, babe, when was the last time we were good together? I've been looking for a way out for a year now, at least. We don't talk. You don't kiss me unless you want to screw. When was the last time we just wanted to hang out together?'

'I wuw wu.' A tear rolled down Alex's cheek.

He looked down to close his eyes, because he couldn't move his arms to wipe the water away.

Alex saw the bone sticking out of his leg again. Pain spread outwards from the wound when he looked at it.

He heaved and passed out.

SIXTY-SEVEN
FERGUS
12:45

I stand outside Alex's building, and try him on the phone a few times. No answer.

It could be nothing. I *want* it to be nothing. Maybe he's in his apartment and hasn't noticed the phone. Or he's on his way back. Or . . . he's been caught by the cops. If Joe had him, I'd know by now, because I'd be in the dock with him.

I'll break in. The lock is an easy enough electronic job. I'll figure out which apartment is his, and, if he's *not* already there, I'll wait for him to come back. We'll have that nice talk about his responsibilities. I work on the lock. People think this type is more secure, but it's easy when you know how. The soft electronic beep sounds out and the door gives inward.

My phone starts buzzing.

What now?

Can't people see I'm busy trying to break into some fud's building?

I ignore it and step into the foyer, but then the phone starts again. I look down at an unknown number on the display, and for a second I'm going to dingy it, but this has been one of *those* weeks. Best not to mess anything up.

'Hello?'

'Do you have a key for that building?'

A female voice. I recognise it straight away. She was on the other end of the phone, in Marxist Martin's bedroom. This was who Dominic Porter dialled.

I play it calm. 'What?'

'Turn around.'

I turn on my heels to look out through the glass door. There's a black car parked on the other side of the road. Tinted windows. Can't see inside.

'Two of my employees are in that car. They've filmed you breaking into that building.'

'I don't know what you—'

'Yes, you do. They'll bring you to me and delete the video. If you're a good boy.'

What now?

I nod at the car and kill the call. There's a button on the inside of the door, so it's much easier to get out. I cross the road and, as I do, the driver's door opens and a tall guy with a buzz cut and a black coat gets out. One of those thick, puffy jackets favoured by private security guys who want to conceal guns. I have three just like it.

'Couldn't you just call me and book an appointment?' I aim for a vaguely pissed-off tone. Which isn't all that hard.

The front passenger door opens and another guy gets out. Same taste in clothes, but this one has longer blond hair.

'Asma Khan doesn't need appointments,' Long Hair says.

Shit.

I know the name. Of course I do. I was doing work for the cartel behind MHW long before I came back to Glasgow. I've heard the name Asma Khan, and that of her brother, Akhel Khan, for years. And I never planned on having to meet either of them. I don't know why she wants me, but it can't be good. I weigh my odds. I can probably take these two if I have to. My adrenaline and endorphins are pumping. As long as I can get to one of them before either pulls a gun, I'll be okay. But I don't know how many other people I'd be pissing off.

I nod. Long Hair waves me toward the car. I settle into the backseat as four messages come through from Sam, and they pretty much ruin my day.

TheSamIreland – Hey.

TheSamIreland – So, I know this is really crappy of me

TheSamIreland – But I need to cancel tonight.

TheSamIreland – Sorry xx

Shite.

It's my fault. I was too pushy. Asking for a second date the night after the first? Who does that? Baws.

They drive me to a bus stop on Argyle Street, right where it joins the pedestrianised Buchanan Street. Long Hair leads the way and Buzz stays in the car, pulling away from the kerb to merge back into traffic before anyone starts to make a scene about him being there.

At the bottom of Buchanan Street, Long Hair stops outside a shoe shop and waves me in. Just before I pass him, he puts a hand out and asks for my phone. When I step back, he promises he'll return it once I'm done. I hand over my mobile and step inside. Straight away, I know something's wrong. The shop is empty.

Not completely, of course.

It's full of shoes.

The staff are standing along the back wall, watching me, and acting like they're too scared to move.

There are no customers. The place has been cleared. I've seen this happen for royalty in London, and I was once in a museum in

New York that had to be emptied out so the President could walk in and look at one exhibit. But I've never experienced it in Glasgow.

I catch movement in my peripheral vision and an Asian-looking woman steps out from behind the nearest rack. She's shorter than I expected, about five two. I'm not sure why, but hearing her name in such revered tones over the last few years had made me picture someone taller, broader. She's wearing baggy jeans and a GAP hoodie. Her hair has blue highlights. Her eyes are what stand out straight away. They're uncomfortably piercing. They make her look like she's staring at you.

'Fergus.' She smiles. 'I've heard a lot about you. Come over here.'

I walk over, and she points down at her feet. She's wearing a pair of tight blue shoes, with high heels and several busy-looking straps.

'What do you think?' she says.

Has one of the most powerful criminals in the country invited me here just to shop for shoes?

SIXTY-EIGHT
SAM
12:45

Crap.

Crap.

As far as we knew, Todd Robinson was Paula's killer.

Hanya pulled the chair over to the door and pressed it below the handle. It wouldn't hold long, but we might only need a few seconds. I climbed onto the dressing table and eased the window the rest of the way open, then lowered myself out.

We were on the ground floor, so it wasn't far to go before my feet hit the grass. I turned back and helped Hanya as she climbed down. Just as her feet hit the turf, we heard someone try and open the door. The attempt was followed by a grunt.

'There isn't a lock,' we heard Sarah say.

The door shook again. This time the chair almost gave.

Hanya and I crossed the yard and climbed the low metal railing onto the street. We ran to the next street over and her car. 'Meet you on the other side of Belahouston Park,' she said sliding behind the wheel.

I unchained my bike and took off after her.

Belahouston is a large public park. It was only a couple of hundred yards away from where we'd been parked, but Hanya was going to have to drive around it, and stop at traffic lights.

On the bike, I cut straight through the park, and got to the other side a couple of minutes ahead of her. I leaned against the railing at the small car park off Mosspark Boulevard, and pulled my phone out while I waited. I'd been thinking about my second date with Fergus all morning. With everything else going on, I needed to cancel.

TheSamIreland – Hey.

TheSamIreland – So, I know this is really crappy of me

TheSamIreland – But I need to cancel tonight.

TheSamIreland – Sorry xx

My heart did a weird thing in my chest as the last message sent. Something I hadn't felt in a long time. I didn't cry when my dad died, yet cancelling a date with a guy made me want to break open?

Crap. Maybe Phil and Hanya were right about me.

Hanya got out of the car and joined me at the fence.

'Want your suit back?' I said.

'After you've washed it.' She smiled.

The joke held for a few seconds, but it couldn't win out against the tension we were both feeling.

'We're in trouble,' I said.

She nodded. 'And if Joe is involved, we really have no idea how high this goes. His party could be involved. The council.'

I pulled the notebook I'd taken from Paula's room and flicked through the pages. Compelling evidence hadn't magically appeared on any of the blank pages.

'We don't have enough,' I said. 'I mean, *we* don't even know what's going on. Not all of it. So, there's a conspiracy, the cops are involved, and Joe is trying to cover it up. There's something about a cartel, and they're going to take something over tomorrow. We've got a vague conversation on tape, and an empty notebook.'

'If we could just get hold of Martin Mitchell or Callum Gibson.'

Hanya hadn't even finished saying the words before we both knew the answer to that particular line of thought.

Crap.

'We'll not find either of them,' I said. 'I've been looking for a dead man. *Again*. Why do I always get into these things?' I laughed, but there was no humour in it. 'Paula was in that room, trying to tape a conversation between Martin and whoever else was there. She runs, contacts me, gives me the package. Joe's people have killed them all to shut them up, and they burned down the building.'

'These people, *my* people.' She made a clicking noise between her teeth. 'They've killed in broad daylight and got away with it. They've buried the CCTV.'

This was all my fault.

As ever.

I pulled on those threads, and the things that came loose hurt the people around me.

'I'm sorry, Han.'

'Don't be. What were you supposed to do? Walk away from seeing Paula die? That's not your style, Sam. Always trying to save people. It's why I like you.' She dropped her voice a little. 'I wish I was like that.'

At any other time, I would have been touched.

I would have buried it under a joke, but still.

In that moment, I was too busy being numb.

A message came through from Fergus.

FergusSingsTheBlues – Okay

That was it. Nothing to say he understood, or that it wasn't a problem.

'What do we do?' I said.

'All we can do is play it normal. They don't know we have the tapes. They don't know we got anything out of the house. I mean, they don't *know* we were in the house.'

'They'll figure it out once she describes us.'

Hanya gave me a look. 'I'm looking for the positives here.'

'Okay, sorry. Positive is good. I'm *with* the positive.'

'Paula was undercover, so she was an easy target. Cal was a criminal, so nobody cares, and Martin Mitchell isn't even known to be dead. They're trying to do this, whatever it is, on the quiet. So, we go about our normal business, we don't make a scene, and we stay around other people.' She gave me one of those looks that said, *This is the important bit.* 'Until we figure all of this out, don't be on your own.'

'Well, I can sit in the office with Phil for the afternoon. I can stall Mike Gibson a while longer, and I've cancelled my date with Fergus, so—'

'No.' Hanya was smiling in spite of everything. 'You're going on that date even if I have to force you there at gunpoint. I can now, you know.' She patted the small of her back. 'I'm locked and loaded.'

'Still carrying?'

She nodded. 'I'm not reporting the gun. Right now we don't know who it belongs to. And if cops are involved in all this, I don't know who I can trust.'

'Why do you suppose Paula left it behind? Why not have it on her?'

Hanya shrugged. 'We're assuming it was hers, for defence. Maybe it was evidence? If it was hers, and she was trained on it, she'd only pull if necessary. Besides, the paperwork? Don't go there. I've shot three people, and my job's been on the line after each one.'

And two of those were my fault, I knew.

I covered with a joke. 'Admit it, you just like carrying one. Playing at Jack Bauer.'

She smiled. 'Maybe a little. Plus,' she turned around and raised her jacket, showing the gun tucked into a small leather-effect holster on her belt, 'I had this left over from the old days.'

We both stood and watched for a while as some children played football in the park. A kid was trying to be Lionel Messi, dribbling the ball past everyone. Until one of the bigger boys booted him to the ground. The rest of the kids celebrated the foul as if it was a goal.

'How about you?' I was packing my bag and getting ready to ride off. 'You shouldn't be alone, either. You don't know who on your team might be in on it.'

Hanya patted the small of her back again. 'I'm fine. I need to go see the Pennan woman in about an hour. She was all kinds of hysterical this morning, so the boss wants me to go back and take another try. You know,' she lowered her voice to impersonate a man, '*You're a woman, she's a woman, maybe she'll talk.* Sexism rules, yo.'

'True dat.'

We did a fist bump to complete our moment of being street. I pushed off on the bike. Hanya called something after me about her suit, but I was already building up speed.

291

SIXTY-NINE
ALEX
14:13

Alex came to again. Things felt easier this time. He could remember most of what had happened. That was a good sign, right?

His legs were stretched out, and he could feel carpet beneath him. Alex opened his eyes to see he was laid out on the ground, with his back against the wall to prop him in a sitting position. His damaged leg had been wrapped up in brown parcel tape, and two of the legs from the chair he'd been sitting on were used as splints, just about visible through the layers of tape.

'I did a day's first aid training at school,' Milo said. 'So you're welcome.'

'And I've seen every episode of *ER* and most of *Grey's Anatomy*.' Kara was kneeling down next to Alex. 'So I was able to supervise.'

Alex realised he couldn't feel the taped-up leg at all. And his other leg was distant; he could feel it only through a wall of ice. His hands were bound behind his back, but he could flex them, so he focused on that.

'You've lost a *lot* of blood,' Kara said. 'I'll need to change the carpet.'

Alex tried to speak, but his mouth wouldn't move at all. 'Wuck wou.'

'That's sweet.' Kara leaned in and kissed his forehead. She waved something in front on him. It was the burner Fergus had given him. 'Someone keeps trying to call you,' she said. 'Maybe the person you were planning to share the money with?'

'You remember what Darth Vader looked like without the makeup on?' Milo said. He was holding a knife. 'Well, you'll see it in the mirror soon if you don't start talking.'

Kara leaned in close to Milo. 'Enough with the geek shit.'

Alex tried to turn to Kara. His movement was limited, and all he could do was turn his head. It sent pain shooting across his neck. 'Wou won web away wib wis.'

'I think we already have. I should thank you.' Kara sounded different, now. Colder. 'You trained me for this. All those friends we fucked over on the way up, cutting off my family when they didn't like you? And you never thanked me for it. Not once. We moved up here and it was all about you. Never looked at what I was leaving behind, did you? I could be running Chelsea or Spurs by now. This is *my* money. I *earned* it.' She took a step back from crazy into unhinged. 'And none of this matters. It doesn't matter what I do to you. It's not really violence, is it? You're not really here; you're in a morgue somewhere.'

Milo got down on his knees and pressed the knife to Alex's throat. 'If I remember right, we each have eight pints, and losing more than four will kill you.' He looked back at the carpet where Alex had been before. It looked like a swamp, with a dark stain and congealed dark goo sitting on the surface. 'I'm not Doctor McCoy or anything, so I don't know, pal, but I think there's more than four over there. You need the hospital, and probably in the next few minutes. So, do you want to live, or do you want to be a dead rich man?'

'Tell us where the money is,' Kara said. 'And we'll get you to a doctor.'

Alex wanted to believe her. Still now, deep down, he wanted to trust what she said. But Kara had already given the game away. She'd said it didn't matter what they did to him, he didn't exist.

He had a simple choice.

Hold out, and die slowly here, but get a few more moments of life.

Or –

Tell them the bank details, and die quickly.

Was there another way? Could he get a message to someone? Maybe Fergus could help. How would he be able to do that? If only his brain wasn't wrapped in this cold water. It was taking so much effort to think.

Maybe he could tell them Fergus had the money? Then they'd call him, and need to keep Alex alive until Fergus got here. If he turned up. Would the hit man care enough to help? Alex had been pretty rude to him. Blackmailed him. Threatened his family.

Shit.

Maybe, just maybe, Alex was starting to think, it would have been a good idea to be nice to a few people.

The doorbell rang. Milo and Kara looked at each other, then toward the door.

'Who is it?' Milo said.

'How should I know?' Kara hissed.

Alex felt a small surge of hope, somewhere down in whatever part of his body was still working. While Milo and Kara were distracted, he started flexing his hands again, feeling circulation coming back.

The rope, or whatever they'd used to tie his wrists together, wasn't as tight as it had been when he was in the chair. Maybe they'd underestimated what was needed, because of all the blood he'd lost.

That thought made him go woozy, but he needed to press on. Push that away. Flex. Pull. Work himself loose.

Kara stood and walked over to the window. She took a look out, then stepped back fast. 'It's one of the cops from this morning,' she said. 'I remember her. Perera, I think.'

'Hanya?' Milo's voice rose. Alex picked up on it.

Kara turned on him, sounding jealous. 'Friend of yours?'

'No, no. She's a, uh.' Milo climbed to his feet fast. 'Sam, you know Sam. They're like best friends or something.' His voice lowered. 'She kind of hates me.'

She's not the only one, Alex thought.

'Get him out of sight.' Kara moved to the door. 'I'll get rid of her.'

The doorbell rang again. Kara stepped over to the living room door and waved her hand in a big circle, signalling for Milo to get a move on.

Milo bent down and took hold of Alex's feet. He lifted them and started to drag Alex along the ground, through to the kitchen area. Alex felt his damaged leg for the first time since waking up. A numb, distant sensation. It wasn't pain, not exactly. More like the time he had a tooth removed under local anaesthetic.

Except, he hadn't been drugged.

He started to realise just how urgently he needed medical attention.

Milo let Alex slump behind the kitchen counter and knelt down over him, holding the knife to his throat. He raised a finger to his mouth in a *Ssshhhhhh*.

Out in the hallway, Alex heard the front door open.

Kara's voice was quiet and controlled, with just the right amount of emotion being held back. The grieving widow. 'Hi detective. How can I help?'

SEVENTY
FERGUS
13:00

'I think they look hard to walk in,' I say, playing it cool.

Khan laughs.

As I stand there, feeling too ridiculous to really let the fear sink in, Khan sits down on the stool and undoes each of the straps. She pulls a sleek red pair off the shelf and slips them on, then stands up slowly, wobbling a little from side to side as she tries to gauge the balance.

'Walk with me,' she says.

We walk up the aisle, toward a mirror. Khan pivots, and we walk back the way we came. Then we do it all over again.

'I have a few problems,' she says. 'And I'm hoping you can help. Do you know Dominic Porter?'

I flinch. Just a little. I look up and see she's watching me in the mirror as we walk toward it. 'The councillor?' I say. 'I voted for him.'

We get to the mirror and turn, walk back down the aisle. At the stool, Khan sits back down, and takes the shoes off. She slips another pair on, and off we go.

'Interesting,' she says. Does she believe me? Does it matter? 'Okay, I'm going to be straight with you, Fergus. I can call you Fergus? Good. I like to be straight. Too many people in the business want to hide behind bullshit or talk in code. We're not in some shitty spy movie, are we?'

'No,' I say.

Her accent is a blend. I know from her background she was born in the Middle East, grew up in England, and studied in America. In each sentence that she says, the words veer off into different accents. Sometimes she has the soft Rs and Ts of England; sometimes she has the purr and roll of the Middle East. The American accent seems to be there at the start and end of everything.

'Good. I don't like that. And I don't like corporate speak. Too many people running things up flagpoles, putting pins in balloons, thinking of blue skies. Fuck 'em all,' she says. 'If I'm going to kill you, I tell you.' She leans into me to whisper, like a friendly aside. 'I'm not going to kill you. I always get someone else to do it.'

I spend a second trying to figure out how to respond, but she cracks a smile. 'I'm kidding,' she says. 'Not about getting other people to do it, but I don't want to get you killed.'

'I, uh, thanks, I think?'

'Here's where we're at,' she says. We pivot and walk the aisle again. 'I have a big deal going through. This time tomorrow? I own this city. All of it. And I don't trust *anyone* not to fuck it up. I got word that someone in Glasgow was moving against me, and Dominic Porter was going to find out who it was. But he's vanished. He called me a couple of days ago, but never spoke. On the line, you know what I heard?'

'What?'

'Two shots. You're the best hit man in town. Hey, that's sexist, isn't it? What should we call it? Hit person? Hitter?'

'Call it whatever you like.'

'Okay. Hitter. You're the best. So I'm thinking, if Dominic Porter was killed, then the person who ordered it will be the person I need to know about. And, since you're the best in town, you're the person most likely to have pulled that trigger.'

I try the same tactic I took with Joe. 'I wasn't hired to kill Dominic Porter.'

She stops walking and peers up at me. Those eyes burn right in. It takes everything I have not to flinch.

'These ones, I think.' She looks down at her shoes, then smiles at the staff against the back wall. 'Yes, I'll take these. And all the ones I tried on. Thank you, girls.'

Khan turns to me again. 'This morning, another man who worked for me got killed. Blown up. Alex Pennan. You believe that? Sky high. Just like in the movies. I hear you'd be the best person for that, too.'

'I didn't kill Alex Pennan.'

My party trick was starting to wear thin.

Khan puts a hand on my arm. 'You're telling the truth there. But there's something you're not saying, isn't there?' When I don't answer she says. 'Okay. I respect loyalty. Maybe if you're as good as they say, and you've been paid, you don't want to break anyone's confidence. Look at it this way, if you *did* get paid to do it, and you *do* know anything else, then if you tell me before 1 p.m. tomorrow, I'll let you name your fee. If you know and you *don't* tell me? Then I'll be making one of those calls to someone else.'

1 p.m. tomorrow.

There's the deadline.

I can throw Joe under the bus right here. I know he's plotting to move on her, and I know who at least two of his accomplices are. But I don't. I've known Joe longer than I've known Khan, and I'm not looking to take sides. Let them do whatever they want. All

I need to do is keep my head down and stay out of it. And now I know how long I need to lay low for.

And it's not just me.

This mess has already taken a lot of people. Dominic Porter. Cal. Paula. If I tell Asma what's really going on, that might lead to Baz and Nazi Steve getting involved, and I kinda liked them.

The only person who knows I killed Dominic is Joe. And he won't betray me to Asma, because that would be turning himself in, too. If I can keep Joe from finding out about Alex, I can come out of this clean.

Walk away.

Kahn slips out of the shoes and gets a couple inches shorter. She nods at the door, where Long Hair is waiting. 'He can go,' she says.

Long Hair hands me my phone on the way out and says, 'Goodbye,' all polite, like this was just a normal everyday event.

I guess for him it is.

SEVENTY-ONE
ALEX
14:28

Milo pressed down on Alex.

They could both hear conversation coming through from the hall in small chunks. Some words were clear, others muffled. Kara was doing her best to keep the cop out there, and her answers were short and polite.

Alex could hear the evasion in Kara's voice, but he was listening for it. He hoped the cop would pick up on it.

'. . . sent the others away,' Alex heard the cop say. 'But I just need to ask a few more things.'

Her voice came closer. She was just on the other side of the door now. Kara's act wasn't working, and the cop wanted to stick around. She intended a longer visit than a quick hello on the doorstep.

The living room door opened. Alex heard the two of them walk in. They were less than fifteen feet away. Would the cop notice the blood? He tried the ropes behind his back. Being dragged along the floor had loosened them. Alex continued twisting his wrists back and forth. He just needed a few more seconds.

'So, there are just a few things we need to follow up on,' the cop said.

'Really?' Kara was playing her role to perfection, trying to sound calm and upset at the same time. 'What is it you need, detective?'

The cop's tone softened, going for friendly. 'Call me Hanya. I just need to go over a few things we didn't get to this morning. Nothing serious.'

Alex heard pages being flipped in a notebook.

'Do—do we really need to be doing this now? Today, I mean? My husband only just—' There was a wobble to Kara's words now, and Alex could picture her starting to tear up. He'd never noticed before, but from the other side of her affections he could see what an actor she could be.

Alex thought about making a noise. Calling out.

It wouldn't do much. He couldn't move his mouth, his throat hurt when he spoke and Milo's hand was pressed tight over his lips. But he knew Milo's knife was a bluff. They needed him alive, and they couldn't risk killing him while the cop was there.

He sucked in some air through his nose and braced himself.

Milo must have sensed what he was doing, and pressed the knife into the flesh of Alex's throat. It didn't quite break the surface, but it would only take one more push. Alex breathed out, showing Milo he was going to behave.

The movement had helped his wrists. They were almost free.

Just a couple more twists . . .

Kara and the cop – Hanya, he remembered – had stopped talking. Was Alex imagining there was a tension in the room? Things felt frozen. Tight.

'Is that blood?' Hanya said.

Yes.

301

Milo stood up. He ran around the side of the counter, raising the knife in his hand. Alex heard an impact, a heavy blow like two people colliding. There were a few grunts.

Hanya shouted, 'Milo? What the fuck?'

Alex pulled his hands free and started to crawl along the floor. It was slow going at first. Hell, it stayed slow, but he grew more confident as he moved. His bound leg was a dead weight, dragged behind him, but he had just enough strength in his arms and the other leg to shuffle forward.

As his head cleared the kitchen counter, he looked up to see what was going on in the living room. Kara and Milo were both on the floor. Hanya was standing over them with a gun switching from one target to the next. Milo was putting his hands over his face as cover from the weapon, and Kara was breathing heavily and wincing.

Alex's first thought was, *I'm saved.*

His second was, *I've seen her somewhere before.*

His third, *Shit, she was the woman talking to Joe at the café.*

Then he looked at the gun again, and it dawned on him that Glasgow cops didn't carry. Shit. Joe had sent one of his crooked cops to take them all out. This wasn't a rescue. He needed to think fast.

If only his brain would play along.

'You shouldn't have that?' Kara said. Halfway between a question and a statement. 'You shouldn't have a gun.'

Hanya hadn't noticed Alex yet. She turned to answer Kara. 'Clearly, you're the brains of the operation. Because wonder-boy here just tried to threaten me with a butter knife.'

'It's still a fucking knife,' Milo said. Alex heard the tremor in his voice.

Alex laughed. In spite of everything. Milo and Kara were both panicking. They were amateurs, and everything about this situation was spiralling out of control. Except for this cop. Hanya. She was cool. She was calm. She was cracking jokes.

The laughter drew her attention and she turned, bringing the gun around expecting a third attacker. Her mouth dropped open when she saw Alex, and she mumbled a vague, 'Whaaat?'

She was surprised to see him.

That gave Alex hope. That meant she hadn't been sent to kill him. He mumbled something that he hoped sounded like, 'Help.'

She pulled out her mobile with her spare hand and started taking a few steps toward him. She typed a number into the keypad, and while her attention was split so many ways, Kara had taken the chance to grab Alex's golf club. She jumped up from the floor and swung it in a wild attack. Hanya sensed the move and, with a precision and strength that Alex would frankly have found hot if his libido wasn't buried under seven layers of pain, she dropped the phone and caught Kara's wrist, pivoted, and threw her across the room and into the coffee table.

Milo grabbed the knife off the floor and again tried to rush Hanya with it. The cop sidestepped Milo again, and used the gun in place of her fist, hitting him full in the face. He flopped backward. And crashed into the bar. Bottles of scotch and vodka rocked, then toppled forward onto him.

'Wait.' Kara had risen to her knees. She was favouring her back where it had hit the table, and her words came in jagged gasps. 'This isn't what it looks like.'

'I don't *know* what this looks like,' Hanya said. '*He* blew up this morning, but it looks like you've been torturing him, and *he* is a footballer who has no reason to be here. Why don't you start telling me what this looks like?'

Milo rose up behind Hanya with a full bottle of Talisker and swung it hard into the back of her head. The sound bounced around Alex's skull. Hanya staggered forward and dropped the firearm. She blinked a few times, and her head seemed to shake in slow motion, like a wrestler trying to sell a big blow. Milo brought the bottle down again. Hanya turned to block it, but wasn't working at full speed, so she only deflected the worst of it, taking the second hit on the shoulder. The bottle fell to the floor and Milo slipped his arm around Hanya's throat from behind, trying to get her into a chokehold.

Kara picked up the gun. She climbed to her feet and aimed, one-handed, at Hanya. She smiled and pulled the trigger. The recoil jerked Kara's hand back, and she yelped in pain. Or at least, Alex assumed she yelped. He saw her face contort and her mouth move. He didn't hear anything, and he realised he wasn't hearing anything at all. The scene remained completely silent at first, then a tinny ringing seeped in through his ears. Thunder rolled in shortly afterwards.

Hanya had sagged, becoming a weight in Milo's grip. Alex watched her push a hand to a wound in her side. Kara aimed again, and this time she planted her feet squarely and gripped the weapon with both hands.

She fired two more shots. Alex heard both of them. Hanya made grunting noises, but so did Milo behind her. They both fell to the floor.

'Y*nnn* . . . you shot me—' Milo called out. He sounded like a hurt cat.

Kara stepped over to them. She looked down at the cop first. Hanya was moving slowly, trying to turn onto her side. Alex saw a glassy look in her eyes, like a UFC fighter who'd taken a big hit. She was moving on instinct. Reaching for the phone. Kara raised the gun to shoot again, but Hanya's movements slowed down, then stopped. The fingers of her right hand twitched in the direction of the phone. She let out a heavy breath. She mumbled something. It wasn't quite a word. It sounded like she was saying, *It's okay*, but Alex couldn't tell if it was directed at him, or at herself. Then her body sagged. One minute she was there, the next she wasn't.

Alex had never seen anybody die before.

He didn't like it.

Kara turned to Milo. He was crying. Alex found the tears more pathetic than anything else. 'You shot me,' Milo said again, through the blood and waterfall.

'At least you won't have to see the next season of *The X Files*.' Kara fired one last bullet, shutting him up.

She turned to level the gun at Alex.

'Now. *Now*. Listen. This?' She waved at the two bodies. '*This* is your fault. You've done this. And now we're probably going to have police here any minute. So. So. What we're going to do is we're going to go for a ride in my car. You're going to tell me where this money is, and we're going to go get it.'

Alex nodded.

Enough.

He had no fight left.

SEVENTY-TWO
FERGUS
13:42

Second time lucky?

I fiddle with the electronic lock at Alex's building, and this time I get it open in seconds. Like a boss.

I take the lift to the first floor. It looks like there are two apartments to each level, one on either side of the lift and stairs. I start going door-to-door, working my way up.

'Hi, do you have time to talk about our lord—'

SLAM.

'Hi, do you have time to talk about—'

SLAM.

'Hi, do you have time—'

SLAM.

'Free pizza . . . is what our lord and saviour—'

SLAM.

Finally I come to a door with no answer. I try a couple more times, and press my ear to the wood, listening for any movement inside. The lock is simple enough, and I ease the door open.

I've been concerned that I might not know when I've found the right apartment. It'll be easy enough if Alex is there, but if he isn't, what signs will there be that it's his place? It'll be under a fake name, so I can't check the mail, and he hasn't moved in yet, so there won't be any giveaway signs of life.

Any doubts vanish when I see the inside of this place. It's tacky as hell. Red leather sofas, metal kitchen, a framed picture of the London skyline on the wall. This is a flat that's been decorated out of a catalogue, by an idiot.

The fridge is full of beer, and the cupboards hold enough different varieties of pasta to feed a bachelor for a lifetime.

I go searching for the *real* proof that this is Alex's place.

The cash.

The flat is arranged over two floors. The living room and kitchen are one large open-plan area, and the bedroom is above, on a small mezzanine. I open closets and cupboards. I look under chairs. Under the bed. I check the bathroom. There's a cupboard under the stairs, and I open the door.

Bingo.

Five large sports bags.

I slide one out toward me. It's heavy. I pull on the zip, seeing the crisp and clean twenty-pound notes stacked in bundles. Alex was right, this isn't just walking around money. There must be millions here. I put the bags back where I found them, and shut the door before I start to come up with any more stupid plans.

I close all the blinds and turn all the lights back off. I settle onto the sofa with a beer. I'll be here when Alex gets back. If anyone else turns up, at least I'll know he's blown it.

I sip at my drink and wait.

This is a mistake.

Something I've noticed, in the hours since I flipped that switch and stopped thinking about killing, is that I'm no longer burying the part of me that says I *shouldn't* kill. That voice has been getting louder all day and, as I sit here in the dark, with alcohol, I can feel something new.

Is this—?

Is this *guilt*?

I pull out my phone and Facebook stalk the guy I took out yesterday. Scott. Even looking at his interactions, I can see he was an arsehole. He shared dodgy memes, cracked rape jokes, total scumbag. But his pictures include birthday parties with a young girl. Maybe a daughter who lives with her mum?

Hell, their lives just got a lot harder.

The guy I wasn't supposed to kill? The councillor, Dominic Porter? He's not married, got no kids, but he does have an elderly mother in a care home. I don't want to think what'll happen to her without the help of her son.

And now I'm sat, in the dark, waiting to talk to someone I've *pretended* to kill. I've helped him steal money off one of the most powerful criminal organisations in the country, and along the way I've lied to two of their key figures.

This is not going to go down as my finest day.

And I'm sitting only a few feet from millions of—

No.

No more complications, Fergie.

If I touch the money, and Alex manages to come back, he'll have a reason to fuck with me. If I can keep him quiet, then we can both avoid pissing Joe off. And if I can avoid any issues with Joe or Asma between now and 1 p.m. tomorrow, then whatever they get up to, I'm out of it.

Just one day without messing anything else up, that's all I need.

My phone vibrates on the sofa next to me.

I have messages from Sam.

TheSamIreland – Hey.

TheSamIreland – Me again.

TheSamIreland – Sorry. I'm having a weird day.

TheSamIreland – Maybe we could just get a takeaway. Watch a movie?

Okay. Maybe the day is improving.

SEVENTY-THREE
SAM
19:30

I made a point of getting to Fergus's place bang on time.

It created a few moments of silliness, because I was ten minutes early, and waited by the front door. Who wants to be *early*? No. I wanted to ring his bell at the exact time we'd agreed.

It was just down to timing. We'd arranged I would pick up the food, and he would sort the movie. I'd opted for Chinese and, remembering my favourite place tended to get busy in the evenings, I'd set off earlier than I needed to. The restaurant cooked the food in record time, and I was at Fergus's door way sooner than I wanted to be.

I'd picked something a little softer to wear this time. The same kind of skirt as our first date, but in a deep blue, and a light, short-sleeved top to match. I wore a denim jacket. A little less *fuck you* than my biker leather.

I watched the seconds count down on my phone, then pressed the buzzer.

Fergus opened the door straight away.

Had he been doing the same thing, on the other side of the door?

What a pair of fannies we were.

Sod it. Go all in.

I held up the plastic bag holding the meal. 'It might be a bit cold,' I said. 'Because I've been standing outside like an idiot for ten minutes.'

He grinned down at me, and I tilted my head back, giving him the room, *Go on.* He took the hint and kissed me. Softly. Nothing serious. It didn't have the charge of our first, but that was fine. Plenty of time yet.

He led me into the living room. His flat was tidy. I was impressed, if not a little jealous. This wasn't a rush job. You can tell when someone had cleaned up just for your visit, because things are way too tidy, and small details will be out of place. A pile of things on a table, a candle burning to cover a smell, all of the TV and cable remotes piled in front of the television. That's the best giveaway. *Nobody* leaves them there.

There were none of those signs in his room. Things were tidy, but looked lived in. The remotes were on the sofa, where people really left them. There were no candles burning. It looked like he actually lived like this.

Fergus took the bag from me and headed into the kitchen. I took my phone out, and switched it off. Like I'd said, all in. Hanya was right. I was going to live a normal life, just for tonight.

I followed Fergus into the kitchen. He already had plates set out on the worktop, and was dishing out the food. He was making no attempts to give me small portions. This man knew his stuff.

'So I thought we could watch *A Life Less Ordinary*,' he said. 'I've got the Blu-Ray.'

I leaned in closer to him and tilted my head a little, hoping it came off as playful. 'Did you buy it specially for this?'

He said that he hadn't, but it came with a telling pause, and I knew he was lying. That was sweet. We already had a *thing*. I watched him move. He's wearing a black shirt. It's looser than the jumper he wore on our first date, but that's just giving my mind more room to play.

And then I'm thinking, maybe the movie can wait?

Maybe the Chinese will be better cold?

When he turned to ask me what booze I'd like, I stepped in close. He took both of my hands in his, threading our fingers together, but didn't make any further move. After a few more seconds I thought, *Sod it*, and kissed him.

Kiss three was still not as good as the first one, but it was getting there. I pressed in a little closer, feeling his back and waiting for him to do the same with me.

He didn't.

Huh.

I *can't* have misread it?

Maybe he just needs a little alcohol to loosen him up. We'd put a fair amount away the first time. Okay. Give him some room, Sam. Back off. Let him ease into it.

Grown up, remember?

SEVENTY-FOUR
FERGUS
19:38

Oh man.

You bottled it there, Fergus.

She leans in, *she kisses you*, and you don't go any further. *She starts feeling you up* and you don't go any further. What the hell is wrong with you?

I want to but—

But what?

I don't know. My gut falls out. I back down. I'd like to blame the stress of the day. But the truth is? I just chickened out.

'I, uh, I've not got gin,' I say, turning back to my cupboard. 'There's beer in the fridge, and I've got rum, also some Jim Beam or scotch.'

'Rum is fine.' Her voice is a little cool. Off. Have I blown it? Shit. 'Rum is my *mistakes* drink, I do silly things.'

There's a flash of that smile again. We're still in the game. I need to earn the moment back, though, because it's gone. Sam walks through into my living room with her food and drink, and I follow.

The place is neat and tidy, and I even tidied away my Blu-Ray collection into their correct cases and onto the shelf.

I hope she's impressed by that. Sam's got these great *eyes*. They just look up into you and, suddenly, you want to have a load of clever answers. But I keep finding I haven't got any.

Sam sits on my sofa, right on the end farthest from me. I figure it's a test to see what I do next, so I settle down right next to her, and she smiles a little to herself.

We start watching the film. At first, we're silent, actually following it while we eat. Then we start cracking jokes at the screen, and turning to each other to talk. Soon, the film is just background noise, and we're talking. Occasionally touching each other's arm or leg.

'Tell me something you hate,' she says.

'Hate?'

'Yeah. I think you learn more about a person from what annoys them than what they enjoy. I mean, aye, I know you like me, and you clearly like films and jokes about Batman. But maybe you just hate black people, and that would be a problem, I won't lie.'

She's needling me. Testing. I like that. I leave a silence for a moment and pull a face that's saying, *Weeeeeeeellll*. Give her a few seconds of thinking she's onto something. Maybe I'm a big hairy racist.

Once I've held it long enough for her face to drop with concern, I say, 'Button-down shirts.'

She almost spits out her drink. 'I wasn't expecting that. What? *Shirts?*'

'*Button-down* shirts. You know them. The ones with the buttons on the collar.'

'Aye, wido, I know what you mean. But why a shirt?'

'Look.' I put my hand up, making this into an important point. 'I'm no expert. I don't do the science or anything. Maybe I'm wrong.

But I think that gravity is already taking care of the issue when it comes to the collar. *Down* is its default position.'

This time she does spit her drink. It goes all over her skirt. She apologises and starts rubbing at it, like that's going to soak up the rum. I touch her thigh at the same time, at first to rub just like she is, but then because, well, it's a great thigh.

She looks at me.

I look at her.

My hand slides up her leg.

Everything else slides out of my mind.

SEVENTY-FIVE

SAM

20:22

He slid his hand up my thigh. Squeezing gently.

I have great thighs.

No point being modest. I spend all day on a bike, I've got stuff going on down there.

His fingers touched the waistband of my skirt, and I felt a little flush, a tremble. He ran his hand across my belly and around the side, to the small of my back. He pulled, not forcing me, but letting me know which direction he wanted me to move.

I sat up, then leaned toward him, moving with his guiding hand.

We smiled, looking from each other's eyes, to our mouths, then back again.

Come on Fergus, I thought. *I've made every move.*

Show me something.

Now.

He pulls me into a kiss. Holy crap. This knocks the first one down a peg. We're strong and warm with each other. I'm not sure when that one ended and the next one began, but somewhere in there our tongues were touching, and it felt like a separate kiss.

I run my hands across his back again. His shoulders, the top of his arms. I let my fingers trace up his neck and into his hair. And finally, he's doing the same. His hands are on me and it feels natural. He can't seem to get enough of my legs.

SEVENTY-SIX
FERGUS
20:30

I can't get enough of her legs.

I keep finding my way back down to her thighs because, man, that cycling is working for her. I come back up to the small of her back, then around to her front, and she gasps a little. I pull at her top, getting it loose from the skirt, then up and over her head. She shrugs it off her shoulders and leans forward as she does, pressing her breasts into me.

I stand up and take her hand, leading her to the bedroom.

Because I'm a traditionalist, right?

We roll around on top of the covers, kissing the hell out of each other's bare skin. Soon I'm inside her, and I start to realise I'm enjoying this a bit too much. I'm going to need to slow down. Her mouth is open in something that's not quite a smile, but looks comfortable, and her cheeks flush a little.

I'm speeding up, pressing harder, the closer I get.

Too soon. I pull back, start to slow down, but Sam wraps her legs around my back and pulls me in. She nods and looks up into my eyes. 'It's okay,' she whispers. I go deeper and harder, she moves with me, picking up our rhythm as she gives me encouragement, telling me to do it.

She gets me there, and I make a soft noise, then laugh at myself straight after.

I slip out and onto the bed beside her. Sam takes my hand and guides me, showing what she wants. We work together until she gets there, too. She breathes, 'Yeah,' a few times, then holds in a breath while she climaxes, letting it out in a happy sigh.

I go to the bathroom to get cleaned up. When I come back to the bed, she's already drifting, half asleep.

I lie down next to her.

Never knew I could feel this good.

SEVENTY-SEVEN
FERGUS
June 9th
06:30

I sleep straight through.

That's the first full night's sleep I've had in years.

Sam's already gone.

I yawn, stretch and head into the living room. My jeans are on the floor, as part of a trail of clothes between the sofa and the bedroom. I fish my phone out of the pocket and check messages.

There's two from Sam. Texts to my number rather than messages through vLove.

Had to go. Something's come up. Talk later XX

And:

Last night was perfect XX.

I've got two voicemails. One is from the burner I gave to Alex. A woman says, 'I think you know who this is. If you want to see Alex alive, call me.'

I have no idea who that is.

Okay. That was the shoe I was waiting to drop. Alex has messed up. Someone has him, and I have no idea what he's told them. The woman on the phone doesn't sound like Asma, and she certainly isn't Joe. Maybe I can still get out of this without involving them.

The next is from Stan asking me to call him back, urgently. I start to make worried connections in my head. Has Alex already spilled too much? It's after 1 a.m. in New York, but when he says urgent, I always take it at face value. I call his number and wait.

Usually he picks up straight away.

This time it takes a while, and he sounds sleepy.

'Sorry,' I say. 'But your message says—'

'Yeah, it's cool. Listen, I thought you should know. There's been a red flag in the UK.'

Red flag is a code. It's an urgent hit, open to all takers. Five hundred grand to whoever takes the target out first.

'Stan, I'm not—'

'I know. But this one's in Glasgow, so I thought you might want a retirement present. Turns out you were right, there are two new hitters in town, and they're—'

'Cops. I know. Alan Dasho and Todd Robinson.'

'Okay. Well, I figured you might want to collect the money before they do. The target is some woman. She's called, hang on . . . Samantha. Samantha Ireland.'

Shit.

PART FIVE
June 9th
Takeover Day

'Well, Sam, you certainly have a type.'

—Sam

SEVENTY-EIGHT
SAM
07:15

I'd woken up early.

Sleeping in someone else's bed is never comfortable for me. It was unusual to have slept as well and as long as I did. I looked at Fergus for a few minutes. He'd rolled onto his side, shedding the covers. It would have looked romantic, if not for his mouth hanging open.

I decided our relationship wasn't at the morning breath stage.

My phone was on the sofa. I padded through in my bare feet and switched it on. I had a couple of messages from a number I didn't know, and four texts from Phil that were all variations on, *Call me. Call me urgent. Sam, where are you?*

I didn't want to wake Fergus up by calling Phil from there. I pulled my clothes on and took a drink of water in the kitchen. My own place was only twenty minutes' walk; I could get a shower and brush my teeth there.

I pulled the front door closed behind me and called Phil.

That was when my world collapsed.

I don't remember the walk the rest of the way home. I don't recall stepping into the shower fully clothed. I know it happened, because that's where Phil found me a few minutes later.

Crying.

For the first time in a year.

Phil didn't say a word. He sat on the floor next to me, and put a hand out, holding mine while I let it all out beneath the warm water.

There was this jagged pain right down the middle of me. I was scooped out. If this was what I'd been holding back for all that time, I wished it had stayed buried. Fergus called me a couple times, but I didn't answer. The phone beeped to say he he'd left voicemails. I didn't want to call him back. The night before had been so good, I wasn't ready to add any problems by talking about where we went next, and I didn't want to talk to him about Hanya.

It felt wrong to load it onto him. Cheap. It was my pain to deal with, not his.

Once I stopped crying, Phil started to tell me what had happened. I knew for a fact he was talking. I could see his lips moving, I noticed his awkward hand gestures and the long pauses between words. Part of my brain was hearing the words, but they were nothing more than the background rumble of a busy road.

He stood up and left the room. I stripped out of my clothes and had a shower for real, washing off the night before. I brushed my teeth but avoided looking in the mirror. I wasn't ready for that.

Two of the words that had leaked through to the front of my mind were *gun* and *shot*.

Was it the weapon we'd found at Paula's place? Hanya had been heading round to the Pennans' either way, but if she'd been killed by something she found because of me . . .

I wrapped myself in my bathrobe and walked through to the living room.

Phil met me from the kitchen with a warm coffee. I took it and sat down. I tried to say *thanks* but it was a croaked noise.

'So they haven't found her yet,' Phil said. 'Hanya's boss was clear that we were to stay out of it, but—'

'Wait,' I said. My voice was raw, but it was working. 'Go back. Who haven't they found?'

'Okay, so at the, the scene, they found Hanya and Milo. And a load of blood that they think must have been someone else, but they haven't tested it yet.'

'Right.'

Alex was dead. Milo was dead. Hanya—

Was dead.

Wait. Milo? Why was—

Of course. Kara hadn't warned me off Milo because our relationship was bad for the team. She'd chased me away because she wanted him. That made everything else slip into place all too easily. She'd been cheating on Alex, so she wanted proof Alex was doing the dirty, too, for the divorce.

So, okay, Hanya and Milo were at the house. That left Kara. 'Kara's the one who's missing?'

'Yep, there's no gun at the scene, and Kara's car has gone.'

'And they said we should stay out of it?'

'Well, yes.' Phil was thinking about his words carefully. 'But I think maybe it was one of those things, like he was telling me the opposite of what he meant. I mean, Hanya's name isn't on the news yet. No details are. But he calls us to let us know. And he's telling me the car's gone, and his words just felt, you know, like—'

'Yeah.' I've played that game a couple of times. They have to tell us not to get involved, but there's a way of doing it that is really saying, *Give us a hand, eh?*

Wait.

Wait.

'Phil, did we ever take the GPS tracker off Kara's car?'

'No, we never got round to it.'

He grinned. I saw the flash in his eyes. I knew it well. The thrill of the hunt. He'd finally caught the bug. He'd found whatever part of our father was buried away deep down. Seeing it on his face, I was caught by how bad it was. I wished we could roll back, and I could stop him falling for it.

Phil picked his laptop out of the bag on the floor and loaded it up. He clicked a few buttons, and our GPS app filled the screen.

There was one tracker active.

The one on Kara's car.

It flashed away in the Merchant City.

SEVENTY-NINE
FERGUS
07:15

The red flag attached to Sam's name means I need to get to her, fast. The problem with Kara and Alex Pennan needs fixing, too, but it can wait. It's only my own neck on the block for that one, I need to help Sam first.

I need to explain. Tell her what's going on. That's also going to entail letting her in on how *I* know about it.

She won't see me the same way after that.

I'll lose her.

But that's something I'm just going to have to deal with. Tell Sam the truth and keep her alive, or keep lying to her and watch her die? That's not even a choice.

I try calling her, but she doesn't answer.

I try again, and leave a voicemail. 'Sam, call me, it's urgent.'

Next up I send a text, same message.

I start calling a third time, thinking at the very least I could leave a warning to let her know she's in danger. Then I realise what I'm doing, and how it's going to look. She's been on two dates with a guy, slept with him and now he's sending her weird needy messages.

You're in danger, don't leave the house. Yeah, right. There's no way that won't sound like a threat.

I look up the address of her office online. It wouldn't be too hard for me to find where she lives, I know she's already said it's not far from me. This feels creepy, but it's better than the alternative, right?

While I'm searching for her details online, Google starts to throw news stories back at me. Sam's way more than a bike messenger. I wonder if she was ever planning to tell me any of this?

Yeah, right, because *her* lies are the bad ones in all of this.

My phone goes off and I answer it out of reflex, not even checking who it is.

'Fergus?' It's my dad. He sounds weird. 'We just had a call. On the house phone.'

My blood runs cold. I remember that Alex had my parents' details, and I know where this is going even before he says it.

'Some woman,' he continues. '*Kara*, she said. She's shouting about money, said if you don't take it to her she'll, Fergie, she threatened us. Yer maw. Zoe.'

Kara?

Kara Pennan?

He gives me the address. As I expected, it's the flat I broke into yesterday. Okay. This changes things. I need to get to Sam, but now my family are involved. I wish I'd killed Alex for real. This is way out of hand now.

'Son, are you in trouble?'

'Don't worry, Dad. I'm sorry she threatened you.'

I heard something that sounded almost like a laugh. 'I'm a union leader, been threatened my whole life. If I didnae back down from Thatcher, I'm no' backing down from this lass. But are *you* in trouble? You need me, just say.'

'I've got it, Dad, but thanks.'

I've spent years keeping my family out of my real life, terrified of what they'd say. First hint of trouble, and my dad's first question isn't, *What the hell have you been doing?* but, *How can I help?*

I leave a message on the answering service at Sam's office number. I give a little more detail this time. *I know this sounds weird, but it's important. Call me.*

I want to get to Sam, but first I need to take my family out of the firing line.

EIGHTY
ALEX
07:15

Alex blinked.

Had he been asleep?

He wasn't sure.

He did this sometimes. He'd been complaining for years of having insomnia. Kara had bought him a Fitbit to monitor his sleep, and the stupid little thing said he slept five to six hours a night.

He just never remembered any of it.

Only one of his eyes would open. What was with that?

And why did his head hurt?

He looked around. Hey, he was in Kara's car. He hated this thing. It was too small, and an automatic. The seats were uncomfortable and she always had her own music on.

Kara was behind the wheel. She looked pissed off.

Where were they going?

Alex tried to speak, but all that came out was a strangled whine. His mouth wouldn't open all the way.

What?

And why was he so sleepy?

Alex blinked.

Had he been asleep?

He wasn't sure.

He did this sometimes. He'd been complaining for years about having insomnia. Kara had bought him a Fitbit to monitor his sleep . . . hang on, hadn't he already been thinking about that?

They were in a room. Alex was on a sofa. It was, wait a minute, he knew this place. It was his bed. His new sofa. The apartment. There was something important about this place, he just couldn't quite . . .

. . . the cupboard under the stairs. There was something about the cupboard under the stairs . . .

And when did he and Kara move in? He didn't remember telling her about this place. It was his secret.

Why was it his secret?

Alex blinked.

Had he been asleep?

He wasn't sure.

He did this sometimes. He'd been complaining for years of having insomnia.

Kara had bought him, wait . . .

Kara? He can hear her. She's talking into a phone.

'*Okay, I don't care about that,*' she says. '*Just tell him to get here, and bring the money, otherwise I'll come find you.*'

Money.

Job.

Wait . . .

MONEY.

Alex remembered. The money. He'd shown Kara the laptop, with all the info, including Fergus's details. He gets a hot flash of memories all at once. Holy shit, she's tortured the shit out of him, and he still hasn't told her the money is in here with them.

Is it really worth all of this pain?

Yes.

Yes, it is.

Alex's body feels distant. He can barely move.

His arms, yes.

He can move his arms.

He can pull himself along the cushions. He can pull himself up, using the back of the sofa for support.

Kara's sitting on the end. She's facing away, talking into the phone, barking orders.

The gun.

Where did that gun come from, again?

Oh yeah, the cop.

They killed a cop.

None of this was supposed to—

Stop. Wait. Alex is getting drowsy. He can't let this— He has to—

He lurches forward and grabs the gun.

Kara turns, her face pissed off. She panics, then, in the second before Alex squeezes the trigger, she wears her *Oh, seriously?* expression.

The gunshot takes Alex off balance. He falls forward off the sofa. The floor rushes up.

Alex blinks.

Had he been asleep?

He wasn't sure.

No, he couldn't have been. He's standing at the altar. Kara's walking down the aisle. She smiles as she draws level with him. A shy smile, despite being the most perfect looking thing in the room.

Alex has hit the jackpot.

Alex blinks.

EIGHTY-ONE
FERGUS
07:45

I'm not messing about now.

I want to blame Alex.

I want to blame Kara.

Truth is, this is my mess, and I know it.

I shouldn't have taken the job. The minute Alex Pennan tried that dick move of threatening my family, I should have dropped him off the nearest bridge without a return ticket.

Now my parents are in danger. My *sister*.

I don't care what state they're in when I get there, I'm shutting both of these fuckers up. My hand shakes on the steering wheel at the thought of it. I wanted to be out. I wanted to walk away. But first, I need to pay my taxes.

I slip my gun out of the glove box and fit the muffler. I strap a holster to my belt, so the weapon can sit at three o'clock, covered by my coat. Usually I like it to be more hidden. I have coats and jackets that have been specially tailored, with extra pockets and straps on the side to conceal weapons, but I want the Pennans to see this coming.

I press the buzzer at Alex's place, but there's no answer.

I don't have time for niceties. I cheat the lock again. I should start teaching classes. I go up in the lift, then knock on the door to Alex's place. I don't hear anything straight away, but then, is that a whimper that comes through the door?

There's definitely someone in there, and they don't sound happy.

I pick that lock, too, a simple Yale, and step inside.

I'm hit by a host of smells all at once, and none of them good. Urine, shite, blood, gunfire, sweat. This place smells like a torture scene I walked in on in Afghanistan. Yeah, that's something that stays with you.

They're both in the living room area. Alex is on the floor between a red leather sofa and a glass coffee table. There's a laptop awake on the table. Someone's been to town on him. His left leg is wrapped tight in brown parcel tape. His head is the wrong shape, and his jaw is off-centre. One of his eyes is swollen shut; the other is already drooped in the half-mast death mask. His skin is almost white.

It's hard to tell which of the injuries did for him, but there looks to be almost no blood in his body, so that's the most likely cause.

'You know, Al, marriage counselling would probably have been easier than this.'

Kara is on the floor at the far end of the sofa.

There's a trail of blood leading back closer to Alex's body, and it looks like she dragged herself across the floor until she couldn't move anymore. Her glassy eyes stare up at me, unblinking. Alex must have tagged her on his way out. The bullet hit her in the gut, but it doesn't seem to have come out the other side. All bets are off when you get shot. Sometimes the bullet goes straight through; sometimes it goes on an adventure inside you. Her skin is cooling, but there's warmth there. Maybe it was her last breath that I heard from the other side of the door.

The laptop has my contact details on the screen. There's another file open, showing the dates and numbers of large financial payments. Alex has been a good boy and laid everything out in one document, in a clear timeline. It shows clearly how MHW set up the deal with the gangs due to go through at 1 p.m. today, and a separate list of deals done by Joe that are meant to win people over to his side in a private takeover.

This is the proof of Joe's big plan.

I open the cupboard door and look down at the bags.

Millions of pounds. Without an owner.

It would be rude not to take it.

Sam can use some of it to blow town, get out of the firing line. I can set my family up for life, and I can even pay off some of my own guilt over the families of Scott Christopher and Dominic Porter.

I just need to get to Sam in time.

EIGHTY-TWO
SAM
08:03

Phil and I watched from across the street as the mortician wheeled two body bags out of the building, past the ambulances and into the back of a waiting van. Phil had driven us into town, and we'd followed the GPS signal to the car. He located our tracker and removed it while I called Hanya's boss and gave him the edited highlights. We had Kara's car, but we didn't know where she'd gone from there.

He gave me the rest of it.

Someone in the building had called 999. The neighbour had heard whimpering and shouting, but said, and Hanya's boss quoted, 'Who am I to judge what couples get up to.' It was when he heard something like a firework or a gunshot that he called the cops.

They found Kara and what was left of Alex.

'Do you have any idea what all this was?' Phil said, as we watched the body bags get lifted into the van. 'I mean, just, what the hell?'

'I'm getting that feeling a lot lately,' I said.

'But I'm not making this up, am I? Alex Pennan has died two days in a row?'

'Weird.'

'Are they sure this time?'

As we watched, a car pulled up at the edge of the police cordon. Alan Dasho climbed out. Todd Robinson wasn't with him. He walked over to the other cops at the scene. He hadn't seen me, and I was feeling grateful for that.

It had been one thing to know about the big conspiracy when Hanya had my back. She'd saved me once before when I'd got in over my head. But now I felt alone. Isolated. I hadn't talked to Fergus, and there was no way I was going to let Phil in on the details.

The less he knew, the safer he was.

'Keep an eye on them,' I said. 'Let me know if the blond guy there turns around.'

'How?'

'*Improvise.*'

I squatted down and made my way along the line of cars. At the bottom, I peeked out to make sure I was still fine, then crawled up behind Dasho's car. I stuck the GPS tracker to the underside.

I wanted to start being ahead of the game.

Wherever these guys went, I needed to know. I didn't have a plan. I had no idea where I would get one from. But I wasn't going to let go. I duck-walked to Phil, and we headed back to his car.

We drove straight for the office. The morning shift had been covered by one of our fastest riders, a recovering student named Dan. He'd never made a pass at me, and I was routinely rude to him, and despite all of that he'd agreed to cover my workload without hesitation.

I had some pretty cool people in my life.

Maybe it was time to start letting them back in.

Phil had been right about all of it.

I wasn't going to say any of that to him, though.

He's my brother.

The office door was unlocked when we got there. That should have set alarm bells ringing in my mind. Dan would still be away on the morning run. If I was the kind of detective I wanted to be, I would have noticed the signs. But my brain was still fogged up with everything that had happened.

Phil walked in first. I followed in behind.

By the time I realised what was going on, it was too late.

EIGHTY-THREE

FERGUS

08:30

I head straight round to Sam's office. It's a professional set-up in a good unit. The rent can't be cheap. Maybe I could make sure they find some money in a bag once all this is over.

I've still got the gun strapped to my waist. If someone comes for Sam, or is thinking about coming for Sam, I want them to see it. Force them to make a decision on how badly they want to try me.

And I hope they buy into the bluff, because my hand trembles every time I touch the gun.

I'm not going to be the greatest bodyguard in history.

I stand outside the office door for a couple of minutes, sucking in the warm morning air. My heart is a marimba. I fight for control.

This is it.

Once I step in, with a gun on my hip like a fucking cowboy, it's all over.

Whatever we've been building, it—

Fuck it—

Shut up and get in there.

I walk in to find the shit is already hitting the fan. The room inside is large: a big open space with bikes, tools and some sofas. Sam is stood in the centre, next to a chubby guy I assume to be Phil. They both have their hands in the air.

On the other side of them, facing me as I walk in, is the big cop from the bridge.

He has a gun pointed at Sam.

His eyes flit to me, and his expression changes for a just a second, trying to figure out how this affects his plan. Sam reads it and turns to see me. Her eyes go wide, and she's just starting to say, 'Fergus, run,' when she notices the gun on my hip as I brush my jacket out of the way, and her mouth forms into a *What?*

'This doesn't concern you, hit man,' the cop says.

Motherfucker. He just *had* to call me that, didn't he? I was hoping to break it to her. Now I won't even get the chance to soften the blow.

That's it.

I'm throwing hot lead at his face at the very first opportunity.

And, I'm hoping, if I keep telling myself that, my hand won't shake when I go for the gun.

I risk taking my eyes from the cop and his gun to look at Sam. And my heart drops. She's fighting not to let something out. Her features are having a private conversation.

'You kill people?' she says. 'For money?'

The room drops away. The threat vanishes. In this second, right here, it's just me and Sam in a big black cave. Her eyes go cold on me. She let me in, trusted me, and now it's been thrown back at her.

'I used to,' I say. 'But I've given it up.'

Phil breaks through the darkness of the cave to bring me back into the room. 'You picked a bad time for it,' he says, the panic coming through in his voice. 'Could you not quit in five or ten minutes, instead?'

I look past both of them to the cop. I can feel Sam's eyes burning into my cheek, but she won't get to be angry for long if I don't deal with the first problem.

I nod my chin at the cop. 'Put that down.'

He doesn't move.

I flex my fingers over the gun. 'I'm going to make this easy, aye? If that gun does anything other than be put to rest on the floor, I'll shoot you.'

He smiles. He already has his weapon trained on a target. Mine is still holstered. He has the drop on me, and everyone in the room knows it. I can see his hand twitch, leading his brain in moving the gun from Sam to me. I shake my head. *Don't try it.*

'You wouldnae make it,' he says.

'You're polis, right?' He nods. 'Since school?' He nods again. I give him the coldest, calmest smile I can. I ignore the nervous twitching of my fingers. 'I joined the military at seventeen. Then SIS. I've stared down people in Afghanistan and Iraq. I've been shot at by people you wouldn't believe, and I outdrew seven mob guys in broad daylight in Manhattan. I can take this gun apart and reassemble it in less than a minute. You really fancy your chances of getting to the trigger before me?'

That thing about the seven mob guys is a lie.

But he doesn't know that.

He also doesn't know my hand is going to shake like jelly the second I go for the gun, and that I don't think I can actually do this.

He doesn't know any of that.

And yet, he squeezes the trigger.

EIGHTY-FOUR

SAM

08:33

I couldn't believe it.

I just—

No. Couldn't believe it. I trusted this guy. I let him in. For the first time in ages, I met someone I liked, someone I wanted to spend time getting to know, and he turns out to be a *hit man*?

Well, Sam, you certainly have a type.

Fergus and Todd stared at each other, either side of Phil and me. These showdowns always looked good in movies. It's a whole different thing when you're in the middle of one. There was nothing fun or exciting about standing between two armed killers.

Especially when one of them was a guy you thought you could . . .

Not now, Sam.

Todd tightened his grip on the gun, which had lowered a few inches while he talked to Fergus. I stared at the barrel. Mostly, I stared at the big black hole in the middle. Would I see the bullet as it came at me?

Todd breathed out, an animal grunt, and squeezed on the trigger.

I heard three shots. The first was the loudest, a metallic sound, slamming a door. The second and third were muffled by my own shock. But I was okay, nothing hit me.

Todd staggered back with each of the first two shots, then the third stopped him in his tracks and he toppled forward, down onto his knees. I looked to where his gun had been, trying to look for the bullets that were making the noise, but all I saw was red meat. His chest was covered in the same sticky mess, and one of his knees was pumping blood onto the floor.

All three shots had come from Fergus.

I turned to him. Phil was already staring. Fergus's gun hand was raised, and his eyes were still locked on Todd. I noticed the gun start to shake, and Fergus shifted his attention to it. He watched for a second, then holstered the weapon. He clutched his chest, then his mouth, but he couldn't stop what was happening, and threw up on our concrete floor.

'Just great,' I said.

Todd groaned. The smell of urine filled the air. Soon it would mingle with the puke, and then we'd have a party. He stared up at us. The gun was a few feet away, on the floor, but I didn't want to pick it up. Fergus bent down and took it. I noticed his hand shaking again as he slipped Todd's weapon into the waistband of his jeans.

Fergus turned to Todd and said, 'I'm trying very hard not to kill people. You're lucky. But that might not last. Did Joe send you?'

Todd glared. Fergus pulled his gun out and pointed it to Todd's head. The cop saw the shake in Fergus's hand and laughed.

'Shot by a guy with the shakes,' he said. 'You getting the blackouts yet?'

Fergus ignored the question. 'I don't think shakes will matter this close. They didn't matter from across the room.'

Todd spat blood on the floor then sighed. 'Joe put out the flag. I told him Sam and the bitch were still sniffing around.' He grinned and looked at me. 'One of those problems is already solved.'

I felt anger surge. I took a step forward to kick him, but Fergus put a hand up. 'And your partner, does he know you're here, cashing the flag in?'

Todd shook his head.

'What's a red flag?' I looked at Fergus, who started to explain. He was only a few words in when I decided, you know what? I didn't need to know. There was a whole side to Fergus that I wanted nothing to do with, and the less he talked, the less I needed to think about it.

I wanted him out of the office. I wanted him out of my life.

But, more than anything, I wanted to know what to do about the dirty cop bleeding out onto my floor.

EIGHTY-FIVE
FERGUS
08:40

Sam keeps switching her attention between me and the cop, and her expression is the same on both of us. She's a lost cause to me now.

'Why would there be a red flag in your name?' I say.

As far as changes of subject go, it's not the biggest misdirect in history, but it's a start.

Sam looks nervous. Off guard. For the first time, I look past my own anger and guilt and see that maybe there's something she was holding back, too.

'I'm a private detective,' she says, not meeting my eyes. 'I've been looking into something big.'

'Is it Joe Pepper, by any chance?' She looks at me and nods. I carry on. 'The takeover?'

'Tell me what you know,' she says. All calm and professional now. She's good at this.

I give enough of the details. The laptop and the trail of proof. Asma Khan and the cartel taking control of the city in a buyout of all the local gangs, including the police. Joe hijacking the deal for himself, and using the corrupt cops as backup. A double cross that would make Joe the most powerful man in the west of Scotland.

Sam nods as I speak. She doesn't seem surprised by any of it. Once I'm done, she fills in the mortar from her own investigation. Cal and Paula, the woman I let go at the start of all this. Mike Gibson. Joe and the CCTV. Everything ties up nicely.

'Joe killed Paula's boss,' I say. 'Or had one of his monkeys do it.'

'Why would she have given me a package to deliver to him, if he was dead?'

I see this as a chance to say something nice. Show some faith in her, maybe earn back some goodwill. 'Maybe that was the point. Maybe she was handing it to *you*, not him. Butler's name was to get you started.'

She nods. For a moment, I think of how well we would work as a team. I've got a knack for this investigations lark, and she has the experience. It could be like an old-school TV show, the two of us, three if we let Phil do the tech stuff, running a detective agency and having adventures.

Then the real world comes back in. Or rather, my brain does, followed by my words, and more tension.

'Well, we can solve one problem,' I say. 'Mike Gibson? He'll want a crack at the guy who killed his son, and we have him.' I gesture to the cop. 'So we have an out there.'

If looks could kill, I don't think Sam would be ending me on the spot, but I'd need urgent medical attention. 'I'm *not* handing him over to be killed.'

'Look, Sam, I hear you. I do.' I try my nicest, most reasonable voice. 'But we don't have a lot of options here. You don't want to kill him. Neither of us want me to do any more killing.'

'I agree with this,' Robinson says.

'I'm okay with you killing him,' Phil says, which draws a glare from both Sam and Robinson.

I carry on. 'And the one thing we know for sure right now is that we can't hand him over to the polis. Mike Gibson is the best way out. Everyone can be happy with that.'

'Not me,' Robinson says.

I raise a fist and say, 'This isn't a democracy.'

'You're right,' says Sam. 'It's not. It's *my* office.'

Sam pulls Phil with her through to the small room at the back for a private talk. Robinson smiles up at me. 'I'm rooting for you two crazy kids to work it out,' he says. 'If it helps?'

With Sam out of sight, I punch him a couple times.

Enough to knock him out.

EIGHTY-SIX
SAM
08:43

In our small office, I settled onto the edge of the desk and Phil took his own seat. We watched each other in silence, waiting to see who would speak first.

'I think he's right, Sam,' Phil said, quietly.

Part of me agreed. The part that would cut a red light on my bike if there was no traffic around. It was a voice that had kept me alive a couple of times in the past, when I'd walked away from cases that could be too big.

Take the easy way out.

Hell,

Take the only way out.

And hadn't this always been where the Gibson case was headed? I knew from the minute Mike asked me to find Cal that the old man would want to beat on his son. But that had felt different, somehow, to handing Todd over to Mike.

But without Hanya, I didn't know which cops I could trust. Handing Todd back to them was most likely a death sentence for me, Phil and Fergus.

And when did I start thinking of us as a trio?

I nodded. Phil understood. We could hand Todd over, but I didn't want to *say* it. Making it verbal was a step I wasn't ready to take. Somehow, leaving it unsaid was easier.

I eased off the desk and walked back out into the main room. Phil trailed after me. I saw him give a small nod to Fergus, who read the same signal. Phil started making a call on his mobile. He stepped over to the doorway to speak outside, where I couldn't hear.

Well, look at what a messed up little team we made.

Todd was unconscious. I thought for a second he might have died. He'd been shot three times, after all. Fergus shook his head, and said Todd was just 'taking a wee nap'.

We had another big problem to deal with. Despite knowing what the whole conspiracy had been about, we were still as trapped as when I'd talked to Hanya at Belahouston Park. There was nobody to turn to.

'There has to be a way out if this,' I said out loud.

Fergus asked, 'How'd you mean?'

'We can't go to the cops. We can't go to the papers. You've got a laptop full of proof, but who could we trust to publish it? The only way would be to put it online.'

'I don't think that would help, anyway,' Fergus said. 'People like MHW, they're all doing bad things all the time, and all the information is available on the net, but it doesn't stop it happening. Most people don't go looking for the details.'

'He's right,' Phil said, joining us. 'Just putting it online wouldn't help. A page full of numbers? Dates? Business deals? Nobody will look. Not without something that's a quick sell, you know, something sexy or sound-bitey.'

'So we're still trapped,' I growled in frustration and dropped down onto the sofa.

'It's not looking good,' Fergus said. 'Aye. The cartel on one side, Joe on the other. One of them has already put a red flag out on you. Between the two of them, we can't go to the cops or the press, and they can make any proof of us disappear. I've got cash,' Fergus turned to me. 'A lot. I can pay for us three to vanish.'

There was no way I wanted to touch anything of his ever again.

'I don't want your money,' I said. I made it as frosty as I could. 'And I don't want to run away.'

'I don't know, Sammy.' Phil sat down next to me. 'Maybe we should. Maybe he's right. If there's no way to win, why don't we just get the hell out of the trap?'

I would never have expected this kind of realism from Phil. He was the dreamer. The geek. The guy with the crazy talk and the stupid theories. 'What about all your usual talk?' I said. 'All your superhero stuff. You'd hate it if they just gave up and hid.'

'I don't think we're in that kind of story,' he sighed. He looked broken. I hated it. 'I think we're in something more like *Watchmen*.'

Todd, who had come to at my feet without us noticing, coughed and spat before saying, 'Forget it, Jake, it's Glasgow.'

Fergus stood up. He pulled his gun. 'In that case,' he said. 'I'll just have to give them what they want.'

EIGHTY-SEVEN
FERGUS
12:00

I'm stood in the doorway of Anderston train station.

It's noon, and we're running late.

It's the perfect place to meet Joe. The station is on a concrete island, cut off on all sides by traffic, and with the M8 motorway above us. Even on a sunny day like this, Anderston is dark and secluded.

Sure, there are cars driving by us constantly, but none of them will notice. Who would be watching out for a conversation between strangers, while driving on one of the busiest stretches of road in Scotland?

All manner of deals go down here. And the cops have learned to keep an eye on the area, but that won't matter to us, because the cops are in on it already.

I'm holding my Ruger. Robinson's weapon is tucked into the small of my back, just in case.

There's movement at the other end of the concrete island, and Joe Pepper steps out into the light, starts walking toward us.

I let him see my gun and he nods an acknowledgement. I press it into Sam's back and say, 'Okay. Time to go. And be scared.'

We walk out to meet Joe in the middle of the island.

EIGHTY-EIGHT
SAM
12:05

I felt the gun at my back.

'Time to go,' Fergus said. 'And be scared.'

In all fairness, he didn't need to prompt me to look afraid. I already had that part nailed. I was method acting. We'd gone over the plan enough times that we both knew our lines. It was the only way that any of us could see out of the situation, but still, it didn't mean I had to *like* it. And the gun at my back was making it pretty easy to look scared as hell.

Phil was parked a few hundred yards away, on the old strip of Argyle Street that had been cut off from the rest when the motorway was built. He had his laptop running in the car, recording everything we said on a conference call, the same way he'd done it when Hanya talked to Joe.

We'd met up here an hour earlier, and each of us had set up our parts of the deal. Fergus had caught the train in from Bridgeton, so he'd be on CCTV if anyone was watching, and I'd cycled here. My bike was chained up next to the train station door.

Once we were both in the doorway, we played out the act, with Fergus showing me his gun and telling me not to move.

Merciful mother of stupid plans, don't fail us now.

EIGHTY-NINE
FERGUS
12:06

I tell Sam to get down on her knees. Sounding like a bastard. She hadn't been happy about that part of it, but we both knew it was for the best.

If Joe does anything unexpected, if he tries to screw us over, I want to be able to draw on him, and it'll be easier if Sam is already down low.

I rest my gun hand on Sam's shoulder, pointed at her neck. She flinches. We've gone over it a few times, but I don't blame her. This is the part I'm not comfortable with, either. Modern weapons don't go off accidentally, but that doesn't make me any happier about pointing it at Sam.

It's a convincer. If we give Joe any sign that we're working together, even something as small as me not wanting to threaten Sam, it's all over.

'You were right. She's figured out about the MHW deal,' I say.

I leave it there. No mention of Joe's own angle on it all.

'You didn't need to bring her here like this,' Joe says. Smooth fucker that he is, for a second it sounds like he's being nice to Sam. 'A photo would have done.'

'I felt like I needed to make a gesture. Good faith, like. I know things got tense between us, and I don't want you holding any grudges after MHW take over.'

Come on, Joe, take the bait.

NINETY
SAM
12:08

The concrete was hard on my knees. I should have worn jeans. Fergus had tried feeding Joe two chances at falling for the trick, and he hadn't bitten either time.

We needed him to explain his plan. Not all of it, just enough to show what he was up to, in his own words.

Come on, Joe, take the bait.

Joe just smiled. The plan wasn't working.

We needed something else to get him going. I decided to go off script. I was going to improvise, and hoped that the man with a gun to my neck could trust what I was doing.

I started to laugh.

Joe's attention shifted between me and what, I assumed, was also eye contact with Fergus behind me. 'What's so fucking funny?' he said.

'Your little puppy here doesn't know the truth, does he?'

Joe stared at me, then a cruel smile ripped outwards from his calm, smug, punchable face. 'No. He doesn't.'

And here we go.

NINETY-ONE
FERGUS
12:09

'Know what?' I say, aiming for a mix of panic and frustration.

Sam's played this perfectly. I was worried when she ditched our agreed lines, but this will work.

'Maybe it's not MHW taking over,' Joe says. 'Or the idiots behind them. Maybe it's going to be me you'll want to suck up to.'

'What are you talking about?'

He steps in closer. I feel like thanking him, because that's going to make his words even clearer on the phones Sam and I have in our pockets.

'This is my Babycham,' he says, looking way too happy with himself at using Cal's word. 'I've set up my own deal. The cartel money goes through in less than an hour, but I've already railroaded their buyout. I'm using their money to make people loyal to me. What's the line? *King Kong ain't got nothing on me.*'

Not only is he a bastard, but he murders movie quotes, too.

'Thanks,' I say. Then, in a higher voice so he knows I'm talking to someone else, 'You get that?'

Long Hair and Buzz Cut, still in their snazzy black coats, step out from the concrete pillars that support the M8.

'Got it,' they say.

NINETY-TWO
SAM
12:10

Joe went through a few different reactions all at the same time. He let out a howl that sounded something like a swear word mashing together with *Whaaaaat?* He tried to bolt and, at the same time, pulled a gun on us. A small revolver that suddenly became the most important thing I'd ever seen.

I couldn't help but stare at it.

Fergus shoved me hard, pushing me to one side while he stepped forward and raised his own gun.

Before any shooting started, one of the two security guys pulled out a taser and zapped Joe, who fell to his knees in a fit of shakes and odd vocal noises.

At the pedestrian crossing that separated the concrete island from the street, we saw Asma Khan and Emma Poole, waiting for the lights to change.

Fergus had called Asma from the office to set up a meet. Once Mike Gibson had turned up to collect his prize, we headed straight to where Khan was waiting. A hat shop. She was a bit of an oddball.

There, we'd explained Joe's plan, and given her the laptop with all of Alex Pennan's evidence.

Emma had examined the information. She was Alex's replacement. In fact, to listen to the way Khan talked about her, Emma had been the brains behind the whole deal. Alex Pennan hadn't been long for this world even if things had worked out differently. Emma confirmed that our story was backed up by the numbers. She followed the trails to each of the gangs that Joe had made private deals with. Khan got on the phone to half a dozen people and threatened them back into line. The coup had been averted.

Khan called off the red flag that was out on my name, but said she'd reinstate it if Joe didn't come clean. Even with all the proof, and with the situation under control, she wanted to hear his confession. She hadn't got to where she was by simply believing everything she was told.

But now Joe's game was up.

Khan knelt down next to him on the concrete.

He looked up at her, still shaking, with wide eyes.

He was a rabbit in the headlights, but it was his own car rushing toward him.

'I've contacted everyone you've made a deal with,' Khan said to Joe. 'And had a quiet chat with them. We're back in control of this. Come,' she checked a Fitbit on her wrist, 'fifty minutes time, we own Glasgow. If you're nice and talkative, I might let you live long enough to see it.'

Fergus helped me to my feet and looked down into my eyes. He was waiting on a cue from me, something to say what we were going to be from there on forward. I wanted, more than just about anything, to tell him things were okay.

To say I could forget what he'd done, and the lies he'd told.

I met his eyes. 'Fuck off.'

Before that moment, I'd never actually seen someone's heart break. He crumpled inward a little, but did his best not to let it show. He touched my arm and whispered a small, 'Sorry,' before turning and walking toward the train station.

I nodded at Khan. I didn't want to linger here. I'd made the only deal available, but that meant I'd still helped a criminal organisation. I didn't want to spend any more time with these people.

'Samantha,' Khan said. She offered her hand in a shake. 'You've done good today. Joseph here might have pulled it off, if you hadn't helped us.' She paused, reading me. 'Your name keeps coming up. I hear it in all sorts of meetings. I can keep you out of trouble for everything you've done so far, I think we owe you that. But don't get up to any more, okay?'

That was perhaps the nicest threat I'd ever received.

Joe spat, but nothing came out. 'Your boyfriend's still fucking dead,' he said.

That was perhaps the emptiest threat I'd ever received.

I turned to walk back toward my bike, but Khan called my name again. When I looked back, she had her hand to her ear, where a Bluetooth headpiece was still connected to the conference call.

'Your brother is asking to speak to you,' she said.

I pulled out my phone and said, 'What?' It came out much blunter than I'd intended. There was a rumble beneath my feet as the train pulled into the station beneath us.

'When Joe turned up alone, I checked the GPS.'

That's right. In all the tension, I'd forgotten one part of our plan. We'd expected Joe would turn up with Alan Dasho in tow. The way we'd sold it to Joe was that Fergus would hand me over to them and then leave.

The GPS tracker was still active on Dasho's car.

'Where is he?'

'The car's parked up by Bridgeton train station,' Phil said.

Shit.

That's where Fergus would get off.

Joe *had* planned a double cross, just not the one we'd expected. Fergus would hand me over to Joe here, then Dasho would kill Fergus when he got off the train, keeping the two deaths on opposite sides of the city.

Your boyfriend's still fucking dead.

The ground shook again as the train left the station.

'Phil, can you get Fergus on the line?'

'There's no signal down there.'

Crap.

He wasn't my *boyfriend*, but he didn't deserve to die.

I looked at my bike.

Bridgeton was three miles away. It was a straight line, if I ignored all the traffic, one-way systems, red lights and people. The train had a couple of stops before then, at underground stations with ticket barriers. Fergus would be at Bridgeton in seven or eight minutes.

Could I make it?

'Keep trying,' I shouted into the phone as I unlocked the bike. I put my Bluetooth earpiece in and kicked off, skidding into the oncoming traffic.

NINETY-THREE
SAM
12:15

I was on the filter lane that directed traffic down from the motorway. I skidded to the left to avoid being hit by a red Ford that wouldn't slow down, then cycled out into the box junction and turned left onto Argyle Street.

'I'm checking the train times,' Phil said in my ear.

I got down close to the frame of my bike, as close to flat as I could make it, then started pumping hard on the pedals.

I overtook one car, then another.

Horns blared.

I blocked the sound out. I was going to be doing a lot of that with the number of traffic laws I was about to break. I drifted into the lane to my right, which gave me a clear run for a few blocks.

'Train's due at Bridgeton at twelve twenty-three,' Phil said.

'What time is it now?'

'You don't want to know.'

A car pulled out from the left and drove straight across into my lane, aiming for the spot straight ahead of me. If I slowed down I would lose momentum. I veered into the left lane, missing the car by inches as we went in opposite directions.

I could check the time myself, but that would take my eyes off the road.

'Phil, time.'

'You've got six-and-a-half minutes, Sam. You need to be doing two-minute miles. You've never managed that.'

'Never tell me the odds,' I said. I knew he'd like that.

NINETY-FOUR
FERGUS
12:15

What next?

Aye, I know it's bollocks to think I could be saved by a woman. Sam isn't the reason I've given up the job.

But still, I'd hoped she could be a part of whatever happened next.

Or at the very least, that we'd have a little while longer to find out that we hated each other.

But now?

Blown it.

I lean back on my seat and close my eyes.

The train is quiet, it could quite easily rock me to sleep.

I tried to picture my next move.

How is it possible to have five million in cash, and still feel like I just lost the best thing that ever happened to me?

NINETY-FIVE
SAM
12:16

I ran a red light at the bottom of Douglas Street. The cars turning onto Argyle Street on the green swerved to avoid me.

No time to wave an apology.

I pushed on.

There was another junction at the bottom of West Campbell Street. That was a real test, as traffic was moving across the road in front of me. I skidded to the right to cut across between two cars, then veered left to avoid landing on the bonnet of another.

Behind me I heard the *whoop-whoop* of a police car, followed by the siren.

Things just got interesting.

Up ahead was one of the worst junctions in the city centre. The corner of Hope and Argyle. On one side of Hope Street sat a row of bars and restaurants, on the other side was Central Station. Every bus into the city from the Southside drove up Hope Street.

As I approached the junction, I didn't even look to my right to see what the dangers were.

Anything I saw would slow me down. I relied on my peripheral vision to tell me of anything bearing down on me, and went for it.

Horns blared. Tyres squealed. I heard shouting. Swearing. One person screamed.

I pedalled on. Under Central Station. The siren stopped briefly, and I wondered what kind of gridlock I'd caused behind me.

I couldn't turn back to look though, because next up was the only junction worse than the one I'd just crossed. After passing under Central Station, you come out to where Argyle Street meets Union Street and Jamaica Street. You come out blind, with no view of the traffic coming down toward you on Union Street. On the right is a McDonald's, and the street outside in summer is always swarming with teenagers. Sometimes they'll throw things at cyclists, try and knock them off balance.

All I could see, as I approached the junction, was the traffic directly ahead of me, and the lights, which were red.

Cars, buses and taxis would be coming at me from the left in a matter of seconds.

The only saving grace was the siren, which had started up again behind me. If my luck held, that would stop the traffic, with nobody able to see round the blind corner to spot which direction the polis car was heading.

'You just did a two-minute mile,' Phil said in my ear.

I closed my eyes again and cycled out across the junction.

NINETY-SIX
FERGUS
12:17

The train pulls in at Central Station.

I watch the people getting on and off. I can read what kind of jobs they do, what kind of days they're having.

I can see the men checking out the women.

The women avoiding the eyes of the men.

I'd been starting to like the idea of being a detective. I've got the skills for it. But maybe not in Glasgow. I could head back to New York. Be a millionaire consulting detective, like in those TV shows. Or just go to New York and be a millionaire, do nothing but drink and watch the city turn over.

I check my phone. No signal, but it keeps trying.

Like that matters now.

I'd got in the habit of checking it constantly, looking for messages. I can stop that.

Right, Fergie, stop being a miserable wee shite. You're getting the train home to five million quid.

You can do whatever the fuck you want from here.

The train pulls out from Central.

NINETY-SEVEN
SAM
12:17

There's a pedestrian crossing where Buchanan Street intersects Argyle Street.

Buchanan is pedestrianised, and in the summer it's full of people. The light was green for them, red for me. The road ahead of me was full of people.

I didn't stop.

I shouted warnings and apologies as I threaded through and around the crowd. 'Sorry.' 'Sorry.' 'Head's up.'

What I got in return was, 'Fuck you.' 'Off it.' 'Jeezo.'

People scattered quicker once they heard the siren behind me.

After the crossing, Argyle Street changes. The traffic turns off, heading north up Queen Street, and the way straight ahead is paved for pedestrians. I rode up onto the pavement and started threading through.

I heard the siren turn north behind me. They could have followed me, but with so many people out on foot, it would be a risk. They could head around the traffic diversion and try to cut me off, if they thought a cyclist was worth chasing.

I felt the rumble as the train pulled into Argyle Street station beneath me.

Next stop, Bridgeton.

NINETY-EIGHT
FERGUS
12:18

At Argyle Street, a drunk tries to get on but slips, and falls back onto the platform.

I get up to help him, and step down off the train.

The doors almost shut behind me, but I shout out to the conductor, and he overrides the signal.

''Hanks, Big'yin,' the drunk says as we step back up onto the train. 'I'd affer ye a drink, but I've ainly got six tinnies.'

I smile and say, 'No worries, pal.'

The drunk makes me think of Cal and his *Babycham*. I can't help but laugh. For all that has happened, for all the death and stupidity of the last few days, our way out of the situation has really boiled down to a variation on Cal's big plan.

We tricked a guy into a confession, and sold him out to a bigger fish.

Cal's *Babycham* has been the right idea all along.

What are the odds?

The doors shut.

The train pulls away.

Next stop, Bridgeton, and home.
For however long I decide to stay.

NINETY-NINE
SAM
12:19

I weaved between two competing buskers and a fruit market stall. As I passed Virginia Street I sent up prayers for Paula. Cal. Hanya.

And anyone else who'd died in the name of this stupid game.

At the end of the pedestrianised section, I cycled out across another traffic junction and onto Trongate. There was less traffic at this end of town, but the roads were only one lane in each direction, so it still got congested.

I hadn't felt the rumble of the train. That was good. At this point, we would be in a straight race. The train ran beneath the road on the route I was taking. If it passed me now, I would never catch it.

Every second that I made now would be precious.

I undertook two slow moving cars, then swerved back in front of them to avoid a bus that had pulled in to pick up passengers.

The road ahead opened up to three lanes as I approached the clock tower.

The lights went the right way for once, giving me a green at the five-way junction. I breezed to the right in a large arc, enjoying the best bit of luck I'd had so far.

The fun wasn't going to last, though.

This was where it was going to get interesting. Because in order to stay on the same route as the train tunnel, and to stand any chance of beating it, I was going to ride the wrong way up a one-way street.

Into oncoming traffic.

ONE HUNDRED
FERGUS
12:19

As we pass beneath the junction at the Trongate, I look out the window.

While I was living in New York, I started reading up on its history and old neighbourhoods. When I came back home to Glasgow, I started doing the same thing for this old city.

There used to be a train station at the Trongate. It was called Glasgow Cross. The station is long gone, and the platforms have been dismantled. But if you look carefully, you can still see the old pillars and, if enough sun is filtering down, you'll get a sense of the large space around you.

Don't get me wrong. I'm no trainspotter. Couldn't care less about them. But once you find out there are hidden spaces beneath your feet, old caves, tunnels or train tracks, it's hard not to want to explore them.

My phone buzzes.

Somewhere at the old station, a signal has got through. I have a message to say I've got voicemail, and half a dozen missed calls from Phil.

I try to listen to the recording, but the signal has gone again.

ONE HUNDRED AND ONE
SAM
12:21

'You lost time on that second mile,' Phil said to me.

'Traffic.' I needed to keep my words short. I needed to focus on breathing. 'People.'

My chest felt tight.

My legs burned. Except for my hamstring – one of the recurring injuries that had made me give up running – which felt like elastic at the end of its give.

'Sam, it's already twelve twenty-one. You're going to need to do *better* than a two-minute mile to get there.'

I didn't answer. No point. I needed to empty out thoughts, words, emotions.

It wasn't a case of aiming for some zen-like plateau, or any other kind of rubbish. No. This was just about needing to think of only one thing.

Pedal.

Three lanes of traffic sped toward me. I got onto one of the white dotted lines that separated the lanes, and stayed on it, riding in a straight line between two rows of angry cars.

At the next junction, traffic opened up to two directions again, but I wasn't staying on London Road. It took a slight detour away from the train's route, and that could cost me too many seconds.

I turned onto Monteith Row, which was deserted, and had a chance to build up a little more speed without worrying about cars.

I could hear my breathing, in and out, sounding panicked.

The whirr of the drivechain.

An intermittent clicking sound that would be freaking me out at any other time.

Nothing else. The world was dropping away. Unimportant. Life was just about the pedals, the ground beneath me and the route ahead.

Until I heard the rumbling sound of the train.

ONE HUNDRED AND TWO
FERGUS
12:22

The train comes out of the tunnel as we pull into Bridgeton.

This is the first station open to the air since I got on the train, and it'll be a chance to find out why Phil's been trying to call me.

I stand up to get off, but there are a lot of other people on the train, so I let them all file out first. It gives my phone time to find the signal and connect with the message service.

I join the back of the queue and walk forward, heading toward the open door.

As I step down onto the platform, Phil's voice barks into my ear.

'It's a trap, man. Dasho's waiting to kill you at Bridgeton.'

I look up, and Dasho is stood right there.

He has a gun pointed at my chest.

I hear a commotion farther down the platform, yelling and pushing. Running. But my world closes in around the barrel of the gun.

He pulls the trigger.

ONE HUNDRED AND THREE
SAM
12:22

The train was behind me. I still had the fragile lead that I'd built up, but I couldn't compete for speed. The rumbling gained on me.

I turned back onto London Road, got my head down again, and just *moved*.

Push.

Push.

Push.

The train tunnel turned back onto the road at the same point, so once again we were in a straight race. Across another junction. A car horn screamed continuously at me as it got near, then scraped by behind me, close enough for me to feel the wind on my back.

Push.

Push.

Push.

For just a few seconds, a few crazy seconds, I pulled away, out-racing a train.

Then my lungs popped, and something flashed white in my vision. Pain barrier. Fine. I'd been there before, and beaten it. I could do it again. I kept going.

The rumble overtook me within sight of the train station. I mounted the kerb at Bridgeton Cross and rode through the bandstand, then down onto the road again. I bunny-hopped back up, and cycled straight into the station.

There were no barriers in this station. Nothing to stop me. I stayed on the bike and made for the steps to the outbound platform. The train had pulled in, and the steps were now full of passengers. I jumped off the bike. It hit the wall with a thud. I hoped it would forgive me.

I pushed down the stairs, through the crowd. No time for apologies or niceties, I just kept shouting, 'Move, move, move, move, move.'

I reached the platform and saw Dasho. He took a step toward the train and raised his hand, showing a gun. People were just standing, watching. Why? *Move.* My legs were turning to rubber. I didn't have anything left in the tank after the ride.

I saw Fergus step off the train.

He noticed the gun.

Dasho raised it higher, looking ready to shoot.

I got to within a few feet of them, but Fergus didn't hear me call his name. Dasho noticed me, however.

His hand started to tighten around the handle. The trigger.

I threw myself between them.

ONE HUNDRED AND FOUR
FERGUS
12:23

My world opens out again as Dasho fires.

A couple of days earlier, and I would have been moving even before the shot. I could have got to him first. As it is, I've been too slow. My brain has switched off. My instincts have dulled.

A blur appears between us.

Sam?

How the hell did she get here so fast?

I hear the shot, and Sam is thrown back into me by the force. We both fall into the open train doors.

She's a dead weight on top of me as we hit the floor. I shrug her off. I want to stay with her, want to see if she's okay. But there's still the issue of a man standing over us with a gun, and if I don't do something about that, we'll both be dead.

The old instincts kick back in.

The professional.

I jump to my feet and spring forward at Dasho. Spread myself wide. Make a big target like a goalkeeper. There's more of me to hit, but that's going to make him indecisive about where to aim.

He hesitates.

I headbutt him, and he falls back onto the floor. His gun skids across the platform.

The crowd are still watching. They're frozen now. Silent.

Number one rule when a gun comes out, is people do the opposite of what you would expect.

In movies, in common sense, they run for cover. They evade. They hide. In real life? No. They freeze. They watch. They wait to be told what to do.

Back in SIS training, we were taught the number one problem in a public gunfight was the fucking *public*. They'll get you killed. They'll get themselves killed.

Okay Fergie.

Keep them alive.

Keep Sam alive.

Hope that she still is . . .

I pull my own gun and fire it into the air. My hand only shakes a little. That gets a reaction. Now people are panicking. Moving. Screaming. They turn as one and head for the stairs up off the platform.

That blocks the exit.

There's only one way Dasho can go, and he takes it. He looks to me, looks to my gun still pointing in the air, then scrambles to his feet and runs in the opposite direction. He hops off the platform and down onto the train tracks, and sprints in the direction of the tunnel to Dalmarnock.

I turn back toward Sam. Her eyes are open, but fluttering. She's losing consciousness. Her face is pale. Almost white.

I start patting her down, looking for the wound. I find blood on her shoulder and pull back her jacket. The wound doesn't look bad. Her paleness is shock, she's going to pass out.

She smiles, weakly. 'Ta da.'

Her eyes close. I let her body relax to the floor of the train. She'll be okay with medical supervision, and I can hear sirens approaching over the shouting and screaming.

Sirens.

Shit.

I'm an armed man.

And there's a guy getting away who tried to kill me. He shot Sam.

My old instincts kick in full force, and I'm off and running. Down off the platform.

Onto the tracks.

Into the tunnel.

I have the gun ready.

My hand isn't shaking.

ONE HUNDRED AND FIVE
SAM
June 17th
15:00

It turned out, getting shot wasn't as painful as I expected.

It probably would have been, if I'd stayed conscious long enough to feel it. The thing is, apparently if you've just raced a train for three miles on a fixed-gear bicycle, then taken a bullet, the thing your body most wants to do is rest.

It wasn't a big hit, to be honest.

More of a graze. The bullet took a little of my skin, and I left a fair amount of my blood on the train in trade.

The cops found Alan Dasho's body face down in the tunnel. He'd made it halfway to the next station, before taking two bullets in the back. Despite the presence of three cameras on the platform, and two in the train carriage, no CCTV footage captured the events. The authorities denied any knowledge of the second gunman's identity.

It's funny how these things keep happening.

I guess it's all down to who you know.

Phil was worried about me, of course. Not about the bullet, because the doctors in the hospital had already told him it was a graze, taking away any chance I had to play it up. No, he kept saying that there still had to be a lot of crooked cops left on the force, ones who had been ready to side with Joe. Phil was convinced they would come for me, and he stayed by my side the whole time I was in hospital.

They never did.

I remembered Khan's words.

I can keep you out of trouble for everything you've done so far, I think we owe you that. But don't get up to any more.

Fergus didn't visit. He never showed up as part of the police investigation, and didn't try and contact me. Our last conversation remained the exchange at Anderston, me swearing, him apologising. I vaguely remembered mumbling something to him before passing out at Bridgeton, but I couldn't tell you what I'd said.

I hadn't hesitated in taking on a moving train to save him. I knew, deep down at first, then much clearer as the days wore on, that I wouldn't have done that if I'd really wanted him out of my life.

But I still didn't send him a message.

I didn't know why. I thought about it, of course. Every other second. But I didn't. I'd hurt him, I knew. But he'd hurt me. And then, well, gunplay. There wasn't exactly a textbook for how to resolve the situation.

I followed the media circus surrounding the Pennan situation. Nobody knew what the hell had happened, but everyone agreed it was entertaining. I talked to the cops at Hanya's funeral, those who could stand to be near me, and confirmed that none of them really understood it, either.

A couple of days after, a video made its way online, along with high-quality audio that must have been recorded on microphones or cell phones much closer to the action. The footage showed the confrontation between Fergus, Joe, Khan and her goons. The sound had Joe confessing, and then Khan effectively doing the same herself.

The cops and press both asked me something short of a million questions about it. I kept my mouth shut and denied any knowledge. The camera wasn't mounted where Phil had been set up, and Khan would have known that.

Our denials kept us alive, but soon the press and public were all over the story. The Scottish government intervened to order an independent investigation, and a special police task force was sent up from London.

'I guess coincidences do happen,' Phil said to me, after the news of the video broke.

'I guess there are always ways to win,' I said with a smile.

Hanya's parents almost adopted Phil and me while I was in hospital. They'd travelled up from London for the funeral and, seeing that we didn't have parents of own, they stuck around and fussed over us.

I think all four of us got something out of that.

The only thing left was to figure out what the hell I would do next.

As fun as it was recuperating at home, watching the whole house of cards collapse on TV news, I needed to get back out into the world. I was famous for fifteen minutes for the second time in my career, and the clients would be lining up around the block.

Phil reported a huge bump in demand for the courier service, too. It seemed like everyone in town wanted to use the most heroic messenger company in the city. We weren't going to argue.

On the day I was discharged from hospital, I found a package waiting for me at home.

A Blu-Ray copy of *A Life Less Ordinary*.

ONE HUNDRED AND SIX
SAM
June 20th
14:00

I was on my last day of bed rest when my doorbell rang.

I opened without checking who it was. I wasn't feeling any threat. Khan had other things to worry about, even if she knew I'd been behind the video.

Fergus was stood in the doorway.

He was dressed in dark blue jeans and a T-shirt, and wearing the same vulnerable, fixer-upper expression I'd first seen on the video. He was holding a Blu-Ray player.

I started to speak, but he shook his head.

'Wait,' he said. 'I've been practising this for a few days, I want to get it out.'

I stepped back and nodded with my chin, *Go on.*

'So, I'm not sure what the rules are for contacting someone who saved your life,' he said. 'When she's already made it clear that she wants nothing to do with you. Here's the thing. If you hate me, if you never want to see me, I'll walk away and respect that. But I think—' He faltered and looked down at the player. 'I knew I'd fuck this up. Look, Sam. I've got a lot of secrets. I've done a lot of things, and I think you'd hate me even more if I tell you about them. But I will, if that's what it takes for you to trust me. I think, you and me? We could have something.'

He stopped speaking and watched for my reaction. Those eyes of his looked so nervous, so broken. My chest did something I'd never felt before. I wasn't sure how to answer him.

'Did I mention,' he said, 'that I'm stinking rich? I have friends in New York. I've always fancied New Orleans. There's a ridiculously flashy sports car parked downstairs.' He smiled. The confidence crept back in a little, maybe bolstered because I hadn't shut the door in his face. 'Fancy coming on an adventure?'

I pushed the Blu-Ray player aside and kissed him.

ONE HUNDRED AND SEVEN
FERGUS
June 22nd
A whole other time zone.

You're only as good as your most recent kill.

Frankly, mine was good.

I'm happy to go out on that. Turns out, I don't want to be a hit man anymore.

That's okay. There are plenty of other things I'm good at. And I'm in no rush to figure out which of them I should focus on.

I'm too busy focusing on Sam.

She smiles at me over her food. I've brought her to The Burrito Box in Manhattan. It's a loving punch to the gut. Sam agrees, too. She says this is the best one we've had yet.

When her smile fades, I catch the little hint of sadness that keeps framing her moods. It's always there, around the edges. She lost her best friend, and she's left behind her brother, her job.

Maybe she's wondering, *How long can this last?*

Does she see the same question in my face?

I stole millions from the cartel. We had shown them proof of Joe's Babycham, but not of what Alex had done. It might take them a while to notice the missing money, but surely they will eventually? I've given most of it away. Sam calls me *The Patron Saint of Whoever.*

And every night I worry, as Sam drifts off to sleep, is this the evening that the dream wears off? Is this the night when she'll wake up and remember her boyfriend is a killer?

I keep wondering, *How long can this last?*

We finish the food and head out onto 9th Avenue and walk hand in hand down the street, like every annoying couple you've ever seen.

Acknowledgements

This book comes out close to the fifth anniversary of my first deal with Thomas & Mercer. I've been thinking back to everyone I've worked with in that time.

Thanks to Andy, Jacque and Rory. They were the first three people I spoke to at the publisher, on a conference call when I hopefully didn't sound as nervous as I felt.

Rory – you're missed, buddy.

In the US, thanks to: Alan (best of luck, writer-man), Anh, Gracie, Timoney, Sarah, Tiffany, Terry, Patrick, Reema and Kate.

In the UK, thanks to: Emilie, Sana, Hatty, Eoin, Neil, Al, Deborah, Molly and Lisa (loved the *Ways To Die* cover).

To anyone I've forgotten on either list, I'm sorry. You guys know I'm an idiot, right?

Thanks to Jane Snelgrove for her passion and commitment to this book, and thanks to Russel D McLean for helping me get it across the line. (GO BUY HIS BOOKS.)

Emotional support through this writing process (I can throw a tantrum, baby) came from Ray, Johnny, Erik, Luca, Eva, Nick, Matt and Dave. Tyler Dilts made me cry, because he's an asshole. Thanks to Jim and Vern.

I wouldn't have a career without the support of Stacia Decker. And thanks to my wife, Lis.

About the Author

Photo: © John Keatly

Jay Stringer was born in 1980, and he's not dead yet.

He was raised in the Black Country, in England, but now calls Glasgow home, and his loyalties are divided.

Jay is dyslexic, and came to the written word as a second language, via comic books, music and comedy. As a child, he spent his time dreaming of living in the New York of Daredevil comics and crime fiction, but as an adult he's channelled those dreams into fiction of his own.

Jay writes hard-boiled crime stories, dark comedies and social fiction. His heart beats for the outsider, and for people without a voice. He's coined the term 'social pulp fiction' to describe his style.